CHAMELEON

A NOVEL

PIP LANDERS-LETTS

Copyright © 2026 Pip Landers-Letts
First Edition April 2026
Published by Rouxmaus Press

Paperback ISBN: 978-1-7385430-1-4
eBook ISBN: 978-1-7385430-9-0

This is a work of fiction.
Names, characters, places, and incidents are the product of the author's imagination or are used fictitiously. Any resemblance to actual persons, living or dead, events, or locales is entirely coincidental.

Editing and proof-reading: **Sophia Blackwell**
Cover Design: **Samantha Sanderson Marshall**

www.pipwritesfiction.com

THE ONE THAT GOT AWAY...

"Wait... it's her in there, isn't it?" Her own voice sounded faint, as if she'd uttered the words from far away or long ago. Pain flared behind Catherine's eyes as the sickening sight of the two of them blurred into focus. They lay in a tableau of tangled sheets and betrayal. Her mind had conjured this image a hundred times — no, a thousand — and even after all this time, it still stung like the first.

The deception.

The humiliation.

The bloody obvious truth of it all.

Catherine had been a fool — careless with her heart, and now it was broken. As their monstrous voices morphed into mocking laughter, she clutched her aching chest and ran. One foot tumbled over the other until she was shivering in the frigid air, hot tears spilling down her face.

Catherine's breath plumed out in ragged gasps as she

lurched through the snow, every step a laboured effort. She stumbled, collapsing onto the ground in a pathetic heap, her hand brushing something soft. With freezing fingers, she dug until she uncovered a pair of scruffy bunny slippers, their once-pink fur matted and filthy.

A raw, guttural sob tore from her throat — the sound of a wounded animal. She scrambled to her feet, retching as she shouldered through the crowd that had gathered around her. They were little more than silhouettes: blank faces with gaping mouths. Their voices blended into a hollow hum, as she turned to run again.

Where was she even going? Before her mind could latch onto an answer, brakes squealed, and someone shouted, "Look out!"

Catherine whipped her head around, but it was too late. Something blunt and hard slammed into her side, tipping her up, over and out.

1

AFTERMATH

PRESENT DAY

The rigid smile slipped from Catherine's lips as Alice left the building.

The buoyant blonde walked away with a spring in her step and a boxful of office plants tucked under her arm. Probably for the best; Catherine and Jeremy would only forget to water them anyway, and the new temp, Stephanie, could hardly be relied upon. More often than not, Stephanie forgot to boil the water before making coffee; adding another task to her meagre to-do list would be futile.

Catherine's chest ached for Alice; after all, she too had once been wrung out by the same pair of hands. Watching it unfold had been like replaying an old movie. Catherine had known how it would end, but she hadn't been able to stop it.

She sighed and stepped away from the window.

Her swift response had been a win-win for everyone involved. She should have been flooded with relief; everything had gone their way when it could so easily have blown up around them. The reputation of Truscote & Dalton remained intact, Alice had received a generous payout and seemed happy to be moving on, and Jeremy had been spared any further embarrassment. Not that Jeremy deserved protecting. What was it Alice had called him?

Depraved.

The word echoed in Catherine's mind, a mocking reminder of her own complicity. She'd defended Jeremy, she'd called him a good man, and now she felt sick just thinking about it. But her reputation was inextricably tied up with his; if he went down, they both would. She'd invested her entire career in this practice, and she wasn't prepared to let the bloody Daltons ruin everything she'd worked for. So Trusty-old-Truscote swooped in to save the day and sweep up their mess.

She glanced at the young woman behind the Reception desk, who sat swiping at her phone screen.

"Stephanie?"

Stephanie's head whipped up. "Hmm?"

"Let's finish up early today."

"What about Doctor Dalton?"

"He won't be back in for the rest of the day... the rest of the week, actually. He's taken a few days off. Personal reasons." Her voice wavered, the euphemism tasting like ash in her mouth. Before Catherine had even finished her sentence, Stephanie was heading out the door.

CATHERINE DETOURED THROUGH JEPHSON Gardens before heading home. She squinted in the glorious afternoon sunshine, a surprising turnabout after the menacing dark skies that had threatened rain earlier. She slipped off her jacket and draped it over her satchel.

Tulips and hyacinths lined the paths, sun-dappled by the light filtering through the canopy of new leaves unfurling above. After a brisk walk around the lake, Catherine bought an oat milk latte from the café and sat, people-watching — a weary-looking mother pushing a pram, an untidy knot of teenagers in school uniform, and a young couple holding hands, swaying into each other as they walked. None of them paid her the slightest attention; she may as well have been part of the greenery — a shrub, unremarkable and blending into the background. But that's how she liked it. *Observing, but unobserved.*

Her phone pinged in her pocket; she pulled it out and tutted at the name on the screen. *Jeremy.* She really should have it out with him properly; unleash the seething resentment that had been bubbling under the surface for years. But despite being her professional equal and business partner for two decades, an unspoken hierarchy remained between them. She had proved to be as much a loyal servant of the Daltons as her father — the family's estate manager of forty years — had been. Catherine didn't want the same for herself — the Daltons until death.

At that grim thought, Catherine slipped her phone back into her pocket. She'd come here to cleanse the palate of her mind, not to stew over the deviant bloody Daltons.

She sipped her lukewarm coffee, wishing now that it were something a little stronger.

An athletic brunette jogged towards her, a high ponytail bobbing with her stride. She glanced down, flashing a smile as she bounced by. Maybe Catherine wasn't such a shrub after all. Catherine tilted her head for a better view from which to admire the perky retreating rear of the jogger.

Another ping from her phone and she tensed, before whipping it out and muting the conversation with Jeremy, while skilfully avoiding the content of the messages.

With a snap decision, she texted Penny.

> I know it's a school night, but fancy a drink?

A little company this evening wouldn't go amiss — less time to pick over her threadbare friendship with Jeremy and less space for Francesca to creep into her thoughts. Francesca wasn't welcome there, or anywhere near Catherine. Full stop.

PENNY:

Sure. Where, and what time?

> El Vino's? We could do dinner as well. I can head there now, if that suits you.

PENNY:

Sounds great. Loz is away, so I won't have to cook for one. Let me dig my way out of these case files, and then I'll be on my way.

Catherine could always rely on Penny. In fact, she used to rely on her for more than just dinner and drinks. They'd enjoyed a long-term casual arrangement that suited them both, until Penny met Lawrence and fell head-over-sensible-shoes for a man.

Catherine was happy for her friend, but the loss of Penny being something more had left her a little hollow; not in a heart-aching kind of way, more like the small grief you feel after finishing a brilliant book. And while it was a shame to lose the benefits, she'd lucked out with one of the best friends she could have asked for, even if Penny came as one of a smug-married pair now. And with Penny being a lawyer, the free legal advice came in handy, particularly with the recent Dalton debacle.

Stop thinking about them. It's done.

The dull ache in her chest said otherwise.

OM-THE-GO

2024

*J*eremy sprang into her office with all the ball-bouncing energy of an entrepreneur on speed.

"Don't be annoyed with me, but I made an executive decision — I hired that consultant to revamp our website."

Catherine shot him a withering glare over her reading glasses. "I still don't understand why we need to revamp our website at all."

"To increase traffic and drive engagement. Things have gone a little quiet now that the post-pandemic flow has ebbed. Maybe we need to move with the times?"

"Do you honestly think psychotherapy needs to *move with the times*? People will always need the kind of help we offer, Jeremy."

"Yes, but we rely on clients to find us, when really we could do more to put ourselves out there." He kneaded the back of the leather chair opposite her desk, as if he were giving it a massage.

Catherine took off her glasses and pinched the bridge of her nose. "And you think a sparkly new website will really help?"

"Yes, it will. But that's not all."

"Christ, there's *more?*"

"This is the good bit!" Jeremy unhanded the chair and practically did jazz hands. "Colin—"

"Colin?"

"The consultant." He gestured for her to keep up. "He's going to set up a feed for you on our new site so you can publish your own micro-blog."

"I only understood two of the words you just said." She pressed her fingers into her eyes, trying to ease the pressure building.

Jeremy chuckled. "Come on, it'll be fun. You're always coming up with little life hacks to help people reduce their stress." He picked up the paperweight on her desk and tossed it between his hands. She'd not seen him this wired about anything in a long time.

"This is exactly the sort of thing that could help to grow our reach," he said.

"Grow our what?"

"Look, it's just a daily thought from you. One thought; I know you have thousands to choose from. A two-minute hack — it could be a breathing exercise, a herbal tea blend to try." He threw his hands up, nearly dropping the paperweight. "I don't know, a bloody rain dance. Whatever. Just give it a try, will you?"

"Why don't you do it?"

"Because it'd be better coming from you." He shrugged. "You know it'll be mainly women reading it, and they usually want to hear from a woman, don't they?"

Catherine pinched her lips together.

"Go on. For me?" His brown eyes pleaded in the way that usually had her giving in to him. *Oh, for Christ's sake.*

"Alright. Fine. But it had better not take up too much time; I'm already pressed as it is. And I can hardly see why we need to increase our..."

"Reach."

"Yes, that."

"Just trying to keep things fresh, Catherine. Alice thinks it's a good idea too, don't you, Alice?" Jeremy called out towards the door.

"Yep, whatever you say, boss," Alice yelled back.

Catherine sighed. Two against one.

Despite her scepticism when Jeremy had suggested the blog, the following day she woke up buzzing with ideas and almost as excitable as he'd been when he was bouncing around her office. After a morning of meetings, she found herself in Snoots, snaffling her favourite corner table by the window. Armed with a pot of tea and a pen, she let her thoughts flow.

A lot of her clients were time-poor people, who struggled to squeeze a moment's peace into their lives. They usually scoffed at her suggestions about meditation and yoga classes — nice in theory, but just another thing to add to the heavy pile already weighing them down. Perhaps if the time commitment were minutes, not hours, then they could create a little space for the calm they craved.

Mindfulness doesn't need a mat; it needs a moment. She uncapped her pen and scribbled that down. That was it — her angle. A micro-blog of mindfulness moments; each post would be like a little pause.

Next, she brainstormed a list of names:

The Pocket-Pause? — *too vague.*

Zenlightenment? — *too lofty.*

The Daily Breath? — *too frequent.*

She stared into the distance, tapping her lip with the end of her pen. Her eyes widened as the perfect name presented itself — *Om-the-Go.* With a happy hum, she jotted it onto the page and crossed through the rejected candidates.

And with the premise formed, and the name decided, the ideas for content flowed from her pen.

Later that day, Catherine found herself eager to pitch her ideas back to Jeremy. This time, she was the one bouncing around his office.

"That all sounds great, but I don't really understand the name."

"Oh, Jeremy! *Om* is the sound of the universe…" She closed her eyes and hummed, "*Ommm.*" When she opened her eyes again, Jeremy stared at her with a blank expression.

Catherine called out for Alice, and seconds later their assistant's blonde curls appeared around the doorway. "Alice, you know about Om, right?"

"Er, do you mean like, *ommm*?" Alice hummed.

"Yes, exactly." Catherine smiled at the confused-looking woman and turned back to Jeremy. "But it's more than just the sound. It's about the vibration and breath. It's tuning into an energy that's bigger than ourselves."

"Right... oohkay." He bulged his eyes.

"I think you're going to have to trust me on this one."

"Of course I trust you." He nodded slowly. "I guess just don't make the blog too out-there." He flared his fingers in the air. "Sure, we want to increase our reach, but we don't want to alienate ordinary folk. I don't want them thinking T&D is just alternative therapies."

"No, but this is holistic practice, bringing effective mindfulness into everyday busy lives. It's a gentle reminder to pause — to tune in, breathe out, and let go. The idea is that you can do that anywhere — standing in a beautiful woodland or closing your eyes on a packed Tube train."

Jeremy's smile widened. "Okay, Trusty... yeah." He nodded more enthusiastically now. "I like it. Perhaps you should call it Portable Peace instead though?"

"No," she said, followed by a look that had Jeremy holding his hands up.

"Om-the-Go it is," he said.

Two weeks later, Colin the consultant — who had all the charisma of a traffic cone, but in Catherine's opinion wasn't nearly as bright — gave her the thumbs-up to post her first blog. She pressed the 'publish' button and looked at the words, now live on the website, just below the fancy banner Colin had designed for the page.

Om-the-Go. Mindfulness for busy people, by Dr Catherine Truscote.

Her new professional photo looked back at her from under the banner; the soft smile on her lips a reminder of her near-miss, almost-kiss with the very attractive, but very married, photographer.

She sighed. She'd done what Jeremy asked; it hadn't taken long and, surprisingly, she'd enjoyed it. She even had a few ideas for the next blog. But what was the point? It wasn't as if anyone would read it.

✦

Life rushes past, but you don't have to.
No mat or mantra required — just you, here, now.
Draw in a deep, luxurious breath. Let it unfurl inside you,
filling your lungs slowly, deliberately.
Let your gaze wander. Name three things you can see,
hear, and feel. Let them tether you gently to the present.
And then, gratitude. Think of one thing, however small,
that you're thankful for right now.
**Mindfulness isn't about slowing life down; it's about
showing up for it.**

✦

CATHERINE TIDIED HER THINGS AWAY, GETTING ready to head home for the evening, when her computer chimed with a cheerful *ding* she'd never heard it do before.

She glanced back at the screen, and the cheerful *ding* pinged again. And again. And then she noticed it.

A little heart at the bottom of the blog post with a number three next to it. Three people had liked her blog, and twelve people had read it. She'd only posted it two minutes ago. *Seriously, how are that many people on the T&D website?*

She shook her head and flicked off the screen, but not before another *ding* chimed.

The next day, she logged in to see twenty-six likes, and nearly twice as many views. She promptly popped her head into Jeremy's office to inform him that Colin must have wired up the website wrong because it was miscounting visitors.

Jeremy chuckled. "Colin connected your blog to another site, so it's like a live feed. It'll help pull traffic through to us. Didn't I mention that before?"

Catherine shook her head.

"Don't look so worried." Jeremy waved a hand through the air. "Traffic tripled overnight, and Alice said we had two new inquiries this morning."

"No pressure, then."

"None at all, Trusty. Whatever you wrote is doing the trick. More of that, please."

2

FROWNY FACE

PRESENT DAY

*C*atherine checked her reflection in the window before venturing inside El Vino y Tapas. Her tired eyes blinked back at her. She fixed her hair where it had been ruffled by the breeze, her fingers easily manipulating the same cropped style she'd worn for years. Only the colour had changed when she finally embraced the grey that insisted on pushing through.

"Striking," Penny had complimented her when Catherine wobbled with insecurity about her new look. Penny, ever the optimist, had a knack for finding the silver lining in every cloud, or in this case, in Catherine's hair. "If anyone can rock a silver quiff, babe, it's you."

"It's platinum!" Catherine had grimaced.

Sitting at their usual table, she pulled out her reading glasses and scanned the menu while waiting for Penny. Futile, as they almost always ordered the same five dishes and a bottle of Tempranillo. But it was something to do with her hands other than look at her phone, which would lead to thinking about the Daltons.

Curiosity nibbled at her about why Jeremy was messaging, but she was allowed an evening off — this whole mess had already consumed too much of her head-space. And here she was, thinking about it again. Now would be a good time for her to swallow her own medicine and practice what she preached on her blog. Advice was easy to dispense, far harder to follow. She sighed.

"Struggling to choose?" A voice pulled Catherine from her thoughts. She glanced over the top of the menu and into the skilfully made-up eyes of the red-haired woman smiling at her from the next table. Catherine hadn't noticed her sitting there before but was now unsure how she'd failed to. Her fiery hair cascaded in loose waves around her shoulders, framing a face both striking and approachable.

The woman twirled the stem of an almost-empty wine-glass between her fingers. "You were frowning so hard I thought you might need help."

"Help?"

"With the menu," the woman laughed.

Scottish. Catherine placed the woman's accent and smiled. "Actually, I'm a regular. I always order the same thing, so I don't even know why I'm looking to be honest." Catherine folded the menu and patted it as she placed it down. "I highly recommend the Pimientos de Padrón."

"Yes, they're delicious!" The woman popped an olive in her mouth, rested her chin on her hand, and fixed her hazel eyes on Catherine.

Catherine swallowed and glanced away, heat rising in her cheeks.

"So, why the frowny face?" the woman asked.

Catherine breathed out a soft laugh. "Oh, tough day... a difficult few days actually, but best not get into all that. I'm waiting for my friend—"

The restaurant door swung open, and they both turned as Penny swept in, instantly filling the room with her presence and the smell of her zesty perfume.

Mateo, the restaurant owner, rushed out from behind the bar and greeted Penny with an elaborate hug and kisses on both cheeks. As the two of them stood locked in an animated conversation, Catherine looked back to the woman, who was now standing and slipping on a bold red coat.

"Trust me, get the Pan Tumaca if you don't usually order it." Her eyes sparkled.

"We don't. Thank you, I'll try it." Catherine smiled politely, surprised by the pinch of regret she felt at their conversation ending so soon. Her gaze followed as the redhead swished out of the restaurant.

"Who was that?" asked Penny with a waggle of her eyebrows as she took her seat.

Catherine looked back to the door. "No idea."

Penny widened her eyes. "Bloody gorgeous."

"Hmm... she was rather attractive, wasn't she?"

"It's women like that who make me seriously question my life choices. Did you get her number?"

Catherine scoffed. "You don't regret Lawrence one little bit. And no, you know I'm not a fast mover, Pen."

"I know, babe, sloths move faster. Now, where's our chap gone?" Penny glanced around for Mateo. Upon catching her eye, he scurried over, notepad in hand.

"The same as usual, sí? With the Tempranillo, you er, want the bottle, sí?"

"Yes, perfect." Catherine unfolded the menu again and ran a finger down the list until she reached what she was looking for. "And we'll try the Pan Tumaca as well, please."

"Sí, sí, Catalan toast." Mateo scribbled on his pad, nodding as he backed away.

Penny raised an eyebrow.

"What? It's good to try new things now and again," said Catherine.

"Sure. So tell me, did everything go okay with your PA?"

"I'm pleased to say she signed the confidentiality agreement, but I still feel awful about the whole thing — poor Alice."

Penny's lips twisted into a smirk. "Poor Alice? I think she came out all right from it all. She enjoyed a sordid affair with her boss's wife, and then got a juicy payout to stay quiet about it. Some girls have all the luck."

Catherine grimaced.

"Too soon? I'm sorry." Penny leaned in and placed her hand over Catherine's. "Truth be told, it's *you* I feel awful for. Babe, if I may—"

Mateo returned to present the bottle of wine, making a grand gesture of uncorking it and pouring a taste for Catherine. She gulped it down and nodded. He filled their glasses and shuffled away.

Penny leaned in again. "I was about to say, don't you think it's time you broke away from the Daltons and all their nonsense? I know you have history, but isn't it holding you back?"

Catherine tensed.

"Look, the last thing you need right now is a lecture, but it could've all blown up and implicated you too."

Catherine held up her hand to stop her friend from venturing on; she already felt foolish enough and hated being seen as an enabler for the Daltons' toxic behaviour. But that's what she was, *wasn't she?* Sweeping everything under the rug and lying to herself about Jeremy being a good man. It made her complicit, at best.

She blinked away the tears prickling her eyes. "Thank you again for stepping in to help; I really appreciate it, Pen."

"Of course." Penny clinked their glasses together. "To fresh starts."

"It's not that easy though, is it?" Catherine frowned as she sipped her wine.

"Change of subject?" Penny asked with a sympathetic smile.

Catherine nodded.

"You won't believe it, but Lawrence has been on about me taking his name again." She swirled her wine before taking a sip.

"Really?"

"Really." Penny glared through wide eyes. "It's like some sort of joke to him. He walks around the house humming that blasted song all the time, so I absolutely refuse."

Catherine chuckled. "Well, Penny Laine has got a nice ring to it."

"Don't you start as well." Penny lifted her glass to hide her grin. "Can you imagine? Penny Laine — lawyer and laughing stock. I will not have my identity reduced to a sappy Beatles song."

"It wasn't their best. But Loz has a point; it's much less terrifying than Penny Weiss. You know how that sounds, don't you?"

"Yes, of course I know how it sounds. I have a terrifying reputation to uphold. It's advantageous for a lawyer to be formidable."

"Hmm, yes, advantageous for homicidal clowns and lawyers alike." Catherine laughed, and Penny playfully nudged her foot under the table.

"There, that's better. You're much hotter when you're laughing, babe."

Mateo bustled over, holding a tray laden with their dishes. He muttered the names of things as he placed them on the table, finishing with a flourish as he set down the Pan Tumaca. "And this dish is from my hometown. Bon profit!"

Penny picked up a slice of the toasted bread spread with ripe tomatoes, garlic, and olive oil. "Oh my God... mmm," she mumbled through a mouthful.

Catherine winked. "I may not have got her number, but I did get her top menu tip."

"You're such a flirt!"

FEELING PLEASANTLY TINGLY FROM HALF A BOTTLE of wine, Catherine let herself into her apartment, kicked off her shoes, and hung her things in the hallway, intentionally leaving her phone tucked away in her bag. She'd charge it in the morning. Why lose herself now in the red-dot deluge from Jeremy? He could do with exercising a little patience, like she had done *all these years*.

Whilst the company of her closest friend had been enough to lift the load and keep her out of her own head for a while, of course nothing had really changed — her professional career was still hopelessly entangled with Jeremy's, another unwitting woman had fallen prey to Francesca, and guilt gnawed at Catherine that it had happened right under her nose.

Catherine padded barefoot through her apartment — her sanctuary. The muted colours and low lighting of her home filled her with calm; a welcome contrast to the often-chaotic inner worlds of her patients, which she spent her days wading through with them.

Catherine liked clean lines and tidiness, and the thought of another person cluttering her space always overrode the waves of loneliness that washed over her from time to time. She slipped into her silk pyjamas and brushed her teeth, chuckling to herself as she recollected Penny's staunch refusal to bend to Loz's will and change her name. Catherine wasn't sure how she would feel about changing her name, not that the situation had ever arisen or was now ever likely to, but she could see Penny's point.

She spat out the toothpaste and rinsed her mouth, meeting the weary eyes of her fifty-six-year-old self in the mirror.

When one reached a certain age, things became more fixed, immutable even, including one's sense of self. No matter what, she'd always be Catherine Truscote.

Yet even her own mind finished that sentence with... *and Dalton.*

For so many years — *too many years* — it had been Truscote *and Dalton.* Could she really extricate herself from that now? Or was it just as fixed as the rest of her?

Sliding between her soft bedsheets, she turned off the lamp and sank into the plush pillows. As sleep tugged her under, all the overwrought emotions and stress of the last few days dissolved into the blackness behind her eyelids.

3

BOYS DON'T CRY

1988

I could almost make out the lyrics thumping through the thin wall; something about boys not crying. I didn't know the song. And even if boys didn't cry, after the screaming match I'd heard between mother and daughter earlier, a girl was definitely crying on the other side of that wall.

My mum's kind face smiled out at me from the photo of us I'd stuck by my bed.

As daylight tipped over the horizon, I peered from the window into the square, four floors below. Scores of fresh-faced students were still lugging boxes and bin bags from cars. Some shuffled through the throng clutching books to their chests, while others guffawed at the high jinks of their new acquaintances. Then there were the worried-looking parents being bundled back into their cars and waved off as if their offspring's newfound freedom couldn't come quick enough.

Turning away from the window, I smoothed my hand

23

over my fresh bedsheets and picked up my mum's blanket. Over time, the comforting smell of her had faded and morphed into my own, but I still liked to hold it to my nose, as if breathing her in might bring her back.

I pushed up my glasses and glanced around my new room. Everything already had its place, including my suitcase, neatly stowed under the bed. The sinking sun glowed against the off-white walls and all their scars from former occupants. There was an odd stain on the carpet by the desk, and the brown curtains smelt musty, but I had a room to myself — thanks to the generosity of the Daltons, who'd forked out extra for a single-occupancy dorm.

"Trusty? Are you in there?" Jeremy's bellow sounded over the thumping bass of a song I assumed was called *Gigantic,* as that was the main lyric repeated over and over. I opened the door and admitted my lanky friend to my new digs. "I've been knocking for ages," he said.

"Sorry, I can barely hear myself think." I tilted my head to the wall shared with my noise-offensive neighbour.

"You could always try to drown it out with your *Orinoco Flow.*"

I playfully hit his arm. "Don't mock Enya. She helps me concentrate."

Jeremy laughed and rubbed the patchy stubble on his chin. He'd been trying — and failing — to grow a goatee for months, but his facial hair appeared in clumps and never where he wanted it to.

"Right then, Fresher, are you ready for the big campus tour? We can start with the library, then grab some supper and swing by the Union for a pint of Purple on the way home?"

"What's Purple?" I asked as I bent to pull on my battered Dunlops.

"Our official campus drink — cider and black." He waggled his eyebrows. "It's disgusting, but it only costs 80p a pint!"

"Why drink it when you can afford something you actually like?" I grabbed my denim jacket from the hook behind the door.

"I'm trying to blend in."

"You'd have far more luck with the girls if they knew you were rich."

"Two things. One: I want them to like me for more than my wallet."

"Fair."

"Two: one of the reasons you're here is to stop me getting distracted by girls. I don't want either of us to have to face the wrath of my parents if I don't graduate with first-class honours."

I grinned. "Good. That was a test, and you passed!"

In the hallway, my neighbour's obnoxious music added to the dissonant blend of slamming doors and spirited conversations. I glanced at Jeremy with raised eyebrows.

"Don't worry, it'll quieten down once everyone's settled in. And failing that, there's the library, or my place — I live with a bunch of computer science geeks and maths nerds. The place reeks of Lynx and desperation, but the liveliest they get is debating the Riemann Hypothesis."

The next door along opened a crack, and the noisy resident popped her head out. Dark hair spilled from beneath the black hooded sweatshirt she'd drawn up tight. With red-rimmed eyes and smudged makeup, she glanced in both directions, then scowled at us, as if we were the ones making all the racket.

Without a word, she disappeared back inside, and the door slammed shut.

"Nice to meet you, too," I said to the closed door.

Jeremy laughed, and I looped my arm through his. "Lead the way!"

MY EYES FLUTTERED OPEN TO THE BLINKING RED digits of the alarm clock on the bedside table. *02:16.*

I reached for a glass of water that wasn't there. Disoriented, I swung my legs out of bed, relaxing as my bare feet settled on the frayed carpet of my dorm room.

My pulse spiked as I caught a whiff of smoke. I flicked on the lamp and put on my glasses, squinting in the harsh glare from the cheap bulb. Wearing my faded pink robe, I shuffled out into the long corridor of closed doors.

A faint metallic rattling came from the direction of the floor's shared kitchenette; a cramped utilitarian space nestled in a nook at the end of the hallway. Hugging my robe around myself, I ventured closer to the source of the smell and peered into the smoky haze.

There she stood — my noisy next-door neighbour.

"Fucking fuck," she said, shaking one hand and

jabbing a butter knife into the smoking toaster with the other.

"Whoa! What are you doing? You'll electrocute yourself."

She jumped, and the butter knife dropped into the toaster, which fizzed with sparks.

"Jesus Christ!" She clutched her chest and glared at me. "Why did you creep up on me like that?"

I leaned over her, pulling the toaster's plug from the socket.

"I didn't creep up on you. I smelt smoke, so..." I turned the toaster upside down and shook out the charred bread. "A little overdone?" I flashed her a half-smile, which she didn't return.

I held out the retrieved butter knife, but instead of taking it, she folded her arms and stared at me with such intensity I thought she might burn *me*.

That's when I noticed her eyes. Beyond the heavy makeup were the darkest irises I'd ever seen, almost as black as the bread she'd cremated. I held her cold gaze until it became uncomfortable, then glanced down, shuffling my feet and wishing they were encased in anything other than my scruffy pink bunny slippers.

When I dared to look up again, her eyes were still fixed on me. Even though I wasn't cold, I shivered and rubbed my arms, gooseflesh prickling under my robe.

"Now that I've saved you from electrocuting yourself and burning the halls down, I'll be getting back to bed."

As I turned to leave, she spoke in a crisp, refined accent, which seemed at odds with her vampy appearance.

"I suppose I should say thank you. I wasn't actually trying to burn the miserable place down on the first night. I was hungry."

She dropped her arms from her chest, and in the dingy yellow light her expression softened.

"Do you want some toast?" A wry smile lifted the corner of her mouth. "I've got jam. It's from Fortnum & Mason's," she added, as if that would be the clincher.

I pushed my glasses up my nose and returned her smile. "Are you asking because you still want toast, but you don't know how to make it without burning it?"

The weird tension before seemed to defuse and she grinned, fluttering her long eyelashes, thick with mascara.

"Okay, well I think you need to turn the heat down a bit." I twisted the toaster's dial, and she stepped closer, peering over my shoulder.

"Oh, is that what the knob's for? I thought that's what made it pop up."

She stood so close I could smell her fruity shampoo; I cleared my throat. "Do you have more bread?"

I watched as she reached into one of the beige melamine cupboards, her hoodie riding up to reveal her milky-white midriff. She retrieved a loaf of pre-sliced bread. *My loaf of pre-sliced bread.*

I sighed. "I guess if you're providing the posh jam, the least I can do is provide the bread."

She bit her lip. "Do you have any butter?"

I rolled my eyes but smirked despite myself. "There's some Flora in the fridge." I untied the plastic bread bag and pushed two slices into the toaster. It smoked a little as crumbs from the last round burned off. Aware of her eyes on me again, without looking up I said, "You better pop the kettle on... and yes, before you ask, I have milk and tea bags."

The sound of her throaty giggle made my insides glow like the elements in the toaster I was now staring into.

"Gadby, by the way," she said while filling the kettle.

"Sorry?"

"Francesca Gadby." She thumbed her chest.

"Oh, right? Hi. Yes... erm, Catherine."

I'm not sure why, but I held my hand out for her to shake. Francesca looked past it and widened her eyes at the sight of my footwear.

"Nice bunnies," she scoffed.

Heat rushed to my cheeks, and I let my unshaken hand flop back to my side. "They were a gift... from my mum..."

The toast popped up, and I left the sentence unfinished. Francesca held out two mismatched plates, and I dropped a slice of toast on each. We stood side-by-side as I buttered, and she jammed. She hoisted herself up onto the countertop and crunched down on her toast as I made tea. Probably for the best that she'd left me to it. I'd already witnessed her toast-making abilities; I wasn't prepared to let her ruin a good cuppa, too.

"I couldn't help overhearing earlier — you seemed upset. Was that your mum dropping you off?"

"Creeping on me earlier too, were you?" Francesca mumbled through her mouthful.

"No, I wasn't creeping. The walls are thin. I overheard—"

"Kidding." She swung her feet, and the untied laces of her battered Doc Martens rattled against the cupboard doors. "University was Richard's idea — he's my mum's latest husband. He reckons a good degree will help me fend for myself. Of course, she's so smitten with the blubbery twat, I just went along with it. But I didn't realise everything would be so..." her lip curled as she glanced around, "communal."

"It's not that bad!" I huffed a laugh as I passed her a steaming mug and leaned against the counter to eat my toast. She fixed her eyes on me again with the same intensity as before. I looked down at my plate, focussing on my food and trying not to think about why her stare stirred something in me.

"Mmm, this jam is delicious."

"It's wild hedgerow. I suspect Mother Dearest was trying to assuage her guilt by dropping me off with an F&M hamper." I watched as she licked jam from her index finger, then picked up her mug of tea and cupped her hands around it. "So, you're actually happy to be here?"

I nodded as I chewed and swallowed my last mouthful of toast. "Yeah, I'm the first in my family to get to uni..." I cast my eyes down to my sad-looking pink bunny feet. "I want to make them proud, so..."

"The older guy coming out of your room earlier... is he your boyfriend?"

"Who? Jeremy?" I honked a laugh and quickly covered my mouth. "God, no. I've known him since I was twelve; he's like my brother. My dad manages his family's estate."

"I see." Francesca tapped her chipped black fingernails

against the mug. She stared into the middle distance, and I took the opportunity to drink her in. The curve of her jaw and smooth white skin — made paler by the makeup she was wearing. My eyes travelled to her full lips, which quirked into a grin, and I realised I'd been sprung.

Francesca levered herself off the countertop and moved towards me, her dark-red lips still grinning. My cheeks burned and I stepped back, rising onto my tiptoes to minimise myself out of her way. She pushed on, confidently taking up the small space. My skin tingled at the brush of her hand on my arm as she reached past me and dropped her dirty plate in the sink.

Oh, she was trying to get to the sink, but — she was standing so close I could smell her shampoo again. Our eyes met, and she opened her mouth slowly.

"Well, I guess I'll see you around campus," she said.

"I... yeah. I'm like literally next door to you... so, I—"

Her gaze dropped to my lips, and my heart raced because, for a moment, I thought she was going to kiss me. Instead, she smiled and stepped away.

When she disappeared around the corner, I exhaled. It felt like a sigh of relief, but I recognised my disappointment. *I wanted it* — I wanted Francesca to take control of the moment and kiss me. I wanted those blood-red lips on mine. I wanted to see if she tasted as fruity as her scent.

Until now, my sexuality had been an abstract concept — a vague awareness that I liked girls generally. But now I desired Francesca *specifically*.

IN THE DAYS THAT FOLLOWED, I COULDN'T GET Francesca off my mind. Even with a full timetable of lectures, my thoughts kept snagging on those dark eyes and red lips. In most of my daydreams, we kissed in the kitchen as I ran my fingers through her soft, fruity-smelling hair. In every daydream, she tasted sweet like jam and hot like tea, but despite all my best efforts to orchestrate a hallway collision, I hadn't seen her since.

I'd heard her, though. Not as loud as the first day, but still at a volume that usually would have driven me mad. Somehow, it became the comforting soundtrack of Francesca. I came to recognise the songs thumping through the thin wall between us; the bass pulsed in time with my heartbeat. I even found myself humming the melodies as I walked around campus, hoping to catch a glimpse of her.

When I knew she was on the other side, I'd pressed my hand to the Blu Tack-stained wall and imagined her, wrapped in her oversized hoodie with knees clutched to her chest, doing the same.

I wished for the courage to knock on her door, to ask if she wanted to hang out or go to the union for a pint of Purple. I rehearsed the conversation in front of my mirror, but I couldn't even look myself in the eye, let alone her.

I leafed through books in the library, failing to find a big enough distraction. All thoughts led back to Francesca. Jeremy must have sensed the shift in me, as he broached the subject when we met for dinner in the canteen.

"Don't worry, Trusty." He squeezed my shoulder. "It

took me a while to settle in and make friends, too. You'll be fine by Christmas break; you wait and see."

Without looking up from my plate, I nodded and prodded a tube of pasta with my fork. "Yeah, I guess."

"Is that neighbour of yours still causing you grief? I can enquire about getting you moved, if that'd help."

"No," I said a bit too quickly. My head snapped up, and I met his startled gaze. "I mean, no, she's fine." I tried to reassure him with a flat smile. "You're right; uni life just takes a bit of getting used to."

"Well, you know you can always talk to me." He squeezed my shoulder again, and this time patted my back for good measure.

"Thanks, Jer. I'll be fine."

Except I was far from fine. I needed to get a certain gothy brunette out of my mind or the next time I saw her I'd likely implode — or worse, pin her to the wall and snog her senseless, which is what I'd done in the fantasy that had swept me away during my Cognitive Psychology lecture.

Later that evening, I nearly jumped out of my skin as I walked back to my room from the kitchenette and Francesca's door sprung open. Hot tea splashed over the edge of my mug, and I swore under my breath. Francesca popped her head out, those dark eyes sparkling with amusement.

"Hi," she said.

"Hi. I was just..." I jutted my chin to my closed dorm door.

"Do you fancy a biscuit with your tea?"

I nudged my glasses up my nose. "I need to do the reading for my seminar tomorrow, so I should probably..." *What the hell am I doing? Yes! Say yes, you moron!*

"Suit yourself." Her head popped back inside, and her door clicked to a close. I stood there internally kicking myself until her door opened a crack. Francesca's hand poked out and shook a tin of Fortnum & Mason biscuits at me.

"They're chocolate chip," she said from behind the door.

I laughed, then gulped hard as I allowed myself to be lured inside. *Sod Psychobiology.*

Behind the closed door, Francesca's room was much the same as mine — mothy brown curtains and odd carpet stains, but the intoxicating smell was all hers. I exhaled a shaky breath and looked down at my steaming mug.

"Welcome to my humble abode." Francesca twirled around. She pushed a button on her stereo, which was smaller than I'd imagined given the noise it could blare out. A drum machine ticked out a tight, syncopated rhythm before a breathy vocal joined the track. Francesca clicked her fingers, sashaying over to the bed and bouncing back onto it. She patted the space next to her. "Come. Sit."

I swallowed and dumbly followed her instruction, clocking the suitcase that sat defiantly at the foot of her bed; ripped denim and faded black T-shirts spewed out and over the floor like a jumble sale for cool people. I wished I were one of those people, but if I wore an outfit like that, I'd look like I'd been mugged.

Francesca opened the tin and pulled out a biscuit before leaning over to dunk it in my tea.

"Oi!" I said, my jaw dropping in mock outrage. She giggled and popped the biscuit into my open mouth. I tried not to spray crumbs as I returned her laughter.

She dunked another biscuit in my tea and bopped her head to the music. The soft motion of her swaying next to me made my heart race, and I tried not to think about the way the bed was moving beneath us. My eyes settled on the poster she'd pinned above her bed, featuring a pale-faced man with unruly hair and heavy eyeliner.

"I love The Cure!" she said, answering my unasked question.

I nodded like one of those stupid parcel-shelf dogs. "I sometimes wish you'd love them a little quieter."

She smirked and nudged her knee into mine. My gaze dropped to a flash of white flesh, her thigh beneath her ripped jeans.

"Don't tell me you like The Smiths? Morrissey is an arsehole. You know he deliberately called the band that just to piss off Robert Smith?"

"Who's Robert Smith?"

Francesca rolled her eyes and gestured to the poster over our heads. I really should have made more effort to find out what other people my age liked. I'd lived in a bubble with my dad and the Daltons — they weren't like other people. No wonder Jeremy had found it so hard to make friends here.

"Who do you like then?" Francesca crunched another biscuit and dropped the tin in my lap.

"Er..." *Don't say Enya. Don't say Enya.* "Enya," I said.

Francesca snorted a laugh. "You're so funny."

I laughed along, making a mental note to hide, or even bin my Enya cassette in the unlikely event that Francesca would ever set foot inside my room.

"I'll make you a mixtape sometime," she said.

"Really?"

"Yeah, of course." The stereo whirred and clicked to a stop. Francesca bounced up from the bed and rattled through a stack of tape cases on the desk before raising one of them in the air like a prize. "The Pixies, now we're talking."

She twisted the dial, and the bassline throbbed from the small speakers. Francesca swayed her arms and then held them out to me. "Dance with me."

"I can't. I mean... I have two left feet."

"You don't need to be good at it." She pulled me up. I groaned but muted my protest when she put her hands on my waist. Heat flared through me at her touch.

"You're all stiff. Try to loosen up." She pulled me closer to her, which had the opposite effect of loosening me up. My nerves pulsed with her proximity. Her hands touched the tender skin around the top of my jeans as she swayed our bodies together. She threw her head back as the song hit its refrain, eyes closed and lost in reverie. "Oooh, Kim Deal's voice," she moaned. "It's so... arousing."

I didn't know who Kim Deal was, so I couldn't speak for the effects of her voice, but Francesca's pelvis rocking into mine was setting me alight. I wanted more but had no idea how she'd react if I made a move, or even what the next move was for that matter.

Francesca threaded her hands behind my neck, and I closed my eyes. When I opened them again, she was staring at me. My heart clamoured in my chest as her lips parted. Her gaze dropped to my mouth, like it had in the kitchen the other night, and the room shrunk to just the space between us.

As she leaned in, I pulled away, breaking the rhythm of our sway. She looked startled and quickly spun away to turn the music off. Embarrassment and shame doused my desire. I'd ruined the moment. Kissing her was all I'd thought about for days, and I'd ruined it. I glanced at my watch, eyes widening at the time.

"Shit — I said I'd meet Jeremy at the library."

Francesca hugged her arms around herself. "Go if you have to."

A loaded silence charged the air, and I felt myself diminish under her penetrating gaze.

"Why don't you come with me? I could introduce you to Jeremy, and the three of us could get a drink together afterwards."

Francesca's left eyebrow arched as if I'd suggested something utterly ridiculous.

"Sorry, I just thought... maybe..."

Her features softened, and her lips quirked into a wry smile. "Alright, I will."

I exhaled, unsure whether I was more surprised I'd had the guts to ask her, or that she'd actually agreed. I mean, it wasn't a date exactly — Jeremy would be there — but I felt like she'd given me a second chance. If the universe gifted me another opportunity to kiss her, I wouldn't mess it up.

4

SPICE UP YOUR LIFE

PRESENT DAY

A loud bang snatched Catherine from sleep. She sat up, blinking in the darkness. After listening for a moment and hearing nothing, she took a long sip of water and nestled back amongst her duck-feather pillows.

When Catherine closed her eyes again, Francesca's face floated behind them — a shimmering spectre of the woman she'd once adored. Those dark eyes bored into her, threatening to pull her in like black holes.

Stop it; she's a ghoul.

Catherine kicked the duvet off her feet and wriggled into a new position, enjoying the sensation of her silk pyjamas sliding against her fresh sheets. She focussed on counting breaths — a technique she often coached her clients with — a good way to occupy an overactive mind and pull herself back from spiralling thoughts... about the goddamn Daltons.

In — one, out — two, in — three, out — four. In — five—

A burst of music pounded through the ceiling and Catherine's eyes snapped open.

What the—? She reached for her phone, tapping her hand across the bedside table where it should have been charging, before remembering she'd left it in her bag at the front door.

Is that the bloody Spice Girls? Catherine tilted her head, making out the words to *Spice Up Your Life* as the song thundered through the floorboards. She pulled a pillow around her ears and let out an anguished grunt.

The upstairs apartment had been empty ever since its former occupant — her dear friend Bridie — had passed away over a year ago. Catherine had grown accustomed to the quiet of the empty space that loomed above her. The music stopped suddenly, yielding to a thick, padded silence.

Catherine rolled onto her side. Sleep had been elusive recently, with all the worries at work and her recurring nightmares starting up again. If only she could close her eyes and—

A splintering crack shattered her short-lived peace; and with a jolt of adrenaline she envisaged a dumbbell being dropped on the hardwood floor. She whipped off the duvet and swung her legs out of bed, imagining the offending article crashing through the ceiling. It didn't, but the noise had rattled her nerves and woken her fully. She couldn't exactly go up there and investigate in her pyjamas — well, she could, but she wouldn't. The thought of confronting a loud and inconsiderate stranger filled her with dread.

Resigning herself to wakefulness, Catherine flicked on

the bedside lamp, shooting daggers at the ceiling as if the noisemaker might somehow feel her wrath through the void that divided them.

She padded into the kitchen. The soft pelmet lighting flickered on, and she tutted at the oven clock. *4:41.* She boiled the kettle and made herself a cup of chamomile — another of her top tips for patients; she'd even written a blog about it. She'd never admitted to anyone that she didn't actually enjoy the flowery taste.

Why is it that often the things that taste bad are good for you, yet the things that taste good are, more often than not, bad? And why must every thought lead back to bloody Francesca?

With that thought came the echo of Penny's mini-lecture about the Daltons and how it was maybe time to let go. Catherine fished her phone from her bag and took her tea through to the bedroom, climbing back into bed and propping up the pillows.

Right, let's get this over with, shall we, Jeremy?

She put on her reading glasses, and after a sharp inhale, clicked into the messages app.

JEREMY:

> I trust all went well with Alice today. You were right. It's for the best that I wasn't there, but I do feel terrible about dragging you into all this. Let me know if there's anything I can do to make it up to you.

Catherine exhaled and scrolled on.

JEREMY:

> Just a thought, why don't you join
> Francesca and I for dinner next week?
> We haven't done that for years, have we?

"Yes, for bloody good reason."

JEREMY:

> Just the three of us, what do you say? It'll
> be like the good old times x

"Absolutely not." *They were not good old times.*

The fresh face of twenty-year-old Francesca surfaced in Catherine's mind again, those dark eyes smouldering with desire as she sank her teeth into her lower lip. Catherine shook the thought away and refocused on her phone screen.

JEREMY:

> Scrap that, silly idea. I've spent the
> afternoon with my good old chum,
> Johnnie Walker. He's a terrible influence.
> If you fancy a drink after work, why don't
> you pop by?
>
> Don't worry, Francesca isn't home!!!

The last message from Jeremy had arrived just after 1 a.m.

JEREMY:

> Sorry to bother you again, Catherine, but
> have you heard from Francesca? Her
> phone is off, and she's not answering my
> calls. Is she with you?

Catherine rolled her eyes. "Why on earth would she be

with me?" She removed her glasses and pinched the bridge of her nose before a soft chuckle escaped her. "Just how drunk were you, Jeremy?"

Penny was right. How and why had Catherine put up with the Daltons for so long?

Of course, it hadn't all been bad. Francesca mainly stayed out of her way, and Jeremy was easy enough to get along with. Even so, it was ironic she'd kept this insanity so close for all these years considering she was a medical psychotherapist. *As is Jeremy.*

Did it say something about her as well as them? *Probably.*

Catherine sipped her chamomile and tried not to think about where Francesca might be and whether she was alright. When Alice had mentioned that she'd seen her earlier in the day, and that she'd seemed upset, Catherine had rather callously scoffed. *Francesca doesn't do upset; she's devoid of emotional intelligence.* And even if Francesca were upset, Catherine really didn't care.

Except she clearly did still care, but that wasn't helpful, so she got up and dressed for her morning walk.

OM-THE-GO

2024

You don't need silence to find calm.
Even here, in the rush of life, it waits for you…
Feel the ground beneath your feet — steady, certain,
holding you.
Lift your gaze. Notice something beautiful you might have
missed — a ray of sunlight bursting through the clouds or
a splash of colourful foliage.
Breathe with your stride – inhale, exhale, let the rhythm
carry you, flowing with each step.
Remember — motion can be meditation in disguise.

To Catherine's amazement, her mini-blog was a hit. Jeremy was delighted. Web traffic and engagement were up for the third month in a row, and even good-natured

Alice complained about all the extra calls and appointments she had to squeeze into their schedules.

"We're having to turn clients away! It's a happy problem," chirped Jeremy. His face only fell slightly when Catherine batted back that it was essentially other people's misery making him happy... and richer.

But she had to admit to herself she was enjoying the blogging experience, especially the little dopamine buzz with every page refresh that revealed a heart-shaped hit waiting for her. The blogs had attracted comments here and there, a little positive feedback adding to the weight of the likes and spurring her on to get creative and write more.

Karen: Amazing! This actually worked.

Sunita_K: Such simple tips, but they always help.

McRainbow83: The feet thing... game-changing!

One particular commenter had caught Catherine's eye. Their tone was different: humorous, with a hint of sarcasm.

Betty77: Who'd have thought breathing would improve my commute? But somehow it does :)

Catherine didn't normally feel the need to reply to comments, but when Betty's name appeared, her fingers twitched, and eventually she caved and sent her a private message.

DR.T:

Maybe don't breathe too deeply while navigating public transport systems.

BETTY77:

Ha! Thanks for the caveat, Doc. Can you imagine me choking on a rogue fart while trying to get my zen on?!

DR.T:

Goodness, that would be a weight on my conscience. Please be careful out there; I wouldn't want you passing out because someone had passed wind.

BETTY77:

Noted. Thanks for the warning x

And the messages went on much like that. Sometimes short, sometimes longer. Frequent, rapid-fire exchanges, lighthearted and fun. Betty teased and Catherine teased back. Ridiculous, really, flirting with this random woman in cyberspace. But it had its appeal, not least because it was contained safely within her devices; she could turn them off and engage on her own terms.

This was a way of getting herself back out there — dipping her toe in the water with zero risk of drowning. And for all Catherine knew, Betty77 wasn't even a woman; *she* was probably a hairy bloke called Malcolm who still lived with his mum. Or, even more likely, a scammer sitting in a fraud factory in Myanmar. As such, Catherine wasn't about to disclose any personal information. And in the instance of Betty asking for her bank details, or anything else along those lines, *"Betty"* could bugger off.

But even from their brief exchanges, Catherine could tell Betty had female energy. *Queer female energy.* Betty was definitely flirting.

Other than a bit of cyber-fun, Catherine couldn't understand what Betty had to gain from their interactions. Nothing would come of it; how could it? So where was the harm in enjoying this *harmless* online flirtation? Yes, it was a professional blog, and there was an ethical consideration, but Catherine couldn't stop her face splitting into a silly smile every time Betty's name popped up in her inbox.

DR.T:

> Alright then, Betty, if my breathing tips have helped with your commute, are there any topics you'd like me to cover in my next blog?

Catherine pressed send. Then, for two whole days, she waited for a response. What on earth was the other woman doing?

Perhaps Betty actually had a life, unlike Catherine. There were only so many times she could refresh her messages without feeling like a complete loser. When a message finally did ping through, it took her so much by surprise she spilled coffee over her keyboard. *Shit!*

BETTY77:

> Hmm, what about mindful eating? I have a mad, busy lifestyle, so I rarely get the chance to enjoy food. More often than not, it's just fuel x

Catherine tried — and failed — not to respond too quickly. Sixteen minutes didn't look too desperate, did it? Perhaps she should've waited two bloody days like Betty had done.

DR.T:

Great idea. Let me see what I can rustle up for you x

BETTY77:

I look forward to it, Doc! x

5

IMPOSITION

PRESENT DAY

eturning from a soggy walk, Catherine shook the rainwater from her umbrella and propped it by the door in the shared hallway.

She stilled as she turned and noticed the shelf above the radiator. She traced her fingers over the now-empty spot, where, for the past year, she'd stacked all the post addressed to the upstairs flat.

So, there actually was a new neighbour, and she hadn't just summoned the Spice Girls in a dream. Standing motionless, she tilted her head to listen out for any signs of life from above, but heard only the familiar groans of the old building she'd lived in for so many years she'd lost count.

Catherine stepped towards her apartment; as she turned her key in the lock, she spotted a pink note slipped under her door. She bent to pick it up, her eyes quickly scanning the words that seemed to have been scrawled in a hurry.

49

Hi!

Just moved in above you — Knocked, but you weren't home. Sorry to ask, but I have to leave town for work for a couple of days. Would you mind popping in to feed my cat?

Food's in the fridge. Key's under the doormat.

Sorry again, J x

P.S. Excuse the mess.

P.P.S. His name is Juniper.

"You've got to be kidding me." Catherine turned over the slip of paper, which looked as if it'd been torn from a fancy notebook.

She shook her head as she re-read the note.

"Absolutely bloody not." She balled the note in her hand, ranting under her breath as she paced inside, banging the door shut behind her.

"SO, HOLD ON, LET ME GET THIS STRAIGHT — you've somehow agreed to look after your noisy new neighbour's cat, and you haven't even met them yet?" Penny's contagious cackle trickled down the phone line.

"No, I'm not looking after it!" Catherine reached the front of the queue and passed over a pre-made cheese baguette to the disinterested cashier. "Two secs, Pen," she said, lifting her phone from her ear to tap it to the card reader. "I just got the note under my door. I can't believe the audacity. First, I get woken up at 4 a.m. with the Spice Girls of all things, and now this?"

"I wouldn't mind being woken up at 4 a.m. by Geri Halliwell."

"Admittedly Geri ticks a few boxes, but—"

A dirty laugh bubbled from Penny. "She can tick my box any time she likes."

"Really, Pen?" Catherine smirked and rolled her eyes. "Back to the topic at hand, I was going to say, who moves in somewhere and expects their neighbour, whom they haven't even met yet, to feed their bloody cat?"

"You don't even like cats!" Penny said through what sounded like a mouthful of salad leaves.

"Exactly." Catherine wove her way through the lunchtime bustle of the Parade. "So what do I do?"

"Well, you can't leave the poor cat to starve, can you?"

She sighed. "I don't see how it should be my problem."

"Look, we both know you're going to feed that hungry pussy—"

"Oh my goodness, Pen. It isn't hard to tell when Loz is away."

Penny released another filthy laugh; the infectious sound was what had drawn Catherine to her when they'd met.

"Well, I'm actually grateful to your new neighbour!"

"Why?"

"Because their little imposition has taken your mind off all that messy business with the Daltons for five minutes." Penny crunched into something that sounded like cucumber.

"Yes, I suppose it has. Anyway, now I've got a busy afternoon of listening to other people's problems, so it's been good to offload mine to free up a little headspace."

"Anytime, babe." Penny pecked a couple of kisses into the phone. "Don't forget to feed the—" Catherine ended the call, smiling as she buzzed herself back into the office, only to be confronted with the sight of Jeremy sitting in the waiting room with his head in his hands.

All the buoyancy she'd gained from chatting to Penny deflated. Jeremy sprang to his feet; his expensive suit hung creased on his tall frame.

"Catherine, you're back! Stephanie didn't know how long you'd be."

Catherine gave him a flat smile and held up her baguette like a trophy. "I told her I was just nipping out to grab a bite. My next appointment is at 1 p.m."

"Mind if I bend your ear while you eat?"

A loud clatter came from the kitchenette, followed by a string of expletives from Stephanie. Catherine drew a breath and widened her eyes.

"I asked her for a coffee, but she's been in there for at least ten minutes; juggling the cups, by the sounds of it." Jeremy's attempt at levity fell flat. His normally bright eyes looked dull and tired, and his mouth sagged, drawing attention to his bristly jowls.

Catherine could feel pity creeping in and nuzzling away her annoyance. *Damn it.*

"Okay, we have twenty minutes."

She strutted towards the kitchenette and poked her head around the doorway. The young receptionist stood slouched against the worktop, her jaw slack as she mindlessly masticated a glob of gum. Catherine cleared her throat, and Stephanie looked up from her phone.

"If it's not too much trouble, we'll take that coffee in my office."

Catherine placed her baguette down, aligning it with her pen and mechanical pencil, both set at a right angle to her notepad. With a long sigh, Jeremy sank into one of the leather chairs facing her desk.

"Please don't let me stop you from eating your lunch," he said.

"It's fine, I'm not really hungry." Catherine's stomach had been growling for food before, but best not to be stuffing her face while he outpoured. "So, did you manage to track down Francesca last night?"

Jeremy tugged at his shirt collar; his throat bobbed as he swallowed. "Yes, a little after two. She's staying at a hotel in the Cotswolds. She asked if I could send a taxi with some of her things... and her Diazepam."

Catherine scoffed.

Jeremy met her stare. "Look, I know how it sounds, but she's really not well, Catherine." Jeremy hung his head again and released an anguished groan. "She's miserable in a way that I... I just don't know how to fix this time."

Catherine couldn't bring herself to feel sorry for Francesca, but Jeremy — even if things between them had soured somewhat over the years — was her oldest friend. He was practically family.

The words left her mouth before she could clamp her lips to stop them. "Do you want me to try speaking with her?"

Jeremy lifted his head, a glimmer of hope replacing the desperation in his eyes. "Would you?"

Christ. Could this day get any worse?

6

WATERMARK

1988

*A*dding Francesca to the mix of our friendship introduced a thrilling new dynamic. She flirted wildly with us both. It quickly became apparent that Jeremy was as smitten with the intoxicating brunette as I was, not that either of us would dare to admit it to the other. Her gravitational pull made us dance around her and compete for her attention. We were satellites in her orbit. Our previously playful banter turned into a sport with actual points to be scored. It all felt good-natured and innocent... until it didn't.

I tried not to notice when Francesca touched Jeremy's chest and he puffed up like a budgie as she laughed a little too hard at one of his lame jokes. Just as he looked away when she traced her fingers over my bare forearm, gazing into my face and hanging on every word I read aloud from a passage of text. *Was that smouldering smile just for me?*

We spent blustery afternoons holed up in the library, Jeremy and I actually studying, while Francesca loudly leafed through books and magazines, attracting frequent reprimands from the librarian. Evenings were passed in the union, huddled in our little trio, sipping pints of Purple. During lecture-free periods, we'd loop arms and breathe in the crisp autumnal air on walks through the cobbled lanes of our university town. Francesca inevitably led us to the local record shop, where Jeremy and I perused posters of bands we didn't know whilst she browsed the cassette tapes.

One afternoon, she slipped a cassette into my coat pocket. I wrapped my fingers around the plastic case and pulled it out, stifling a laugh and pretending to be appalled when I glanced at the cover — Enya's latest release. Francesca leaned into me and planted a soft kiss on my cheek. I raised my hand to it, still feeling the warmth of her lips long after they'd left my skin.

Occasionally, we'd hang out in Francesca's room with the volume of her stereo cranked up. We'd pretend to enjoy the music while Francesca swayed her limbs, dancing with abandon as our eyes drank her in. One night, she pulled me to my feet and, like a puppeteer, commanded my reluctant limbs until I was slow-dancing with her to a song I didn't know and could barely hear over my galloping heartbeat. The sensation of her arms around my waist was almost too much to bear.

I stole a glance at Jeremy. Red blotches crept up his neck as he tapped his loafer-clad foot and stared out the window. I closed my eyes and wished him away. I wished I were alone with Francesca. I'd capture her lips with my own and kiss her like she'd never been kissed. Not that I'd ever been kissed, but I'd spent so much time thinking about it, I'd convinced myself I knew how. And this time, even my thundering heart and breathlessness wouldn't be able to stop me.

Who needs breath anyway?

Francesca nuzzled into my neck, and my hopes soared.

A couple of days later, I was still riding high. Francesca had chosen *me* to dance with and *my* cheek to graze a kiss against when we said goodnight, and it was all I'd been able to think about since. I sat through a lecture on Homeostatic Processes, but instead of taking notes I'd written Francesca's name over and over on my notepad, like it was the only word that mattered.

The flat light of the December day had already leached away by the time I stepped out of the lecture theatre. I squeezed my books to my chest, hoping the pages might offer some warmth, and hurried across campus to our halls, guided back to Francesca by the warm orange glow spilling from her window. I pictured her wrapped in her hoodie, a deep frown etched between her dark eyebrows as she scrambled to finish her overdue assignment. We'd planned to hang out in her room later... *without Jeremy.* I'd make her a cup of tea and bring her biscuits to help her push through, because the sooner her assignment was done, the sooner she could return her focus to me.

I took the stairs two at a time, but my stomach plummeted back down all four floors as I saw Jeremy at our end of the hall. He pulled Francesca's door to a close and glanced around, spotting me with the startled expression of someone caught with his fingers in the pie.

Jealousy burned in my gut like a hot rock.

"Alright, Trusty," he said with a wolfish smile as he slunk past.

They'd been alone together, without me. Perhaps it had been completely innocent, but I couldn't shake the look on Jeremy's face. It was the same expression he wore when he beat me at chess or tennis, or any of the games we used to play together during those languid summers on the Daltons' estate. He'd won, and just when I thought I was about to score.

I quietly let myself into my room and flopped onto my bed. My stomach churned. This was all my fault. I'd collided them together when I should have kept my two worlds apart. Staring at the ceiling, I blinked away the hot tears welling. When Francesca's music bled through the wall, I wrapped my pillow around my head and curled up under my mum's blanket.

7

JUNIPER

PRESENT DAY

*S*adness plucked at Catherine's chest as she climbed the wooden staircase to the apartment above. For so long, she'd avoided even looking up the stairs, let alone ascending them. She hadn't set foot inside Bridie's apartment for well over a year. An unsettling stillness lingered in the wake of her dear friend — not just in the building, but inside Catherine.

An octogenarian Scot with a razor-sharp wit and a cast-iron poker face, Bridie was the formidable matriarch Catherine had longed for, and finally got. They'd lived a floor apart for over ten years, exchanged pleasantries in the entranceway, but only bonded in a bubble during the pandemic. Late-night card games and a mutual love of whisky — Scotch specifically — sealed their unlikely friendship.

Two winters ago, Bridie picked up a chill on her chest, coughed through the night and complained to Catherine that her lungs were "Blawin' like broken bagpipes."

Ignoring Bridie's protests, Catherine drove her to hospital. "You're in the right place," she'd said, squeezing the old woman's mottled hand. "Let them fix you up and you'll be beating me at cards again in no time."

The next day, Catherine returned with a bag of Bridie's things, only to crumple into a plastic chair when they told her she'd gone.

"They said it was pneumonia. I'm so very sorry." Catherine broke the news to Bridie's long-distance daughter over a long-distance phone call.

"Thanks for letting me know," the daughter said. "She always said she wanted to be scattered in the loch. I'll arrange it." Static fizzed in the silence. "You should come. I mean, I think she'd have—"

"Sorry, I have work. Let me know if there's anything you need from her flat." Catherine hung up before emotion could fray her voice. She refused to own this pain; she'd already lost her mother. This pain had someone else's name etched on it; she wanted to box it up and post it to the long-distance daughter. She didn't hear from her again about the funeral or the flat.

Now, following the instructions on the pink note, Catherine rummaged under the doormat for the key and let herself inside. What struck her first was the gauntlet of unpacked boxes and suitcases blocking any clear path from the hallway into any of the rooms. The new neighbour must have moved their stuff in whilst Catherine had been at work, as she'd have noticed this much stuff being carried up the stairs.

She squeezed between the boxes and into a small

clearing in the lounge. In the centre was a semi-constructed bookcase and a screwed-up instruction manual. Catherine wondered whether the job being abandoned halfway through had anything to do with the empty wine bottle on the coffee table. The glass beside it had red lipstick smeared on the rim.

She looked around, trying not to dwell on the mess that loomed above her own tidy living space. Bridie would be horrified. The old woman may have had way too many knick-knacks for Catherine's liking, not to mention a penchant for doilies, but she'd kept the place spotless.

Catherine whirled around at the sound of rustling behind her, eyes widening as one of the smaller boxes toppled over, setting off a domino effect around it. As she leaned to peer over at what might have caused the boxes to fall, something brushed her leg. Catherine screamed and stiffened. The small creature at her feet sprang away, fur on end. Catherine clutched a hand to her chest and released a breathy laugh.

"Oh my goodness, you gave me quite a fright!"

Big round eyes filled with dilated pupils peered up at her.

"You must be Juniper. I live downstairs. Your owner asked me to pop by and feed you."

Why am I explaining myself to a bloody cat?

Juniper slunk behind a bulging suitcase. Catherine knelt and held out a coaxing hand. She rubbed her fingers and thumb together, making a soft shuffling sound, which must have been instinctive as she'd never interacted with a cat before. After a moment, a tentative paw stepped out from the shadowy space.

"I'm sorry I scared you."

As if accepting her apology, the full fluffy grey form of Juniper emerged. He arched his back and softly mewed as he took in her face with his bright green eyes.

"Oh, so you do want to say hello."

Catherine reached out to him, and Juniper purred as he pressed his head into her palm. His fur was surprisingly soft, almost like velvet.

"Right, well, I suppose you want your supper?" Catherine stretched to her feet, and Juniper rubbed against her shins, purring louder still.

"I'll take that as a yes!"

Juniper twisted his slender body like a helix between Catherine's legs as she edged around the boxes, stepping over a slumped carrier bag stuffed with electrical cables and the spewed-out contents of an overflowing laundry basket.

"What a mess," she muttered, dreading what she was about to face in the kitchen.

The light flickered on to a relatively tidy room. Aside from a few dishes stacked in the sink, the space was clutter-free and at least looked clean. Catherine opened the fridge and easily identified Juniper's food amongst its sparse contents. Besides a bottle of tonic water and a bowl of waxed lemons, the only other item was cat food; an entire shelf of it. Juniper meowed at her feet, and Catherine smiled down at him.

"Alright, impatient one." She took a can of shredded

chicken from the stack and emptied the unappetising contents onto a saucer she found in a neatly packed cupboard — the new tenant wasn't a completely lost cause, after all.

Juniper effectively pounced on his food when she placed it down. She watched for a moment as he hunched over and hoovered up his meal like it might be his last.

Catherine's curiosity about Juniper's owner was piqued again. She wasn't nosy, despite her job, which essentially involved picking through people's problems and asking them pointed questions. But she was intrigued by her new neighbour. What sort of person moved in and then left with their life in such disarray? Not to mention leaving a dependent without a proper care plan. How could they be so confident that Catherine would step in to help?

As Juniper licked the saucer clean, Catherine glanced around the room again, her gaze settling on a grainy photo held to the fridge door with a magnet. In her hurry to feed Juniper, she hadn't noticed it before.

From a rural, Mediterranean-looking vista bathed in hazy sunshine, two smiling faces beamed out. A topless, tanned man with neatly trimmed facial hair and a woman with a large, floppy sun hat. She wore oversized sunglasses, which covered most of her face, but there was something familiar about that red-lipstick smile.

OM-THE-GO

2024

Taste life… one bite at a time.
Let your next meal seduce your senses:
First… inhale deeply. Allow the aroma to linger, to tease, to stir anticipation.
Then… drink in the details. Admire the colours and textures of the sumptuous food before you.
Now… savour. Let the flavours unfold slowly, feel the weight of each bite on your tongue.
Eating mindfully is not restraint.
It is presence. It is connection. It is pleasure.

BETTY77:

Wow. Should I be eating the food or making out with it?

The response had Catherine grinning like an idiot at the screen.

DR.T:

Haha, well, if making out with it helps you enjoy it more, then go for it!

BETTY77:

Your professional advice is that I should snog a sandwich?

Catherine laughed out loud.

DR.T:

No, that's not quite what I was getting at.

BETTY77:

Haha, okay. Well, I must say, this latest blog is a little less Yoda and a little more Nigella.

DR.T:

I think that's a good thing? I mean, physically I'm less like Yoda (green and fuzzy) and more like Nigella (human… though that's where the similarities end).

BETTY77:

I was thinking more in terms of their vibes, actually. You're a perfect blend of both x

DR.T:

Oh. Thank you, I think?!

BETTY77:

Haha, it's a compliment. I'm sure I'm not the only one who's told you that.

DR.T:

You might just be the first.

BETTY77:

Well, in that case… I'll say it again. I think you're both wise and sexy, Catherine.

And one day, I would very much like to take you out for that mindful meal you so beautifully described x

Shit, shit, shit! Catherine snapped the lid of her laptop shut. With those words, it was as if Betty had jumped into the room and was standing before her. It was a reminder that she was talking to a real person out there somewhere — and real people wanted real things.

That conversation had been both exhilarating and terrifying, but a line had been crossed. Catherine was neither wise nor sexy; it was just a good act — easy enough to pull off online.

But the way Betty had used her first name. Yes, it was readily available on the top of the blog page, but she'd never used it in their messages before. It felt very personal, like she was looking into Catherine's eyes and seeing her, really seeing her. And Catherine didn't want to be seen, *did she?*

8

SPELLBOUND

1988

The last two weeks of term slipped by in a wintry blur as an Arctic gale howled across campus, stripping the last brittle leaves from the trees. Through the grey filter of my mood, everything looked dull and desolate.

Rather than confront Francesca about the unreasonable volume of her stereo, I invested in a Walkman from the record store. I buried myself in coursework and did my best to distance myself from Francesca and Jeremy. When I needed to leave my room, I'd put my ear to the wall first to make sure Francesca was out. I ignored the invitations and small taps at my door, or else I called back and declined with excuses about stomach bugs or deadlines. Then, I'd watch from my window as Jeremy and Francesca walked across the square together, arm in arm, pressed in close to one another for warmth. I watched her throwing her head back, laughing at one of his jokes, and how he inclined his head towards hers, their breath misting as one in the cold air.

I thought she liked me.

My imagination ran wild with everything they were doing alone together. Had Francesca kissed Jeremy on the other side of the wall to where I slept and dreamed of her?

I imagined her pushing him back and straddling his lap. Or was it Jeremy who'd taken the lead? I swallowed the lump in my throat as I thought about his rough hands running up her soft thighs. Had she let him touch her where I'd been longing to touch her? I couldn't bear the thought, and, at the same time, I couldn't stop thinking about it. My stomach knotted as I imagined the two of them laughing about how pathetic I was — *a love-struck loser.*

By the last day of term, I'd dodged Francesca for almost a fortnight, yet her presence still invaded my senses. Her pulsing music haunted me. Her fruity scent lingered in the hallway. Sometimes I swore I could feel her heat emanating through the flimsy wall between us; I loathed myself for wanting to press my body against it just to feel closer to her.

Despite the December drizzle, the campus buzzed with end-of-semester excitement. Assignments were in, lectures were finished for the year, and people were getting ready to head home for the Christmas break. The collective mood lifted my spirits. I even surprised myself by smiling at the pucker-faced librarian when I checked out the books I needed to get a head start on next term's reading list.

My smile fell as I stepped outside and Jeremy called my name. *Shit.*

He panted like he'd jogged to catch up to me.

"Hey." I clutched my library books to my chest.

"We haven't seen you for ages…"

We. That tiny word slammed into me, and I redirected my gaze to my boots.

"I've just sorted out our train tickets for tomorrow," he said. "Sorry, it's an early one, we'll need to get going by 9 a.m. Shall we get a taxi to the station, save lugging all our stuff up the hill?"

My mind was still stuck on *We.* I couldn't look at him again, so I just nodded.

"Great. Well, that's that then." Jeremy shuffled his feet. "I'm just heading to the union. It's the end of term, which means half-price Purple until the bar's dry! Why don't you join us?"

Us! I winced. "Sorry, I have to go." With my head down, I charged past him, ignoring the concern in his voice as he called out, "Are you alright, Trusty?"

He followed up with something about Francesca, but thankfully I didn't catch it as I sped away from him.

So, they're officially a 'we' and an 'us'. I already felt foolish enough about my misdirected feelings for Francesca, I didn't need Jeremy seasoning the wound. *Of course it was him she was interested in and not me. Why am I so stupid?*

After the train journey, I could go back to avoiding him again. The sprawling grounds of his family home were easy enough to get lost in. For as long as my dad had worked for the Daltons, he and I had spent quiet, cosy Christmases together in our little cottage, enjoying the ease of each other's company. The only social obligation we had every year was the Daltons' Boxing Day buffet. I imagined this year would be no exception unless I could dream up a good enough excuse.

I'd have a month to get over my silly unrequited crush, *because that's all it had been, hadn't it?* Once I'd had time to recalibrate, I'd smooth things over with Jeremy and we could get back to how we were.

Back in my room, I packed the small stack of books I was bringing home into my rucksack, folded my clothes into a neat pile and pulled my suitcase out from under the bed. Then I sat for a moment, hugging my mum's blanket like it was her. I wasn't very good at confronting my problems. I recalled the way people had tried to get me to talk after my mum had died. But my grief was just that — *mine.* So I swallowed it down. The irony of studying psychology hadn't escaped me — I was figuring out the keys to unlock others, whilst learning how to bolt myself more firmly shut. I imagined speaking to my mum about my feelings for Francesca. I was sure she'd have understood and helped me make sense of it all, but I wasn't ready to come out to the hostile world, at least not for a girl who didn't even want me.

With my suitcase packed, I clicked Play on my Walkman, gathered up my dirty dishes and shuffled to the kitchenette in my bunny slippers. I hummed along to Enya as I plunged my hands into a bowl of soapy water.

A pair of arms wrapped around my waist. I caught the sweet scent of her and froze.

Francesca buried her face in my hair and inhaled.

I swallowed, my throat suddenly dry. "What are you doing?"

"I'm hugging you."

"Why?"

She answered by squeezing tighter. I squirmed around in her arms, hands dripping as I reached for a tea towel.

"Francesca, I don't know what you're playing at, but—"

"Shh!" she said so close to my face I could smell the Purple on her hot breath.

"You're drunk."

"No, you are." She giggled and pressed herself against me, pinning me to the sink. Her lips and tongue were stained deep red. *My God, I want to kiss her.*

"Let me get you some water."

She dropped her arms from my waist and stepped back. "What's your problem?"

"Nothing, I just... I'm just trying to..."

I dried the glass I'd washed and filled it with cold water. She took it from me and gulped a mouthful, all the while glaring at me through makeup-smudged eyes, like the first time I'd met her.

"Why haven't you ever kissed me?"

My chest lurched. "What?"

"You do want to kiss me, right?"

I had to tear my eyes away from the droplets of water glistening on her top lip.

"I... what about Jeremy? Aren't you two dating?"

"Noooooooo." She drew out the word until her lips settled into a cocky grin.

"But..."

"But, what?" she hiccupped. "You've been the one acting all aloof."

"Yeah, because... I thought..." I frowned, staring down at the sticky linoleum as I tried to figure out what I'd thought because now it all seemed so hazy.

What I had seen was Jeremy exiting Francesca's room looking smug and shifty, that was all... and then I'd avoided spending time with the two of them. I really had leapt to something, hadn't I?

With my psychology hat on, I considered that maybe I was looking for an excuse not to deal with my feelings for her. Perhaps believing Francesca was with Jeremy was easier than confronting my sexuality; it was easier than coming out.

When I looked up at her again, her dark eyes were boring into me.

"I... er..." I squeezed the back of my neck and blurted, "I think I'm a lesbian."

Francesca snorted a laugh, and I bowed my head, feeling ridiculous for having said what now seemed so obvious. But then she stepped into my space, her voice a husky whisper as she said, "If you're not going to do it, then I will."

Next thing, her lips were on mine, and her tongue slipped into my mouth in a frantic, hot, wet kiss that tasted of cider and faintly of cigarettes. Neither of those were things I particularly enjoyed, but now I would savour them, because they tasted like her. We backed into the countertop, and I banged my head on a cupboard.

"Shit!" I rubbed the spot, and we erupted into giggles.

A clatter came from down the hallway, followed by a burst of rowdy voices.

Francesca bit her bottom lip. "Shall we go to my room?"

The heat in my already-flushed cheeks intensified, and I gulped, envious of her confidence, but still hungry for more.

"I should, er... finish my dishes."

Francesca tugged the sleeve of my sweatshirt and breathed into my ear. "How about you join me when you're done?" She flashed me a wicked grin. "You should lose the bunnies first, though."

As she drifted away, I glanced down at my pink slippers. *Fuck!* I'd forgotten I was wearing them.

I finished my dishes at the speed of light, uncharacteristically leaving them draining on the board. My body thrummed as I returned to my room to shed my slippers and run a comb through my hair. I exhaled a shaky breath, feeling like nothing more than a jittery bag of nerve-endings. *Is this really happening?*

I knocked before pushing into the room and closing the door softly behind me. Amidst the mess of discarded clothes and dirty cups, Francesca had lit a handful of tea light candles. Soft music played from her stereo — a woman's voice singing a haunting song I hadn't heard before. Francesca lay on her bed with her hands behind her head. She rolled onto her side and patted the space beside her. I swallowed hard as I stepped toward the bed. Her face was the plainest I'd ever seen it; she'd scrubbed the make-up from her eyes and tied her hair back. She looked so unbelievably beautiful I had to stop myself from rubbing my eyes to check she was real.

"You're nervous," she said as I settled next to her.

My stomach flipped. "Yeah, I…"

Francesca reached up and removed my glasses. She tucked some loose strands of hair behind my ear before cupping my jaw and softly steering my face towards hers. "Do you want to kiss me again?"

I didn't trust my voice, so I just nodded dumbly. She crushed her lips to mine, parting them with her tongue. This time she tasted of minty toothpaste, and I couldn't believe we were actually kissing on her bed. Francesca's hand began to roam, at first over, then under my sweat-shirt, her fingers making me gasp as they blazed a trail across my bare skin.

Jeremy came crashing into my thoughts, as well as everything I'd imagined happening on this bed while lying awake on the other side of the wall. I pulled back, breath-less, and Francesca frowned.

"What is it?"

"I… I was thinking about Jeremy."

Her eyebrows knitted together. "Why? You just told me you're a lesbian."

I exhaled a laugh. "No… I mean, yes, I am. It's just that… there's really nothing going on between the two of you, is there?"

Francesca cocked her head and pursed her lips into a tight line.

"I'm sorry for asking, but you've been spending a lot of time with him lately and, if I'm not mistaken, he's keen on you."

She hooked a leg over mine and pulled herself up until she was straddling me. My body ached for her, and I cursed my mind for thinking about Jeremy when the hottest girl on campus was trying to get off with me. But a nagging part of my brain needed to know.

Francesca stared into my eyes with a heart-stopping intensity. "Well, I'm keen on *you*, soooo… I don't want to think about Jeremy, or anything other than this, right now." She dragged a finger over my lips and traced it down to the hollow of my throat. "Perhaps we should put your lesbianism to the test?"

I swallowed. She looked so beautiful in the sway of the candlelight. I arched up to kiss her again, but she pulled back.

"Hold on, it's rather hot in here. Why don't you take this off?" She tugged at my top.

I sat up between her legs and whipped my sweatshirt over my head, revealing nothing but a plain white bra underneath.

"There. That's better." Francesca gave a satisfied smirk and pushed me back onto the pillows. My breath hitched as she traced her tongue down my neck and along my bra strap until she reached the cup. She glanced up at me, her dark eyes full of want. "May I remove this?"

How was she so confident and hot, when I was nothing

but a very un-sexy mess melting beneath her? My jelly-like limbs couldn't comply, but before I knew it, I'd rocked forward so she could uncouple the bra hooks. She cupped my breasts in her hands. I moaned as she flicked her tongue over my nipple and took it into her mouth.

The ache between my legs grew so strong my hips bucked involuntarily beneath her. *Oh God.* Mortification dropped like a ball in my stomach. I felt Francesca's smile spread across my skin.

"Getting impatient for more, are you?" She sat back and unfastened my jeans, pushing her hand past the waistband and into my underwear.

"Francesca, I haven't done this—"

"Shh! Just relax," she said, wriggling her fingers under the thin cotton.

I gasped as she dipped into me.

Of course I'd touched myself there, and over the last few months it had always been while thinking of her. But now here she was, inside me, taking everything I had to give.

I lay mesmerised and panting, her dark eyes urging and curling fingers coaxing, until I crested and came — hot, flustered, and a bit embarrassed that it had happened so fast.

She sat back and licked my wetness from her hand, staring into my eyes as her tongue flicked between her fingers. She settled down next to me, my arm under her head and her arm around my naked midriff.

"Is there anything I can do for you?"

She responded by kissing my cheek and nuzzling into me. "No, but this is nice. Will you stay?"

"Yeah, of course." There was nowhere else I'd rather be. I kissed the top of her head. My nipples stood to attention in the cool December air as I lay grinning at the ceiling, listening to the soft rise and fall of Francesca's sleeping breath.

What felt like only a few hours later, light yawned into the room through the thin curtains. My eyes shuttered open, and my heart thumped at the warmth of Francesca still sleeping next to me in the narrow bed. At some point she'd pulled the duvet up over both of us and turned away from me. In the stark, sober daylight, nerves twisted my stomach as I thought about last night. I didn't regret it; it had been the best thing that had ever happened to me. *But would she regret it?*

Francesca stirred and pulled the duvet over her head. "Keep it down, will you? I can hear you over-thinking from here."

I laughed. "How on earth can you hear me thinking?"

She twisted around to face me. My God, she even looked gorgeous with mussed bed hair. I imagined mine, on the other hand, would look like I'd lost a fight with a gorilla.

"You breathe loudly through your nostrils when you're thinking too hard." Her mouth split into a wicked grin.

"I do not breathe loudly through my nostrils."

"Yes, you do." She reached over and squeezed my nose. Laughter erupted between us, quickly dissipating my worries. Her hand dropped to my bare chest where she traced lazy circles over my nipple.

"What we did last night... have you... done that before?"

Francesca puffed out a small laugh. "Couldn't you tell?"

"Well, yeah... you seemed to know what you were doing."

"Let's just say I know how to make you feel good, and next time you'll know how to make me feel good, or at least you'll have an idea where to start."

I grinned stupidly. "Next time?"

"You're going to have to return the favour, of course." She leaned in and captured my lips. I was self-conscious about my morning breath, but she didn't seem to mind. The faint taste of me lingered on her lips and stirred my arousal again. I dared to let my own hand wander, moving it slowly under her oversized T-shirt, feeling my way over her skin, which was as smooth and soft as I'd imagined it would be. I paused when I reached the curve of her breast.

"May I?" I whispered.

"I insist," she purred. I slid my hand up, gently cupping the fullness of her, and she deepened our kiss. The alarm clock on her bedside table interrupted, chirping until Francesca reached over me and knocked it onto the floor. The alarm wheezed a final chirp as the batteries popped out.

"What time is it?"

"Eight," she said.

"Shit. I need to leave in an hour. I haven't finished

packing, and I should probably take a shower." I jumped up and scrambled for my bra and sweatshirt. "You probably need to pack too." I glanced around at the mess.

Francesca groaned her dissatisfaction and flopped back, sprawling into the space I'd vacated.

"I'm sorry I have to go..." And I truly was. If I had my way, I'd never leave this room. "I promise I'll make it up to you."

She arched an eyebrow. "Oh, you will alright."

Her confidence whipped the fluttering in my stomach into a swarm.

I leaned over to kiss her again, and my smile spread over her lips. "Merry Christmas, Francesca."

"Humbug," she pouted before gripping the back of my head and sliding her tongue into my mouth.

AS THE TRAIN RATTLED OUT OF THE STATION, I wrapped my hands around a polystyrene cup of coffee. My face ached from the grin I'd tried, and failed, to bite back all morning. Avoiding Jeremy's inquisitive gaze from across the table, I focused out the window at the stark frost-ravished landscape rolling past.

"You're looking awfully chipper, Trusty. What's got into you?"

"Francesca, Francesca, Francesca," my mind sang. I tried to temper my smile as I glanced at him. "Just looking forward to getting home and seeing my dad."

"Fair enough. It's always good to get home for the holidays and spend a little time with the folks." Jeremy threaded and unthreaded his fingers on the table. "I do feel awful for Francesca though."

Her name sounded strange on his lips now, like he was saying a word only I understood the meaning of. I really didn't want to share her with him anymore.

"Hmm... how so?"

"The poor thing's spending Christmas on campus. Her mother's away on a Caribbean cruise with her ghastly new husband."

My heart sank. "I... I didn't know." *Why hadn't I asked about her plans?*

"You know what she's like, brave face and all that. She said she didn't care, that she doesn't even like Christmas anyway. But I feel bad, us off having our jollies while she's stuck there all alone." Jeremy's mouth stretched into a grimace. "That's what I tried to talk to you about before you dashed off. I was hoping you'd be able to persuade her to come with us. I'd even asked my folks, and they were fine, delighted in fact. You know, with the idea of me finally bringing a girl home!"

"Yeah, but it's not like *that*, is it?" I blinked rapidly, as if my eyelids had just learned Morse code for 'back the fuck off, Jeremy'.

Colour flushed Jeremy's cheeks. "No, but... maybe. I think there's something between us. I mean, she's not disinterested. And..."

"And, what?"

He glanced around to check no one was listening in,

then leaned forward over the table. "We nearly kissed a couple of weeks ago."

I almost snorted out my coffee. "You what?"

The train rounded a bend, and the carriage rattled over the tracks.

"I popped by one day, but you were out. I knocked on Francesca's door, and she was super stressed about an assignment, so I offered to help. Afterwards, we loafed about, listening to... you know, her music."

I rolled my eyes. "Yes, I know her music. I hear it through the wall most days." I gestured with my hand for him to continue. "So..."

He huffed out a laugh. "Yeah, well. We had a moment."

I narrowed my eyes. "What sort of moment?"

"She rested her head on my shoulder, and so I leaned in."

"Right. And?"

Jeremy frowned and fixed me with a curious gaze. "Why are you suddenly so interested? You all but disappeared on us over the last few weeks."

"Did you kiss or not?"

He huffed and slumped back in his seat. "Not."

I realised I'd been leaning in too. Relief seeped through me as I sat back in the musty seat.

"But it almost happened." He chewed his thumb. "I think she wanted to, but she got shy."

I pressed my tongue to my bruised lip, recalling how it had felt to finally kiss Francesca. She'd been far from shy with me. I took a sip of my now-lukewarm coffee.

"I don't think she's very experienced," continued Jeremy.

This time I spluttered the coffee back into the cup. "And you are?"

"No," he said, flustered, "but I'm the chap, and I'm older, so I should take the lead."

I widened my eyes at him. "Perhaps you should leave those views in the 1950s, where they belong."

Jeremy waved my suggestion away. "You know what I mean."

I focussed on the bare bones of a tree in the distance and cleared my throat. "Maybe you should set your sights on someone else?"

He squinted, scanning my face for the rationale.

Shit, I've said too much.

"You're not jealous, are you, Trusty?"

"What? No!"

He grinned. "You know you'll always be my favourite girl, right?"

"Shut up, you idiot." I laughed despite myself. "I'm not jealous." Not in the way he thought I was, anyway. My mind settled back on Francesca sitting alone in her room, and my chest tightened. "I feel awful that she's on her own. I wish I'd known."

"If it's any consolation, I'm not sure you'd have been able to talk her around. She seemed pretty adamant about staying put."

I swallowed. "I could've tried." My mind conjured the way she'd groaned when I'd left her high and dry, and how

I might have tempted her to come back with us, but I quickly shook that thought away. Now that Francesca and I were on intimate terms, I hated the idea of sharing her with Jeremy, especially on the grounds of *his* family home, where he'd spare no expense trying to impress her.

9

SCHADENFREUDE

PRESENT DAY

Catherine's polished brogues crunched into the gravel as she stepped out of her Boxster. Her eyes trailed up the limestone facade of the exclusive Cotswolds hotel. The wisteria creeping around the doors and windows was starting to bloom, emitting a heady floral scent in the early afternoon air.

Catherine took a deep breath as a sudden swell of anxiety gnawed at her resolve. *Why on earth did I suggest this to Jeremy?*

She smoothed her hands over her white blouse and tugged at the hem of her blazer. She had nipped home after work to get changed, but any effort she'd made was entirely for herself. She enjoyed cutting a smart figure and making a good impression. None of this was for Francesca's benefit. Especially not the liberal spritz of Penhaligon's Halfeti Leather, which Catherine reserved for special occasions. Although seeing Francesca unravelled did feel like a special occasion.

The spiteful part of Catherine's brain twisted her mouth into a half-smirk, which she eyed in the reflection of the hotel's sliding doors before they swished open. *No, this isn't about schadenfreude.* Catherine was here to check in on Francesca's wellbeing. This was a favour to her business partner... *her oldest friend.* And Catherine was a professional, if nothing else. She wasn't here to gloat at Francesca's misfortune; she was here to... *Oh, to hell with it, I might gloat a bit. Penny will be proud.*

For a moment, Catherine thought about texting her flamboyant friend with this latest development, but she'd already caught the eye of the bubbly blonde receptionist, who was smiling and beckoning her towards the desk.

"Hi, I'm here to see Francesca Dalton," Catherine said in the sort of whisper reserved for libraries and funeral homes.

"Sure, let me see." The receptionist tapped away at her keyboard and frowned. "Ah, Mrs Dalton has asked not to be disturbed."

Catherine's fixed smile didn't falter. "Well, I'm her doctor, so..."

"Right, okay. I can pop a call through to her room, if that would be..."

Unblinking, Catherine nodded and looked on as the young woman cradled the phone receiver on her shoulder and dialled.

"Afternoon, Mrs Dalton. I'm ever so sorry to disturb you...

Yes, I realise that, but...

Okay, sure, but she says she's your doctor...

Yes, *she*...

No, sorry, I didn't catch the name..."

The receptionist glanced up at Catherine and then lowered her voice slightly. "Yes, white hair."

"It's platinum," Catherine hissed.

"Okay, yes. I'll send her right up."

CATHERINE TUGGED HER BLAZER AGAIN AND puffed out a breath before tapping the door of room 201. She waited for a response, but none came. She rolled her eyes and knocked again. After a beat, she hunched in closer to the door, her mouth barely an inch away from the wood grain.

"Look, Francesca, I know you're in there. You literally just spoke to the receptionist and told her to send me up, so... are you going to let me in or not?"

She waited for what felt like five minutes — long enough to check three times that she was standing at the right door. As she turned away, the door swung open, as if Francesca had been watching through the peephole all along.

A blast of stale air spilled out of the room. Catherine hadn't been entirely sure what to expect, but she almost gasped at the sight of Francesca. Her normally perfectly styled hair hung lank, her skin looked pallid, and a stained white bathrobe hung limp around her shoulders, making her look smaller than she really was.

"Fine, come in if you have to." Francesca's voice croaked like she'd barely used it for days.

"Francesca, you look—"

"Terrible, I know." Francesca gave her a vacant glare before turning away. "No need to rub it in. Is that why you came here? To gloat at the state of me?"

"No!" Catherine said a bit too quickly, and followed up with a softer, "Of course I'm not here for that. I wanted to see how you were doing. Jeremy has been worried sick about you... and I've been worried about you, too."

Francesca shrugged and shuffled sloth-like back towards the four-poster bed, where, by the looks of it, she'd wallowed for the past few days. Clothes lay strewn from the door to the bed, as if Francesca had shed a skin before slithering into it. Dirty cups cluttered the bedside table, and empty food wrappers fanned around the indent Francesca had left in the sheets.

"Shall I make us a cup of tea?" Catherine asked, grasping at the default British response to any crisis.

"Good luck finding a clean cup." Francesca slumped back onto the bed.

"You know they'll come and clean the room if you let them." Catherine looked around at the mess and shuddered. It looked like Francesca had polished off the contents of the minibar, but there wasn't evidence of much else. "When was the last time you ate?"

"Why do you suddenly care?"

Catherine puckered her lips. "I don't, if I'm honest."

Francesca let out a laugh that sounded like a balloon popping. "I appreciate the honesty."

"But I'm here. And I feel a certain — duty of care, should I say?"

"You know you're not actually my doctor, Trusty?"

"Well, neither is Jeremy, but you still get him to prescribe you sleeping pills, so…"

Francesca opened her mouth, but instead of protesting, she licked her top lip. "Alright, I'll eat. What's on the menu?"

Something flickered in her dark eyes that made Catherine look away.

"Well, why don't you get yourself cleaned up, and—"

"I'm in no fit state to go out!" She threw her arms back and dramatically clutched at the pillows.

Catherine held up her hands. "I wasn't going to suggest that… I just thought it might make you feel better, and while you're at it, I'll order some food and tidy up a little in here."

"Oh, I do like it when you take charge," Francesca growled and sat forward. Her gown fell open ever-so-slightly, revealing that she was wearing nothing underneath.

"I'm not playing games, Francesca. I can just leave, you know?"

"You're no fun anymore," Francesca pouted. "Fine, alright. I'll go take a bath." She stretched up from the bed, like Sleeping Beauty stirring from slumber. Then she made a show of letting the robe drop from her shoulders and dip down her back as she flounced into the bathroom and shut the door behind her.

Although she seemed brighter than when Catherine

had first walked in, Catherine knew better than to trust Francesca's mood; it'd be like trusting an angry ocean not to drown you in a storm — everything could change in an instant.

Over the sound of running water, Francesca called out, "Do you want me to sing whilst I'm in here, so you know I haven't topped myself?"

"No. If you do that, I might top *myself.*"

Francesca responded with a hearty laugh, and Catherine hated that the sound still caused a swell of affection inside her. She opened the window to let in some fresh air and busied herself folding Francesca's discarded clothes, gathering the wrappers and tissues into the bin before collecting up the dirty cups and glasses and popping them outside the door for housekeeping to ferry away. Finally, she straightened the bedsheets, smoothing out Francesca's indent, like she'd once done with her life. *Christ, why am I dredging that up now? It's been decades.*

Catherine swept a satisfied glance around the tidied room before calling through the bathroom door, "Are you alright in there?"

No answer came, so she tapped loudly on the door. "Francesca?"

There was another long pause before a loud splash of water, followed by a dramatic gasp.

"Is everything okay in there?"

"Come in and see for yourself, if you like."

"No, I'm quite alright, thank you."

Catherine reclined in the small lounge area and returned to frowning at an unfinished Sudoku puzzle on her phone. At the sound of the bathtub draining, she called an order through to room service — a chicken club sandwich, a side of house fries and a large pot of tea. She'd have a cup, make sure Francesca ate something and then excuse herself. No reason to prolong *whatever this was*.

Steamy, fragrant air gushed from the bathroom, and Francesca came out dressed in a clean white robe. Catherine struggled to tear her eyes from the alluring stretch of Francesca's swan-like neck, exposed as she towel-dried her wet hair.

She swallowed and forced her eyes back to her phone. "Feel better?"

"Mmm, yes. As much as it pains me to say it, you were right."

"I've ordered some room service. It'll be here soon."

"Good, I'm starving. You were right about that, too."

Catherine bit back a grin, which faded as Francesca threw her wet towel on the bed. She reclined at the opposite end of the sofa, her arms spread wide and draped over the edges.

Catherine tried her best not to psychoanalyse the woman in front of her, but it was hard not to — Francesca was a fascinating subject, after all. Catherine had wondered if that was what had kept Jeremy so rapt all these years. The irony hadn't escaped her that they, two qualified medical psychotherapists, had once both fallen for someone they should have actually been studying.

Francesca's lips twisted into a grin. "You're looking at me and frowning. What?"

"Sorry, I was thinking about... Jeremy."

Francesca rolled her eyes. "Of course you were."

"Well, one of us should."

"What are you implying? I love my husband dearly."

"Let's be real, Francesca; you love his wallet."

"It's his finest feature."

"You're unbelievable."

"You're uptight."

Catherine sniffed, ending their ridiculous rally.

Francesca smirked as if she'd won. Over thirty years had passed, and she still knew how to get a rise out of Catherine. *Why am I here?* Catherine uncrossed her legs and clapped her hands to her thighs. "Right, well, your food will be here soon, so…"

As Catherine rose from the sofa, Francesca's smirk fell away, and a deep line appeared between her eyebrows. "You're leaving?"

"I came to check that you're okay, and…" she waved a hand in Francesca's direction. "You're obviously fine, so there's no reason for me to stick around."

Francesca sat up, an emotion registering on her face which, if Catherine didn't know better, could have been mistaken for vulnerability. Her voice came out small, and almost unrecognisable. "Don't go."

"I don't see how my being here is helping you. I came to see if you wanted to talk and whether there was anything I could do to help, but it was clearly a fool's errand."

Francesca's shoulders hunched. "I have this constant pain, right here." She pressed her hand to her breastbone and rubbed it in a way that made her look fragile, like a tiny bird fallen from a nest.

Despite everything she thought she'd feel seeing Francesca like this, Catherine felt the urge to hold her. She shook that thought away and tried to focus. "What sort of pain?"

"It hurts to breathe sometimes."

Catherine moved closer, peering into her face as if it might help make sense of the symptoms. "Does it hurt to breathe now?"

Francesca nodded. "You're not going to make me do those silly breathing exercises from your little blog, are you?"

"Well, that might... wait, you read my blog?"

Ignoring the question, Francesca continued to knead a clenched fist into her chest. "There's a constant ache right here... and I want to cry all the time. I've never been a weeper, but I can't help myself lately; the tears keep coming."

"And did these... *symptoms* start when things ended with Alice?"

Francesca drew another ragged breath and nodded. "Jeremy took me to the hospital before I asked him to bring me here. They hooked me up, did some tests, but everything came back normal. The pain hasn't gone away, though."

Catherine sat back and crossed her legs. "The problem isn't in your chest," she said with quiet confidence.

A long time ago she'd worked out that Francesca had all the hallmark traits of a personality disorder. After some back and forth, she'd settled on psychopathy. Francesca's constellation of behavioural traits seemed like a textbook case — with enough charm to snap a snake into a coma, she sparkled like a rare gem when she was the centre of attention, but she was also alarmingly manipulative, entirely self-absorbed, and prioritised her own needs above all else.

But, no, she could see it now. Catherine chuckled lightly and picked a piece of fluff from her trousers.

"What?" Francesca twisted around, her anguished look from before replaced by a narrowed gaze. "What are you laughing at?"

After all these years, Catherine realised she'd got it wrong. Unlike someone with purely psychopathic tendencies, Francesca was capable of forming genuine emotional attachments. And the keen sting of rejection would always bite hardest for a narcissist.

"I think you're suffering from a broken heart."

Francesca blanched. "Don't be ridiculous."

"You were in love, but it was unrequited. You've had your heart broken."

"It wasn't unrequited. Alice loves me. She needs me, but I wasn't prepared to give my lifestyle up. I thought she'd see sense and compromise, but no—"

"Did you ever compromise for her?" Catherine asked, but already knew the answer from her own experience.

"I was willing to look past all the silliness and carry on as we were. That's a compromise."

Catherine threw up her hands. "You need help; real psychological help."

Francesca sniffed. "I'm married to a therapist, the last thing I need is help."

"Jeremy is blind to how you are. You're capable of causing real hurt, Francesca. You hurt Alice, don't you see that?"

"I offered her things she could never afford. She hurt me when she threw it all back in my face."

Catherine laughed and shook her head. "Oh, Francesca, not everyone has a price tag."

"Don't you *'Oh Francesca'* me, like you're some authority on matters of the heart," she snarled, her chest pain seemingly forgotten. "You're a shrivelled old spinster, consumed with jealousy."

Catherine threw her head back as genuine laughter bubbled up from inside her.

Francesca's eyes bulged. "What are you laughing at now?"

A tap at the door interrupted. Swiping a tear of laughter from her eye, Catherine stood to let in the room service. A young porter set out the dishes on the low table and Catherine closed the door behind him. When she turned back to Francesca, she sat staring at the plates like she didn't know what to do next.

"Are you going to eat?" Catherine asked.

"Will you have some too?"

Catherine laughed again. "You just called me a shrivelled old spinster, so I'm not about to sit down to dinner with you."

Francesca waved a hand between them. "You know I say things sometimes in the heat of the moment. Please.

Sit with me a while longer." She shuffled forward, picked up a chip and blew on it before popping it in her mouth. "Look, there's plenty for us both. We'll call a truce over chips."

Catherine flicked her wrist to look at her watch. "Okay, I'll stay a while longer, but then I have to get back to feed the cat."

Francesca arched an eyebrow. "That's not exactly challenging the shrivelled spinster stereotype, you know?"

"It's my neighbour's cat. I seem to have a way of getting myself into these... situations." Catherine retook her seat and poured herself a cup of tea from the pot as Francesca took bird-like pecks from the club sandwich.

"It's the first time I haven't been hit by waves of nausea," she said between mouthfuls of fries.

"Waves of Nausea," Catherine mused. "Sounds like it could be an Enya album."

Francesca laughed; a proper laugh that split her mouth wide open and creased the corners of her eyes in a way she'd hate because she'd given too much away. But it made her look so human, so stunningly flawed.

"You know, I thought you were joking the first time you said you liked Enya. There was me with my cool gothic post-punk rock, and you obsessed with a middle-aged Irish woman and her grandma music."

Catherine's mouth gaped in mock-outrage. "Enya wasn't middle-aged in 1988."

"Yeah, but *you* might as well have been."

They both laughed, and something shifted between them. For the first time in a very long time, Francesca's company didn't feel discordant. Here they were, getting along. Laughing together like old friends with a shared history and in-jokes.

When the light of day drained away outside, Catherine got up to leave, but for some reason, she paused to see Francesca into bed. And for some reason, Francesca let her.

Francesca's eyelids drooped, and Catherine brushed away her still-damp hair and kissed her forehead. As she quietly made her way to the door, Francesca's sleepy voice croaked behind her, "Trusty?"

Catherine spun back around, softened by the sight of the small woman swallowed up in that big bed. "Hmm?"

"Thank you," she murmured.

ALL THE PIECES

*C*atherine leaned against her front door, letting it click to a close behind her. She breathed in the familiar scent of her apartment, grounding herself in the enveloping stillness.

A laugh bubbled up from somewhere inside her. Her amusement stemmed not so much from seeing Francesca so completely unravelled — the schadenfreude had been far less thrilling than she'd imagined — more at the unexpected sense of resolution she'd walked away with. A lightness washed over her, as if she'd been unburdened of a weight she hadn't realised she'd been carrying.

It wasn't as if Catherine had spent the last three decades consumed by Francesca and the scars of their past, but like Penny had said, something had been holding her back. All along Francesca had been lurking in the back of her mind, like a puzzle she'd never quite managed to solve. But Catherine felt like she'd lifted the veil — *Narcissistic Personality Disorder.*

For the first time, Catherine had witnessed the other woman having a genuine emotional response to something. Catherine wasn't a sadist — seeing Francesca wounded was far from pleasurable, but seeing Francesca for who she really was vindicated her own heartache.

Francesca wasn't a psychopath, after all — incapable of love and merely emulating emotion for her own gain. She was a narcissist, craving validation to inflate her fragile sense of self-worth, and now her supply had run dry, she lay in a crumpled heap like a withdrawing addict.

Catherine heeled off her brogues and bent to tuck them into the shoe rack. She padded through to the kitchen, reached for a crystal tumbler from the cupboard and poured herself a double measure of Balvenie; the eighteen-year-old she reserved for special occasions. Neat — no ice, just the way Bridie had taught her to appreciate it.

She leaned back against the countertop and swirled the leggy liquid around before raising the glass in a toast — to herself for decoding the enigma of Francesca? Or to Francesca for being cracked open enough that Catherine had finally glimpsed all the pieces? Or was it a toast to her younger self because she hadn't bled in vain?

Maybe all three. Catherine tipped her head before bringing the amber liquid to her lips. As the warm rush of alcohol hit her chest, her fingers twitched, restless with unspent energy. She moved through to the lounge, flicked on the table lamp, and set her drink on a coaster.

From under the sofa, Catherine pulled out a puzzle mat. She unfastened the Velcro straps, rolled it out and smoothed it down on the coffee table. She settled on a cushion on the floor, back against the plush sofa and legs stretched out under the table. The half-finished puzzle was a tricky thousand-piecer; a fresco of Sappho holding a stylus and tablet — or at least it was a high-society Greek woman commonly alleged to be her. It had been an ironic Christmas gift from Penny, who found it hilarious that Catherine enjoyed jigsaw puzzles. But Catherine refused to be embarrassed by her hobby, no matter how much her friend teased. She'd always found calm in the ordering of chaos — that satisfying click when an elusive piece slotted into place.

Catherine sipped her drink and rifled through the box. She picked up a piece with three blanks and a tab that looked like it was the curve of a cheekbone or the crook of a finger. She popped it into the 'Sappho pile' and spotted a section of the background, part of a loop from a swirling mosaic pattern. With satisfying ease, she pushed it into place, finally anchoring two sections together. As she rewarded herself with a warming sip of Scotch, a dull thud sounded from above. Catherine glanced up, her eyes widening with realisation. *Shit.*

With a sigh, she drained the dregs from her glass before stretching up from her spot on the floor. She slipped on her mules and put her door on the latch. At the top of the stairs, she retrieved the key from under the doormat and entered the flat. The streetlight outside dimly lit the hallway, casting eerie long shadows from the boxes and her new neighbour's scattered belongings. Unlike the shy cat who'd greeted her the day before, Juniper pounced over and threw himself at Catherine's feet, stretching and rolling around, exposing his furry belly. Catherine bent to pat him and he arched up, pushing his soft head into her hand.

Something inside her lit up — all this time she'd seen cats as arrogant and aloof; she'd never witnessed a display of affection like this. And yes, she realised it was probably because she could open the fridge... but even so.

Juniper chirped, and with his tail held high, the end of it beckoning like a curled finger, he sauntered down the hallway. Catherine followed him into the kitchen and set about getting his dinner as he wove his lithe body around her ankles, in what she supposed was some sort of ritualistic food dance. Catherine read the label of the can she'd pulled from the fridge.

"Shredded chicken tonight; does that sound good?"

He chirruped, which Catherine took as a yes.

Whilst Juniper devoured his food, Catherine returned to the photograph on the fridge, wondering which of the two smiling faces was Juniper's *neglectful* owner, if indeed it was either of them. Perhaps it was both?

Catherine's eyes drifted back to the woman's smile. She squinted, again struck by the familiarity of that grin. If only the photo were a little clearer. She glanced down at Juniper. "You don't mind if I have a little look around, do you?"

Juniper chirped but remained engrossed in his food, which Catherine took as authorisation to go ahead. Perhaps the Scotch had emboldened her, but her curiosity about her new neighbour (*plural?*) suddenly had her flicking on lights as she moved into the lounge. The Scotch must have numbed her senses too, because the mess wasn't spiking her anxiety the way it had before.

A small stack of postcards sat at the top of one of the open boxes. Catherine shuffled through them.

New York City. *The Village isn't the same without you. Miss you, babe. Will x*

Buenos Aires. *This fucking place! Why aren't you here when I need you? Depressed without you. Will x*

Dublin. *Hey, slut bag! Miss you so much. Big sloppy kisses, Will x*

Lisbon. *It's three months until we get married. I CAN'T WAIT!! Love you, Will x*

The date stamp on the Lisbon postcard was from last year. *Ah, so the smiley pair on the fridge are a couple.* The photograph was probably from their honeymoon.

Great. Just what Catherine needed; newlyweds with their bedroom stacked right over hers. And this Will character sounded like a treat. *I mean, who calls their fiancée a slut bag?...* on a postcard of all places, for anyone to read. Catherine tutted and went to toss the cards back into the box, but an envelope caught her eye, specifically the name peeking through the plastic window — Ms. J. McPherson... *McPherson?*

Bridie's last name was McPherson. *What was her daughter's name again?* Catherine tried to cast her mind back to their many late-night chats, from most of which she'd staggered down the stairs after Bridie's liberal pours of Scotch.

"Christ!" Catherine started as Juniper nudged at her ankles again, demanding attention.

"I really don't like cats, you know?" She reached down to fuss him and he leaned in as she ruffled her fingers through his soft fur. "You can schmooze me all you like, but I won't change my mind about you." He purred as she rubbed his chest and chin.

She really should get back to her jigsaw and think about microwaving something for dinner, but she didn't feel hungry yet and Juniper seemed to be enjoying her company. Almost as if she were looking for an excuse to stay longer, Catherine's gaze landed on the abandoned flat-pack construction project taking up the middle of the room.

What's flatpack furniture if not a giant jigsaw puzzle?

Catherine unbuttoned her shirt sleeves and rolled them up to just above the elbows. She picked up the screwed-up instruction manual, smoothed it onto the coffee table and regarded it for a moment. But the empty wine bottle and dirty glass kept looking at her, as did Juniper, from the tower of boxes he'd climbed onto.

"How am I supposed to work in these conditions?" she asked him.

Juniper slowly blinked.

After ferrying the offending articles into the kitchen, she returned with a tall glass of water, took a sip, and perched on the sofa to give the instructions a thorough read. It was always harder starting a project partway through. She'd experienced it from time to time with Jeremy, when she'd taken on a patient of his; she felt off-kilter because she hadn't done the groundwork herself. But as on those occasions, she took the time to assess and order the parts, putting all the pieces into neat piles for ease and efficiency.

When she'd gathered up the scattered screws from the floor, everything was accounted for, except a packet of dowels. She emptied the remaining big parts from the box and stacked them in order, then she turned the box upside down, and a small packet tumbled out.

"Ah-ha!"

Juniper hopped down from his perch to investigate and then leapt into the empty box in one lithe jump. Catherine laughed and teased him with one of the cardboard straps. He snatched at it with his claws and pulled it into his mouth when he caught it.

"Stop distracting me," she said through a grin, and turned back to studying the instructions.

Time slipped by as she absorbed herself in the task, stopping only to refill her water glass or to shoo Juniper away when he tried to bat the fixings off the coffee table.

It had gone midnight when, with a satisfied sigh, Catherine clicked the final shelf into place and rubbed her hand along the smooth woodgrain as if she'd cut and sanded it herself.

"Et voilà!"

With wide eyes, Juniper stared up at the finished construction standing proud in the centre of the room.

"What do you think?"

Juniper answered by rearing back and launching himself onto the highest shelf.

DESPITE HER LATE-NIGHT FURNITURE-BUILDING exertions, and the Francesca Dalton-related breakthrough, Catherine did not sleep well. Too hot, she kicked off the duvet, but then too cold, she groped for it, pulling it around herself, only to be prickling with sweat moments later. In her more lucid wakeful moments, thoughts raced through her mind, and even with all her techniques, she ended up giving over valuable sleeping time indulging them.

Should she try to talk to Jeremy about her discreet diagnosis of Francesca? Maybe he could get her some help. *Maybe it's none of your business, and you should leave well enough alone.* She'd got what she needed from it, right? Closure, of sorts.

But just when she'd settled that, she had a sudden rush of regret concerning her evening's activities. Would her new neighbours think it weird that she'd taken the liberty of constructing their flatpack furniture when she was only meant to be feeding the cat?

Oh God. It was weird. She stared into the swirling blackness, as waves of mortification washed over her. Should she go back up there now and take the bookcase apart before they returned?

No, that'd be even weirder. Leave it and claim it's a neighbourly gesture — a moving-in gift, a wedding present?

Ugh... she may as well get used to having no sleep with newlyweds moving in above her. Maybe that's what all the banging was the other night? They were having weird Spice Girls sex right above her head. *But what sort of people have sex to the Spice Girls?*

Perhaps she should offer them some therapy on top of the flatpack construction.

A dull thud came from above — *Juniper*. She didn't like cats, but she could make an exception for one. *Maybe.*

Next thing she knew, she was chasing Francesca with a chicken club sandwich. Francesca sprinted away, somehow faster than Catherine even in preposterous heels and a sequinned cocktail dress, but still she followed until they reached a tall bookcase. Francesca turned and laughed at her before scaling the furniture like a sparkly spider-woman, climbing up and up as Catherine watched helplessly from below. "Wait!" She reached her arms up, but Francesca lashed out and clawed at her skin until Catherine fell and jolted awake in her bed.

It didn't take a psychotherapist to work that one out.

Catherine's eyes strained against the bright sunlight pouring into the room. She'd been so exhausted she'd forgotten to draw the curtains before flopping into bed, then failed to notice they were still open during the night. Resisting the urge to let the residual fug of a fitful sleep weigh her down in the bed any longer, she rose and stretched her neck from side to side. Her shoulders were surprisingly achy, probably thanks to her shelf-building efforts.

Perhaps she would see whether Penny fancied a wild swim; it'd been a while, and the weather was clement, at least according to her app. Penny would be up for it if Loz was still out of town; perhaps they could make an afternoon of it — an early pub dinner.

With the seed of a weekend plan sown in her mind,

Catherine got dressed to head out for her morning walk. Pulling her front door to a close, she stepped to the building's main door and stopped in her tracks — it was open. Not wide open but unlatched and slightly ajar. She could have sworn she'd locked it last night. Apparently not; she had been a little distracted after all the Francesca *fun*.

Stepping outside, she pulled the door firmly closed behind her, giving it a little shoulder budge just to make sure the latch wasn't on the fritz. She squinted against the sun and turned her collar up against the wind, still sharp with the receding bite of winter.

She strode amongst the early-morning joggers and dog walkers — a brisk canter around Jephson Gardens, with its glorious blooms battling against the bluster. On her route home, she intentionally detoured to Snoots, smoothing her hands through her wind-ruffled hair as she stepped inside to the buttery aroma of freshly baked pastries and the hiss of the espresso machine.

She joined the queue of customers and glanced up at the hand-written chalk board, even though she knew her order by heart — a tall oat milk latte and a croissant. Shuffling forward with the queue, she pulled out her phone to text Penny about weekend plans, but a voice grabbed her attention — that soft Scottish lilt. Catherine lifted her head, peering around the shoulders of the tall man in front of her.

There she was — the redhead in the red coat, ordering a double espresso to go.

Catherine's fingers were back in her own hair again, feathering the strands this way and that, wishing she'd thought to wear a clean shirt and brush on a little mascara before leaving the house. But she always returned home to get ready for her day after her walk, so why would she have thought to do it before?

Her mind scrambled to find something to say, but would the woman even remember her from the other day at El Vino's? The room seemed to brighten as the redhead turned from the counter, tiny cup and scrunched paper bag in hand. She was even more striking than Catherine remembered her — all hazel eyes and cheekbones. She squeezed past the queue, and before she could stop herself, Catherine reached out and touched her arm. The woman looked startled until her eyes settled on Catherine and softened with recognition.

"Oh, hi." The woman's painted lips quirked into a smile, but something else flickered across her face. Catherine was good at reading people — *she was trained to read people* — but she struggled to read whatever that was.

"It's me... from the restaurant." Catherine pointed at herself. "Frowny face."

"I'm pleased to see you don't look so frowny now."

Catherine realised she was smiling a bit too hard. "No, I'm, er... much less frowny today." *Christ, Catherine, say something else. Anything else...*

The woman raised her eyebrows, her lips twitching with a grin.

"Oh, er... thanks for the recommendation, by the way, the er, Pan..."

"Pan Tumaca?"

"Yes, it was delicious. Thank you."

"Good. You're welcome." The woman took a breath as if she were about to say something else, but she just smiled instead.

"Next, who's next?" the barista called out, an edge of impatience in his voice, because it was obviously Catherine, and she was obviously holding up the queue.

Catherine looked at him and put her hand up. "It's me, sorry." When she turned back, the woman was already a blur of red heading out the door. *Damn.*

OM-THE-GO

2024

"Trusty! Is that a hangover you're nursing?" Jeremy's voice boomed into her office.

Catherine winced and lifted her head from her hands.

Jeremy grimaced. "Christ, you look a fright."

"I'm fine," she croaked. "What do you want, Jer?"

"Er, I was just going to ask whether you'd mind popping another blog up soon. We'd been going great guns, but traffic has really dipped these past couple of weeks. Colin suggested it might be because—"

Catherine scrubbed her hands over her face. "Sorry, I haven't been in the mood lately." Her voice cracked, and she swallowed. "I'll try to post something later."

After Betty's kind-but-creepy words, Catherine had decided to leave it a while before posting another blog. She'd only meant to dip her toe in those waters, but she'd waded too far out of her comfort zone. After the last message, Betty hadn't sent any follow-ups, which was fine because surely meeting an internet stranger would be ill-advised, regardless of how tantalising the conversation was. The online flirtations with Betty had, however, piqued Catherine's interest in dating again. She'd even mentioned it to Bridie, who'd clucked out kind words of encouragement.

Jeremy's face crumpled with concern. "You really don't look so good. Are you unwell?" He stepped closer and squeezed her shoulder.

"My neighbour died," she blurted, as if the weight of his hot palm had lanced out the words. "We were friends." Catherine swallowed around the lump in her throat. "And now she's gone, and I feel so…"

"God, Trusty. I'm so sorry. That's awful. Do you want to talk it through properly? I'll ask Alice to make us some tea, and we'll shut the door."

Catherine glanced at her watch, the numbers blurring slightly. "I've got a client in ten, so…"

"Let me get Alice to cancel; you're in no fit state. You should—"

"Thank you, but no. I'm okay. I'll be okay." She raised her hands. "Work will take my mind off it," she said, not really knowing how she was meant to help other people get through their difficult times while she was wading through the thick of her own.

"Are you sure?" He sucked in a breath and bobbed his open palms as if weighing the air. "It's one of the perks of having a practice partner, isn't it? Free therapy when you need it."

Catherine forced a smile. "I'll get another blog post up soon."

"No rush. Whenever you feel up to it." He turned to leave, but glanced back. "You know where I am, okay?"

CRADLING A STEAMING CUP OF CHAMOMILE, Catherine settled into bed with her laptop propped on a pillow. She hadn't set out to write about grief; it wasn't the obvious choice of topic to cover for a mindfulness blog, but whilst staring at the flashing cursor on the blank screen, that's what came to her in a tidal wave of sorrow demanding expression.

She'd been touched by Jeremy's offer to talk, but the last thing she wanted was to unravel in front of him. Penny had checked in and offered to come over, but Catherine craved the soft solitude of her bed cocoon. She needed quiet time to find the right words to soothe and rationalise the raw emotions that had chafed inside her ever since the nurse said, "I'm so sorry — she's gone."

Catherine spent hours crafting the blog post, taking so much care over so few words, she scrutinised each one until they blurred and danced around her screen. With a deep sigh, she hit the 'publish' button, snapped her laptop shut, and slid down between her soft sheets, letting the darkness fold over her.

**Grief arrives quietly, but reshapes everything.
You don't need to silence it — only to meet it,
moment by moment.**

First... breathe. Let the ache rise and fall with your breath.
Exhale the sorrow.

Then... notice. A memory, a trace, a presence that still
glows in the quiet corners of your heart.

And finally... hold onto small comforts, however fragile —
a nickname they had for you, a recipe they taught you, an
old jumper they wore. These things endure beyond
absence.

**Loss is a weight to be carried with patience,
reverence, and the quiet knowledge that love doesn't
die.**

THE FOLLOWING MORNING, SUNLIGHT STREAMED
through the gap in the curtains, painting a stripe across
her duvet. She woke to the biggest response she'd ever had
to a blog so far. Notifications flooded her inbox — likes
and comments from names she'd never seen before,
strangers offering condolences and sharing their own
experiences of loss.

And Betty.

Catherine's heart stuttered.

BETTY77:

Hey. I saw your latest blog. Beautiful
words, thank you for sharing x

P.S. I hope you're okay. x

DR.T:

Hi. It's been a tough few days. I lost someone I really cared about. It's always difficult to say goodbye, isn't it? Thanks for reaching out x

BETTY77:

I'm so sorry. Be gentle with yourself x

Catherine drew a shuddering breath and pushed back the covers. *Enough moping.* What better way to shake the sadness from her bones than a walk?

11

GLASSHOUSE

PRESENT DAY

A headache blistered behind Catherine's eyes. She flicked off the computer monitor, unable to stand the glare any longer. With its muted green walls and warm lighting, her office wasn't an unpleasant space, but she'd been in the room so long the walls felt as though they were pressing in. A light breeze flapped through the vertical blinds, which clattered against the window ledge, beckoning her toward the bright afternoon beyond the sash frame.

Fortunately, all her appointments were done for the day, but there were some fairly urgent case notes to type up, a diagnostic summary to send over to the university hospital, and a progress report to submit to a client's insurance company. These were all tasks the very capable Alice would've handled before things had gone tits-up. Thanks to the Daltons, now she only had Stephanie, who was about as much use as a saddle on a snail, so Catherine would have to do it all herself.

She removed her reading glasses and cradled her pounding head in her hands for a moment, but before slipping into another negative thought pattern, she drew a decisive breath — sometimes she just needed to swallow her own advice... *fresh air and a change of scenery.*

Later, she'd pour a glass of something nice, pop dinner in the oven and power on through, but first she needed to get past the blinding pain behind her eyes. Scooping up her satchel with her laptop stowed safely inside, Catherine set out.

"I'm off for the day. See you tomorrow."

Stephanie grunted an acknowledgement, but barely lifted her head, which prompted Catherine to take a mental note of another task: hire a new PA. *Preferably someone with all Alice's skills but none of her looks. At least that way the Daltons won't get any more funny ideas.*

Catherine shivered against the unexpected chill — the sunlight promising summer was being undermined by a breeze that still whispered winter. *Damn,* she'd left her jacket hanging in her office. Not wanting to turn back, she buried her hands in the warm comfort of her pockets and strode towards the park. Avoiding the high street, she took her favoured route past the row of Regency townhouses, their gleaming facades striking against the backdrop of blue sky.

Pink blossom from the cherry trees flanking the park's main avenue drifted in the air like confetti. Catherine passed the fountains and the Jephson Memorial, then found herself gravitating towards the Glasshouse. She'd only been inside a handful of times as it was closed during her early morning walks and too busy at the weekends. But now, it stood quiet, like a giant glass lung holding its breath.

Inside, the fragrant air wrapped her in a warm hug, and the door swooshed closed behind her, trapping in the humidity. She wandered over the bridge and stopped to admire a greedy ficus, which had tried to swallow its surroundings by growing up and around the railings. Calm washed over her amid the vibrant green ferns and tropical plants, a few of which she could name without looking at the plaques — orchids, birds of paradise, pink powder puffs, *and is that a banana tree?*

Then, in the corner of her eye, a flash of red.

Red coat, red hair. *It's her.* She sat on a bench over-looking a slate rockery packed with flowering cacti. Catherine's stomach swooped.

Seriously? Get a grip! Her self-flagellation must have spilled into sound, disturbing the other woman's peace as she turned around. For a second, Catherine wanted the greedy ficus to swallow her too, but that feeling evaporated when the woman's lips lifted into a smile, and she waved.

"Hello, again. Are you following me or something?" Laughter laced her lovely voice.

Catherine shook her head as she walked towards her. "You keep turning up everywhere I am lately."

"Well, I've recently moved here, so..."

"In that case, welcome to Leamington. It's a beautiful spot."

"So far, so good." The woman's eyes smiled as well as her lips.

Catherine swallowed. "It seems you've found all my favourite haunts at least."

"Do you come here often?" The woman released a short laugh, as if realising how that sounded. "It's lovely here. I mean, in the Glasshouse."

Catherine grinned. "No, I don't usually come in." She motioned her arm in an arc around them. "But I do spend a lot of time in the park. I live close by, so…"

The moment stretched between them. There was something known within the hazel eyes of that unknown face. Catherine couldn't shake the feeling they'd met before. She realised she was staring and broke eye contact, which seemed to snap the woman out of her own spell too.

"God, I'm sorry. Would you like to sit down? Here, let me…" She moved her handbag to make space on the bench beside her.

"Oh, are you sure? I'm not disturbing your peace, am I?"

"No, not at all. I just came in out of the cold for a bit. It's bloody Baltic out there."

Catherine laughed. "Granted there's a chill, but it's hardly Baltic!"

"It is when you've moved here from warmer climes."

"Scotland?" Catherine teased.

The woman shot her a withering look, but her lips battled to pinch back a smile. "Barcelona."

"Wow! That's quite the move. I can see why you're more comfortable in here." Catherine chuckled. "So, why the big move to the Baltics then?"

She shrugged. "It's a fresh start, I suppose. A new job

opportunity came up, and a place to live, so it seemed the universe was pulling me back to the UK after all this time."

Catherine surprised herself by asking another question, reservations overcome by the desire to dive deeper into this stranger whose name she didn't even know yet. "What do you do?"

"I'm a flight attendant, at least for a few more days, anyway. I've got a couple of shifts to cover, but after that I'll be making the switch to ground staff."

Catherine pictured her up in the sky, all red curls and lipstick as she swooped down the aisle flashing her bright smile at passengers. "How very glamorous."

"No, really, it isn't. The hours are shite, the jet lag is brutal, and don't get me started on passengers who press the call button for a bag of nuts during takeoff!"

"Right, I hadn't really considered any of that."

"Don't get me wrong. I've loved it, and it's taken me places I never thought I'd go. But I'm beyond done with my life being measured in landings and layovers, drifting from one soulless hotel room to the next. I think it's all caught up with me. I'm not getting any younger."

"That's a universal truth." Catherine puffed her cheeks out before letting loose a laugh. "Good on you for figuring out what you want and going for it. It's not always easy to see the path ahead, let alone find the courage to follow it."

"You sound like a therapist."

Catherine cocked her head.

"Ach, you are!" The woman bit her bottom lip. "I can see why; you're very easy to talk to when you're not frowning."

"Ha! People pay me good money to listen, frown or no frown."

"But this was free, right?" She traced a finger through the air between them.

"I don't make a habit of charging for unsolicited conversations, particularly if I'm the one gatecrashing someone else's peaceful moment."

The distant sound of laughter pulled the woman's attention. She glanced at her watch and jumped up.

"Sorry, I have to dash. It was really lovely chatting to you—"

Catherine stood. "Yes, lovely to meet you again."

"Likewise," she said, before focusing on something above Catherine's head. Catherine looked up but saw nothing aside from the vaulted glass ceiling.

"What is it?"

"You have a little..." She plucked a pink petal from Catherine's hair and held it out on her fingertip.

"Oh!" Catherine took the petal. "Thank you."

A smile rose on the woman's lips. "I'll see you around, then?"

"I hope so."

She turned, her red coat swishing like a brushstroke sweeping off a canvas before she disappeared. Catherine stared after her, the petal still perched on her finger.

I didn't ask her name.

AFTER THE PINK PETAL ENCOUNTER WITH THE LADY in red, Catherine practically floated home. She swung by Snoots to treat herself to a coffee and mid-afternoon snack — a little incentive to help her power through her to-do list.

Coffee cup balanced and paper bag clenched between her teeth, she felt around for her keys in her pocket. As she moved to slot the key in the lock, she found the door already open.

What the—

She took a tentative step into the entrance hall, peering around the door for an intruder. It was a small space with nowhere to go, other than her apartment off to the right, the shared storage and meter box cupboard under the stairs to the left, or straight up the stairs to the apartment above. Catherine tiptoed in, quietly placed her coffee on the radiator shelf and grabbed an umbrella from the stand. She gripped the newel post and craned her neck, squinting into the shadows.

There's no one up there.

She stepped towards the cupboard. Perhaps a homeless person was living under the stairs, jimmying the lock to get in and out as they pleased, poor soul. Eyes wide and alert, she tensed and reached for the door, but it was latched from the outside. She clicked it open anyway, umbrella at the ready, but the only things living in the cupboard had eight legs and she wasn't about to argue with them.

She turned back to check her own front door — definitely locked. *I must be losing it,* she thought — but she distinctly remembered double-checking the main door when she'd left that morning. She shook her head as she replaced the umbrella in the stand and grabbed her coffee and croissant from the shelf. Her heart lurched when she spotted something on her doormat — a white envelope, pushed under the door. Innocuous enough, but evidence that her marbles were not yet lost. She scooped it up, closed the door behind her and strode through to the kitchen.

Catherine placed the envelope on the counter and stared at it while she sipped her coffee, her brain working overtime. Someone had been inside the shared hallway even though she'd locked — and checked — the door. Someone had placed an envelope under her door. And that someone knew her name. She traced her finger over the sloping letters in blue biro. Should she open it? Should she take it to the police? What would she say? *Someone has broken into my home — with no sign of forced entry — and left me a note.* Ridiculous.

Curiosity wrestled her restraint to the ground, and she tore the envelope open. Inside was a single sheet of pink paper.

Thank you so much for taking care of Juniper. He's a clever boy! In my absence, he's managed to assemble flatpack furniture!! Did he learn that from you?

I'm sorry to ask for another favour. Please

can you pop into Juni again? It's just for two more nights.

Yours gratefully, J x

P.S. Can you let Juni know that there's a chest of drawers waiting to be assembled in the bedroom xx

Catherine exhaled a laugh as she re-scanned the words. It was cheeky, but there was something undeniably endearing about it. Just as there was something endearing about Juniper — *Juni.* Catherine wasn't entirely displeased that she'd get to spend a little more time with him. The flatpack was a bonus.

But she'd have to have a word with her new neighbour about leaving the main door open and scaring her half to death.

As Catherine drained the coffee cup and tucked into the croissant, it occurred to her that the note was just signed 'J'. Where was the W for Will? Was he no longer on the scene? The postcards she'd read were recent, so that must have meant they'd only been married for a few months. *Surely it hadn't ended already?* Catherine had seen enough relationship drama in her career to dismiss that naïve question. Sometimes people got married to fix something that was already beyond repair.

Perhaps that was why J had moved here — to get away from crass, globetrotting Will.

God, she was spending far too much time thinking

about these strangers, which was a sure sign that she needed to — as Penny would phrase it — *get a life.*

She picked up her phone, because now was a respectable time to text her friend.

> Are you free for a swim tomorrow? Breakfast afterwards? I've lots to fill you in on x

A response pinged through immediately.

PENNY:

> Sounds perfect x

12

HERE COMES YOUR MAN

1988

I woke to Dad placing a cup of tea on my bedside table.

"What time is it?" I said through a yawn.

"It's early. Go back to sleep if you want, kiddo. I'm heading out with Jasper and Jeremy for the shoot."

I sat up and reached for my glasses, blinking as my eyes focussed. "Do you really have to kill those poor birds?"

Dad dusted my forehead with a kiss. "You used to make decorations with the feathers." He pointed at the dust-collecting dreamcatcher that hung from the end of my curtain pole.

"Yeah, because I didn't want them dying in vain. It's macabre." I glared at him. "Boys will be... brutal," I muttered, half-grateful that it was pheasants, not foxes, as I would've struggled to make something from them. The thought of eating game, or any meat for that matter, turned my stomach.

"I'll be back around noon. I've got the fire going, so chuck another log on when you're up."

"Have fun murdering those innocent creatures," I called after him.

"Yeah, yeah, we will," he chuckled. I smiled at the sound, the faintest hint of happiness. I hadn't heard him laugh properly since before Mum died. He wore his grief like armour, sealing everything in, and everything out.

Even on cheerful occasions like Christmas, sadness lingered in the air. Dad's grief was a constant, blinking in the background like the fairy lights strung around the fireplace. Impossible to miss, but completely ignored, because we didn't talk about Mum, lest something crack open and pour out. No one wants to clean up a sticky mess, especially not at Christmastime. So Dad held it together for me, and I him; both hoping that our wounds would magically heal themselves. But the more I studied the subject, the more I realised this strategy would be as effective as cooking a turkey without putting the oven on.

I cupped my hands around my mug of tea, and once again my mind returned to Francesca and the last night of term; the night I'd lost something but gained everything. I yearned for her touch, to stare into her eyes and to be ravished by her hunger. I couldn't shake the thought of her alone in her sorry little dorm room, starved for affection, with nothing but her moody music for company. I'd left her. I'd let her down when she needed me. But how was I supposed to know she wasn't going home? I swallowed my guilt with a gulp of tea.

I settled back under the duvet with Margaret Atwood,

who'd I'd joyfully found in my Christmas stocking. Time easily melted away in Atwood's words, but before I'd had the chance to become completely absorbed, there was a knock at the door. Perhaps Dad had forgotten something, including his keys.

With a sigh, I placed my book face down and open, careful not to crack the spine. I loathed it when people cracked the spines. *Monsters.*

I padded through the lounge in my bunny slippers, still clad in my plaid pyjamas, with the bottoms tucked into woolly socks. The fire crackled in the hearth, red-hot embers glowing as the flames died out because I'd forgotten to put another log on. I'd get it going again, make another cuppa and then settle back down with Margaret for a while...

A gust of bitter air rushed in as I opened the door to Jeremy, standing tall in tweed with a half-grin cocked on his face.

"What are you doing here? Aren't you supposed to be out murdering things with our fathers?"

He ducked under the lintel to step inside. "I gave it a miss."

"Oh! Well, why are you dressed like that?"

Jeremy's smile faltered, and he looked down at his tweed ensemble. "I was going to go, but then... I got a phone call."

I looked at him blankly as he rocked on his heels, as if he was trying to contain whatever was trying to fizz up out of him. "How fast can you get dressed?"

"What — why? I'm not planning to go anywhere." I

gestured to my bedclothes.

"Come on, Trusty! It'll be fun. No sense in moping around here."

"I'm not mop— *what* will be fun?"

"Get dressed, and you'll see," he said, eyes wide. "It's a surprise. A good one."

"Ugh. Fine."

I pulled on jeans and a warm jumper, dragged a comb through my tangled mess of hair and brushed my teeth. The whole while Jeremy paced in the lounge, or at least that's what it sounded like from the creak of the floor-boards under his feet.

He lifted his head and beamed as I re-entered the room. "Good to go?"

"Sure, but where are we—"

"All in good time."

Parked outside the cottage was Jane Dalton's vintage Porsche — the one she'd promised to Jeremy if he graduated with first-class honours. Jeremy strode toward it, bending to hold the door open and closing it behind me when I'd folded myself into the car.

The country lanes blurred by as he pushed a mixtape into the deck and Francesca's music blared from the speakers, bands I wouldn't have been able to name three months ago — The Cure, The Pixies, Siouxsie and the Banshees, My Bloody Valentine. A fist of jealousy squeezed tight in my gut. "Did she make this for you?"

"What?"

"The tape. Did Francesca make it for you?"

"No, it's on loan. I'm trying to get into her music, you know, so we'll have more in common."

Try all you like, it's me she's into. I wanted to say the words and watch him flounder, instead I bit my lip to hide my smile and looked out the window at the frost-dusted landscape stretching beneath the pastel sky.

Before long, Jeremy pulled up in front of the train station. The usually busy spot was empty of other cars aside from a couple of waiting taxis. I turned to look at Jeremy. "Why are we—"

He waggled his eyebrows. "We're picking someone up."

Occasionally, the Daltons invited other people to their Boxing Day Buffet; an odd aging aunt or distant cousin and, once or twice, people from the country club who Jane and Jasper had become friendly with. But these people always arrived under their own steam, and never by train.

A tiny flicker of excitement sparked in my stomach. *It couldn't be, could it?*

I didn't want to give myself away, because I didn't yet have the words to explain what I was or who she was to me; what we were together. It was easier to keep up the clueless charade and just hope. *Hope.*

As we waited on the platform, I frantically chewed the spearmint gum Jeremy had offered, while he whistled an annoying tune and flicked his wrist to check his watch every twenty seconds. His frenetic energy was making me nervous. It had to be Francesca we were waiting for because I'd never seen him act this way around anyone else. I looked down at my muddy boots and regretted not taking more time to get ready.

And then, Jeremy was effectively hopping on the spot. I lifted my head and sighted the shimmer of a train on the horizon. I tugged at the hem of my jumper and adjusted my scarf, enduring the agonising wait as time seemed to suspend itself.

The train stopped with a hydraulic hiss, and for a moment there was no sign of anyone getting off. I realised I'd been holding my breath when one of the rear carriage doors opened and Francesca appeared. My heart squeezed at the sight of her. Jeremy darted over to help lug her suitcase down to the platform.

We hugged an awkward hello, then stood back, looking at each other. She'd cut her hair, and it now hung soft and shaggy just below her jawline, with a fringe that made the angles on her pale face look sharper.

"What? Why are you both looking at me like that? Can't a girl change her look?"

"Yeah," I said with a breathy laugh. "You look…" *Gorgeous, stunning, perfect.*

"Great!" said Jeremy.

Francesca smirked, then looked at me through her eyelashes before looping her arm through mine. "Come on, let's go. It's bloody freezing standing around here."

Francesca and I walked ahead, her leaning into me, squeezing my arm, and me feeling like my heart might burst right out of my rib cage. Jeremy trailed behind us, carrying her suitcase and muttering to himself. When we got to the car, he insisted I climb into the back, which was only fair, but felt like his small revenge.

Jeremy revved the engine and winked at Francesca. "Got to warm the girl up before taking her for a ride."

I felt the milk from my tea curdling in my stomach.

"Fancy a swift one at the pub before we go back to mine?" he asked.

"Sure, why not?" Francesca smiled.

"Not The Stag, Jer? It's an old man's pub."

"I don't know where else will be open. Besides, Francesca will brighten the place up."

"That's a mammoth task to put on anyone."

"I can drop you home first if you like, Trusty."

"No," I said a little too quickly.

"Yeah, thought not." Jeremy flipped the cassette tape and pushed it back into the deck. *Here Comes Your Man* by The Pixies started up and Francesca nodded her approval, drumming her fingers on her knee; her usually chipped black fingernails had been perfectly manicured with bright red polish. I couldn't stop looking at them and thinking about how she'd brought her fingers to her lips to taste me. I loosened my scarf as heat rose up my neck and into my cheeks.

I COULD'VE SWORN THE SAME COLLECTION OF corduroy-clad men were sitting in the same seats last time I'd visited The Stag. Every silver head turned to look as the three of us entered the pub, eyes lingering on the newcomer before turning back to their tankards. I had

NO IDEA WHY JEREMY WANTED TO BRING Francesca here, of all places. It smelt of stale beer and old men.

"Here, look, there's a table by the fire. I'll go get the drinks in."

I led the way, undoing my scarf and tucking myself into the bench seat. Francesca shucked off her coat and squeezed in next to me rather than taking one of the two empty chairs opposite. The fire crackled, and I rubbed my hands together before daring to glance at her.

"So, how have you been?" I asked, my lips summoning a shy smile.

"Yeah, okay. It's been quiet." She nodded.

"I didn't know you were staying... you know, on your own."

"I didn't tell you."

"But you told Jeremy."

"He asked."

Shit. "Sorry, I didn't think to. You always seem so—"

"It's okay. I like being alone."

"I've missed you," I blurted. "I've been thinking about you... and, you know, everything else. I've been thinking about it a lot."

A sexy half-smile tugged at Francesca's lips. "Yeah?"

"Yeah."

"Good," she said, and I swallowed.

The fluttering in my stomach batted all my words away, and now Jeremy was striding over, tongue poking out in concentration as he carried three purple pints between stretched fingers.

"Here we go! A little taste of uni in case you're missing it." He unbuttoned his jacket, revealing a pressed white shirt and tweed waistcoat.

Francesca took a tentative sip from her pint. "God, it's truly awful."

For a split second Jeremy looked crushed, but then he released a hearty laugh. "It is rather, isn't it?"

"Disgusting," I added, dipping my tongue into the pink froth.

Jeremy raised his glass. "Well, cheers anyway."

We clinked our glasses together, and all took a sip.

An awkward silence stretched out. This was the first time the three of us had been together since Francesca and I had... I couldn't think about that now, but my body thrummed with the proximity of her, and Jeremy must have been able to sense it too; the shift, the gear change. I needed time to find my footing in this uncertain terrain, which felt impossible when I couldn't feel the ground.

Jeremy gave in first. "Ma's had Bunty make up a guest room for you. You'll be just up the hall from me... so, if you get lonely, you know where I am." Eyebrows raised, he brought the pint to his mouth. A moustache of pink froth clung to his top lip when he pulled the glass away.

I shifted uncomfortably in my seat and Francesca turned to look at me.

"How about you? Where do you sleep?"

"Oh, with my dad..." my whole body cringed. "No, not with... I mean, we have a cottage on the grounds. Dad is the groundskeeper."

"Right, yes, I remember... but you're coming to this

party, right?" Her leg pressed into mine with far too much pressure to be accidental.

I nodded.

Francesca cradled her chin and peered at Jeremy across the table. His cheeks reddened, and he took another slow sip of his drink.

"Well, it's not really a party. It's just a casual sort of soirée. Drinks, dinner, and whatnot." After a beat, he tore his eyes away from Francesca to look at me. "The Beaumonts are coming again this year."

"Please tell me you're kidding."

"Nope, Hugo's home from Oxford. And he's very much looking forward to seeing *you*, or so I've heard." Jeremy smirked.

I sank into the seat with a groan.

Hugo Beaumont. It'd taken the entire evening to get Handsy Hugo to back off last year, eyeing me across the dinner table and, later, needling me with questions I didn't want to answer. I told him I wasn't interested in dating anyone because I was concentrating on my studies, but he kept touching my arm with his porky fingers like I'd given him permission and standing so close I could smell his rank breath. I'd made wide eyes at Jeremy to save me; then, like a knight in shining Armani, he waded in and draped an arm around my shoulder.

"Hassling my girl, are you, Hugo?"

Claret-faced, Hugo held up his meaty hands and backed away. "Oh sorry, JD. I didn't realise she was taken. I'm not one to piss on another chap's picnic."

And if I hadn't already known I didn't like men, that

very moment would've been enough to turn me off forever.

With Francesca here, it'd be unlikely Jeremy would prop up the lie for my benefit this year.

"I've heard Hugo joined the rugby team and has been getting himself into shape."

I shot him daggers.

"He's not so bad once you get to know him. There are worse chaps out there, Trusty. You know the Beaumonts are one of the wealthiest families in Berkshire?"

Francesca shifted slightly beside me.

I shrugged and shook my head. "Why would I care about that?"

Jeremy held up his hands. "Just thinking that maybe the four of us could double-date?"

"Piss off, Jeremy." I sprung up, almost toppling the table. Jeremy's eyebrows shot up as he grappled to steady the glasses. I glanced at Francesca for support, but instead of being outraged, her eyes flickered with amusement.

"Steady on, Trusty. I'm only kidding about."

"Yeah, well... it isn't funny." I huffed out a sigh, feeling a little foolish for taking the bait.

Francesca tugged my hand, and I sat back down. She squeezed my knee under the table and left her hand there, the warmth of it creeping up my thigh.

"You know... a double date could be fun." Teasing laced her voice, but something about the way she said it made me think she was seriously considering it.

I turned my pointed glare on her. She tilted her head as

if waiting for a response to a perfectly legitimate request. My mouth gaped with the words I couldn't say...

Even if Hugo wasn't objectively grotesque, I came out to you. You're literally the only person I've come out to, and you actively put my lesbianism to the test. So, why would you want us to date other people, when all I want to do is kiss you, and hold you, and touch you, and... I thought that's what you wanted, too?

"Don't you start, as well," I said, pushing her hand off my leg and crossing my arms.

Jeremy chuckled and slapped his palm on the table. "Right, better drink up. We have a party to get ready for."

"Soirée," I muttered under my breath.

Jeremy downed the dregs of his purple pint and grimaced as he gestured his empty glass to me. "C'mon, you'll need plenty of time to look your best for Hugo."

Francesca nudged a playful elbow into me as she got up. If it was meant to reassure me, it didn't. All the elation I'd felt at her arrival dropped like lead in the pit of my stomach. This new terrain was rockier than I'd imagined.

13

DON'T YOU WANT ME

When we arrived back at the manor, I made my excuses and left them to it. The brittle sound of Francesca's laughter echoed behind me — the laugh she always used around Jeremy.

I crunched along the gravel track until the manicured lawns gave way to the more rugged, untamed beauty of the surrounding landscape. Our cottage sat nestled in its own private garden, framed by imposing conifers and a low picket fence, marking the boundary of our little world — a world away from all the pretensions of the manor.

An evening curled up with Atwood and her Handmaids suddenly seemed preferable to the thought of an evening of Francesca and Jeremy laughing at me as I tried to swat Hugo away like a persistent blowfly. But with the fresh air and distance between us, I could see that their conversation was just banter. I could see how silly I was to question Francesca's feelings and motivations when just last week she'd been the one to seduce me, to pull me into her bed and consume me like a Fortnum's hamper.

Jeremy was winding me up and Francesca was playing along, that was all. Of course she liked me and not Jeremy. Of course she didn't actually want me to date Hugo Beaumont. She'd sat next to me, touched me under the table, and flirted when I told her I'd missed her. Things between us were good. We hadn't yet had the chance to define our relationship, and perhaps *relationship* was too formal, but what we had was something special, and everything she'd said hinted at more to come. Yet something about her that afternoon had sown a seed of doubt.

Cold air and an earthy smell followed Dad into the cottage when he returned from the hunt.

"Alright, kiddo," he called, waving a gloved hand in my direction. He peeled off his waxed jacket and wrestled with his muddy wellies, leaving them in a haphazard pile in the porch.

"Good timing. I just brewed a pot," I said as he shuffled into the room, all ruddy-faced, hugging himself to warm up.

"I was about to have a bath, but you can go first if you like?"

"God, I really don't feel like socialising tonight," he said, blowing into his chapped hands as he bent by the fire.

Me neither, I thought. But I didn't say that, because I didn't want to give him an excuse to back out of it. He needed this; it was one of the few social occasions he still went along with, probably because it felt like duty wrapped in obligation. The Daltons were not only his employers, but his friends.

"You'll have a good time once we're there and we don't have to stay late." I handed him a mug of tea. He smiled up at me, appreciation softening the lines etched onto his face.

"Go on, you get in the bath first, love. Leave the water in, and I'll add some hot."

After a soak in the tub, where I strategically dunked myself every time I let my mind wander to Francesca and Jeremy, I took my time getting ready, deciding on a white blouse to tuck into high-waisted black trousers. I blow-dried my hair, scrunching mousse through to give it more volume. I even brushed on a little mascara and a swipe of pale lipstick before standing back to take in my look. *Not too bad.*

Dad poked his head around my bedroom door. "Ready, love?"

I turned to face him as he slowly stepped into the room.

"You... look..." he said, wearing an expression I didn't recognise.

I turned back to the mirror to try to see what he was seeing. He closed in behind me and rested his hands on my shoulders.

"You look beautiful... I mean, you actually look like..." his voice cracked. "Your mum."

"Oh," I said, searching my reflection for any hint of her, but I couldn't see it.

Before the sadness bloating between us squeezed all

the air from the room, he said, "She'd be so proud of you, kiddo." He planted a kiss on the top of my head and turned to leave.

"Dad?"

"Yeah?" He looked back, eyes glistening.

"Do you really think she'd be proud of me?"

"I know she would."

FESTOON LIGHTS LIT THE SINGLE TRACK TO THE manor house. I linked my arm through Dad's and squeezed into him against the biting chill of the crisp evening. As we neared the manor, the front door swung open and Jasper's voice boomed out.

"Michael, Catherine. Come on in."

We stepped inside, stamping away the cold and shucking our outerwear. I folded my peacoat over Jasper's outstretched arm as he pecked a kiss on each of my cheeks. Jane popped her head out of the drawing room; her elegant face split into a smile when she saw us.

"Catherine, look at you. You look lovely, darling. So grown-up... You're all so grown-up now. Come, come, let me fetch you a drink, and you can go find the others in the snug."

I turned to check on Dad, but he was already lost in conversation with Jasper, both men hunched over, chatting like conspirators.

I smiled as I looked back to Jane, who was chuckling at the same thing, and I was hit with a genuine rush of affection for the Daltons. They'd been good to us; they treated us as equals even though Dad was on their payroll. We'd lost so much before we came here, but the Daltons had been a glorious light at the end of a dark tunnel. They were friendship and warmth. Plus, they'd been more than generous with my education, which Dad never would have been able to afford otherwise.

In the kitchen, Jane poured me a glass of Champagne and clinked it with her own. "Before you go in to the others, may I speak with you for a moment?"

I took a sip and tried not to wince. It was still a taste I hadn't acquired, despite Jeremy sneaking bottles and sharing them with me throughout the summer before I started uni.

Jane leaned in, looking at me through her fluttering false eyelashes. "What's your take on this Gadby girl Jeremy's brought home?"

The question caught me off guard. "Oh, Francesca. Yeah, she's..." *Where do I start? She's bright, funny, sexy, can do magical things with her fingers...* "She's really great."

Jane laughed, and her diamond earrings sparkled as they swayed. "Phew! Jeremy's besotted, but he's my baby boy and I don't want to see him hurt. Girls can be so cruel, and he's the sensitive sort, as you know."

I bit my lip and nodded.

I *knew* this is what they'd think. Jeremy knew exactly what he was doing when he'd orchestrated this. *"Me, finally bringing a girl home,"* was what he'd said on the train.

I must have been frowning as Jane touched my arm

and peered into my face. "Oh gosh, I'm sorry. That was awfully insensitive of me, Catherine. Sometimes these chaps can't see what's right under their noses, can they?"

I tilted my head until the penny dropped. "Oh, wait. You don't think that I like—"

"It's quite alright. I get it. It took me years of flaunting my ankles before I finally turned Jasper's head. If it's meant to be, it's—"

I squawked a laugh. "No, really. Jeremy and I are just friends. He's like a brother to me."

Jane pressed a hand to her chest in an exaggerated flap of relief. "Thank goodness. You looked crestfallen. I thought I'd shoved my foot right in it then."

"No, not at all. I guess the three of us are close friends. I was just thinking how it'll change everything if..." *If Francesca and I were to come clean about how we spent the last night of term wrapped in each other's arms.*

"Ah, yes. I see," she grimaced. "You don't want to be a third wheel. Look, don't worry, you'll meet the right chap soon enough."

I broke eye contact and stared down at my polished shoes.

"And if you don't, then eager young Hugo Beaumont will be waiting in the wings. If rumours are to be believed, he has quite a crush on you." Jane chuckled but then widened her eyes as if struck by an important thought. "The Beaumonts are one of the wealthiest—"

"Families in Berkshire." I finished the sentence with her, and we both laughed. "Yes, I know. I'll bear that in mind."

"Right, well you better go see what they're up to, and I'll go rescue poor Camilla before the chaps bore the poor woman into a coma. Supper's at eight."

I nudged open the door to the snug, where a tense concentration hung in the air. Jeremy leaned over the back of the chair where Francesca sat, holding a fanned hand of playing cards. I couldn't tear my eyes away from her black dress with its plunging lacy neckline and ruffled cap sleeves. Her makeup was pared back, but immaculate. Subtle kohl around her eyes, and dark lips which made her skin look pale, almost ethereal. She looked stunning, not that she didn't usually look that way to me, but her outfit was a far cry from the clothes she wore around campus.

Here, there wasn't even a hint of the vampy goth-girl I knew. She not only looked different, she held herself differently, moved differently. It was probably just the new hairstyle and change of clothing; I hadn't seen her in a dress before. But something about it felt off — almost like the same machine with a different operator who hadn't quite figured out the controls yet.

Francesca's forehead crinkled in concentration as Jeremy leaned in close to her, whispering and pointing at the cards. The air crackled with a low hum of anticipation, punctuated by the clinking of ice.

Hugo and his younger brother, Archie, reclined on the Chesterfield opposite, their own cards fanned out and face down on the coffee table. Hugo swirled an amber liquid in his glass. "Oh, come on, JD. Quick game's a good game; how long's it take to teach her?"

Jeremy scoffed. "Why are you in such a hurry to lose, Hugo?"

I laughed too, and they all twisted around to the doorway where I stood.

"Catherine," Hugo beamed, his round face shining like a glazed gammon. His legs flailed as he struggled to pull himself up from the low sofa. Jeremy scoffed and jumped up to give him a hand before moving over to me.

"You've scrubbed up well, Trusty." He leaned in and kissed my cheek. "We're showing Francesca how to play Bastard."

"Teaching hcr how to cheat, more like it," said Hugo. He gripped my shoulders and pressed a flaming cheek to mine. "Lovely to see you, Catherine. You look delicious."

"Good to see you too, Hugo." I looked past him and held up a hand to Archie, who bobbed his head in return.

Hugo leaned in, the smell of bourbon sickly on his breath. "I can teach you if you like; we can make it doubles. Give these two a run for their money."

I looked over at Francesca, her dark eyes sparking like flint, lips puckering against a grin.

"Thank you, Hugo, but I think I'll sit this one out."

"Suit yourself, but I'd be happy to show you a few tricks whenever you're up for it." He gave me a leery grin. The guy had confidence; I had to give him that.

I perched on a stool at the edge of the table, as far away from Hugo as possible, and took a sip of Champagne every time Jeremy touched Francesca, the sharp liquid adding to the stab in my gut. Twenty minutes later, quiet young Archie threw down his last card.

"Bastard," he said smugly, and Hugo looked like he wanted to slap him.

"Right, well, that concludes that." Jeremy gave Francesca's shoulder a consolatory rub before he stretched up from the back of the chair. I shuddered at the sight of his skin touching hers, but she was looking right at me. I lingered as the boys went on ahead, catching Francesca's wrist as she moved to follow them. She spun, her eyes flashing as she looked down at my hand, still holding her wrist.

"You two looked cosy." The words came out more accusatory than I'd intended. I released her hand, and she pressed it to my chest, pushing me back into the wood-panelled wall.

Her dark-red lips twisted into a grin. "Jealous?"

"Of course I am." I pointed vaguely toward the dining room. "They think you're his girlfriend."

"So what?" She leaned into me, her eyes dropping to my lips.

"I thought we were..." Again, I stumbled to find the right words.

"Go on."

"*A thing?*" The question almost squeaked out of me.

Francesca stood so close, I could feel her breath when she laughed. She fixed me with a stare so penetrating she could've nailed me to the wall with it.

"I fucked you, and I'm going to fuck you again. We have unfinished business, remember? So if that's what you mean by *a thing*, then yes. We're *a thing*. Are you..." she slid a hand down between us, palm up and applying pressure as she reached between my legs, "...okay with that?"

I nodded dumbly, transfixed by her eyes. My brain still screamed with questions, but I wilfully ignored the red flags, instead focussing all my energy on not grinding myself onto her hand.

She must have felt me holding back as she cupped her hand tighter, squeezing me through my trousers and the now-saturated fabric of my underwear. She smothered my gasp with a kiss, soft at first and then rough, nipping at my bottom lip until it hurt.

Seemingly satisfied with herself, she pulled back and patted my chest with the hand that had been groping me just seconds ago.

"I'm starving!" she announced, as if she'd just woken from a strange dream. Her eyes raked over me, then she dramatically flounced out of the room. I stood, rubbing my bruised lip with my thumb as I caught my breath, echoes of *I'm going to fuck you again* bouncing around in my head.

Yes, I wanted that; I *really* wanted that, but I couldn't help noticing she hadn't denied she and Jeremy were an item. I didn't want to be a bore about it, but I needed to clear that up. I nodded to myself in shaky resolution before making my way to the dining room.

14

CLOSE TO ME

The clatter of cutlery and Jasper Dalton's booming voice competed to fill the lofty space of the dining room. A banquet of dishes sprawled across the table, and the only remaining seat was between Hugo and my dad. Francesca didn't even look up from her leaned-in conversation with Jeremy. Hugo beamed and patted the chair beside him.

"Saved you a seat, Catherine."

I summoned a gracious smile and sat. Hugo took the liberty of unfolding my napkin and placing it on my knees. Normally I'd have slapped his porky hands away, but I was too distracted watching Francesca touching Jeremy's arm and giggling. I bunched the napkin in my fists.

When the din died down, Jasper turned his attention to Francesca — *Jeremy's guest of honour,* as he called her. He quizzed her about her background, university life, and plans for the future. Jane squeezed his arm and stage-whispered, "It's not a job interview, darling."

Francesca politely smiled and performed beautifully, not only answering Jasper's many questions, but embellishing her answers with stories and earning genuine laughter from the Daltons and the Beaumonts. All the while, Jeremy looked at her like an eager puppy, ready to roll over on command. His pride was palpable — he'd brought home this bright young thing. Jeremy and Francesca were of the same calibre; they were in the same league — *how could I compete?*

A mishmash of food was passed around the table: vol-au-vents, quiches, mini prawn cocktails, stuffed potato skins — Jane's attempt to be on-trend seemed to have delighted the other guests but turned my stomach. I picked out a couple of items and prodded at them with my fork, while my mind chewed over everything with Francesca and Jeremy, and whether it would be too needy and desperate to ask her to be clearer about *us*, about what I was to her. Or should I just try to relax and go with the flow? I'd been accused of being uptight before now; I didn't want to scare her off by pushing too hard.

"Penny for them," Hugo said, leaning into me more than was necessary.

I jolted back to myself and lifted my eyes, momentarily feeling sorry for him. None of this was his fault. "Sorry, I just feel a bit—"

He placed a hand on my back.

"If I may..." He inhaled as if preparing to say something profound, then leaned over, speared the vol-au-vent on my plate, and popped it into his mouth whole.

Too much; it was all too much. I needed some space

because my thoughts were as tangled as my limbs had been with Francesca's just a few days ago. I whipped the napkin from my lap and stood. My chair scraped across the parquet floor, and every head turned to look at me.

"Sorry," I said, my voice sounding breathy and pathetic. "I—"

"Everything alright, Catherine?" Jasper's brow furrowed.

I glanced around at the questioning faces, my eyes settling on Francesca, who stared back, one eyebrow arched in cool appraisal.

Dad touched my hand. "What's up, love?"

I looked down at him and mustered a smile. "I'm fine. I just need some air."

"Shall I come with you?"

"No, stay and have fun."

Dad nodded, and I paced out of the room with their conversation following me.

"What did you do, Hugo?" asked Jeremy.

"Nothing! Well, I ate her vol-au-vent, but she wasn't eating it, so…"

A burst of laughter chased me down the hall.

By the time I'd reached the front door, tears were tracking down my cheeks. I felt ridiculous, particularly because Francesca had kissed me before dinner. She told me that she still wanted me, that she was going to have me. That should have settled the churning in my stomach. But it hadn't.

I stepped out into the freezing night air and wrapped my shivering arms around myself. *Shit.* I'd forgotten my coat, and the door had locked behind me. I couldn't ring the bell; I felt stupid enough already.

As I charged along the track with my head down, sleet began to fall — wet, icy and soaking my thin blouse. I rolled my eyes to the sky as if there were some malevolent force at work doing this to spite me. By the time I'd reached the cottage, my shirt was wet through, and my hands shook as I tried to unlock the door with the spare key in the porch.

"Why did you leave like that?"

"Fuckin' hell," I screamed and dropped the keys.

Francesca puffed out a laugh behind me. I didn't look around because I didn't want her to see me like this — no doubt looking as pathetic as I felt. I picked up the key, but my hands were shaking so much I couldn't get it in the lock. I wanted to scream.

"Here, let me." She took the key from me, opened the door, and invited herself in. The warmth of the cottage enveloped me like a hug. I grabbed a towel from the bathroom to dry my wet hair and returned to see Francesca glancing around. The space was humble compared to the manor house, but it was cosy and warm, and it was home.

She wrinkled her nose. "It's like a little hobbit house."

"It's a cottage," I said flatly. "Why did you come after me?"

Francesca narrowed her eyes. "Why did you leave?"

Almost as if the cold had snapped some sense into me, I realised I was bored with this bullshit. "Because I can't bear to watch you and Jeremy act like a loved-up couple. Because I felt sick listening to the Daltons fawn over you like you're Jeremy's girlfriend." The words spewed out of me, and the release felt good, like lancing a boil. "Can't you see what it looks like?"

Francesca poked her tongue into her cheek. "Fuck Jeremy," she said in a low growl.

"Have you? Have you fucked Jeremy?"

"That shade of green is very unbecoming on you, Catherine." She laughed, and I wanted to launch myself at her. I wanted to slap her smug face and kiss her at the same time.

She was confusing, and this was exhausting.

I slumped onto the sofa and stared into the fireplace as a burst of embers crackled from a blackened log. Francesca removed her coat and crossed the room. She perched next to me and placed a warm hand on my knee, then spoke softly, her voice coaxing, like she was luring prey.

"It's all theatrics. I'm just having fun."

"Well, it's not fun for me. I wasn't acting. I thought this was real."

Francesca moved a finger between us. "This…is…real," she said, each word deliberate.

Tears sprang from my eyes again, and the next thing I knew, I was sobbing into her lap. She wrapped her arms around me and rocked me slightly. A long moment passed before she spoke again.

"You're freezing. I think we need to get you out of these wet clothes."

I looked up at her, aware that my face would be a messy fright, but she cupped my cheeks and gently rubbed the smeared makeup from under my eyes with her thumbs. I met her gaze, and she bent, covering my mouth with her own. Her tongue pushed past my flimsy defences, past all the red flags and barbed words, until I was disarmed and lying on my back.

She hitched up her dress and knelt above me, unbuttoning my wet shirt and peeling it from my damp skin before casting it across the room. She kissed my neck, her breath hot as she traced her tongue along my collarbone. As I arched up, offering myself for her to consume, my eyes flicked to the door.

"My Dad will be home—"

"Where's your bedroom?"

Our mouths fused together, hot, wet and hungry, as we crossed the room in a tangle of limbs. Behind my closed bedroom door, she turned her back to me, peering over her shoulder with an incendiary stare.

"Unzip me," she murmured.

I swept aside her hair and slowly lowered the zip of her dress, revealing the porcelain flesh of her back. I ghosted my fingers over her skin, almost afraid to touch her, but I needed to know this was real, that she was really here, and we were really about to do this... again.

She turned, dark eyes on me as the material fell from her shoulders and slipped down her body. She stepped out of the dress, now pooled at her ankles, and moved towards my bed, catching my wrist and pulling me with her.

She knelt before me and unbuttoned my fly. I released a gasp full of want as she roughly tugged down my trousers and underwear. I didn't have time to be embarrassed or unsure, because after a quick glance up she gripped my arse and pulled me into her mouth. I released a guttural groan as she plunged her hot tongue into my wetness. Instinctively, I reached for her head, bunching fistfuls of her hair in my hands as the sensation of her tongue sent pleasure rippling through my core. Each movement was a desperate, primal response, a need to hold on, to deepen the connection, to drown in the overwhelming tide of desire crashing over me.

"That's it, fuck my face like a good girl," she panted, moaning as she dived into me. My hips bucked, seeking more pressure until she was right on the spot, flicking the tip of her tongue and sucking my...

"Oh, fuck," I gasped. Francesca continued to lap, holding firm arms around me as my orgasm pulsed and turned my legs to jelly. She gripped my hands and got to her feet.

"Feel better now?" she grinned, the slick of me glistening on her lips.

"What are you doing to me?" I threaded our fingers together.

"I do believe they call that cunnilingus. Want to try it?" Her lip hitched in a half-smile.

"I want to try everything with you."

"Good," she purred and pulled me down onto the bed.

Beneath the covers, she twisted around until she was straddling one of my thighs, and as we kissed, I moved my hand, reaching between us and daring to touch her through the barrier of her silky underwear. She moaned into my mouth and reached her own hand down to tug her knickers aside.

I paused, hesitating. It wasn't that I didn't want to touch her; I just didn't want to get it wrong. She pulled back to look at me, confusion etched on her face.

"What are you waiting for? I want to feel you inside me."

I swallowed. "Okay, but will you tell me if it's not—"

"Use your instincts, and remember confidence is sexy. Here, like this." She reached for my hand and pressed it between her legs, guiding two of my fingers with her own until they dipped inside her. "That's it. God, yeah..." She groaned, arching into me and throwing her head back. I continued to move slowly inside her as she rocked onto my hand. It was insanely erotic to see her like that, and I was captivated watching her yield to the pleasure I was giving her. Her eyes were on me again, dark with desire, and something almost feral flickering in them.

"I want you to fuck me like you've been starved and I'm your final meal."

"Sorry, wha—"

"Harder and faster. Show me how much you've wanted to do this to me."

I closed my eyes and did as she asked. I concentrated on rhythm and speed until my forearm ached and my skin was slick with sweat. I kept going until she tightened around my fingers and her moans reached a crescendo. She collapsed onto me, breathless and hot. And for a moment, I lay smiling at the ceiling and glowing with pride.

"Stop looking so pleased with yourself; there's definitely room for improvement." Her criticism was laced with gentle teasing, but I rolled into her and buried my face in her hair.

"I'm willing to try again. And again. And as many times as it takes to perfect doing that to you."

"Good, because I'm not done with you yet." She smothered my mouth with her hungry lips and trailed her fingers over my bare skin, stirring my arousal again. I wanted to feel her everywhere; every inch of me ached to be claimed and consumed by her.

"I want you to eat me now." She whispered her desire into my ear and chased it with her tongue; the combination set me alight and rendered me wordlessly compliant, sliding down between her legs, removing her saturated underwear and diving into her like I knew what I was doing. And by the unholy sounds she made, I'd been a quick study.

Rather than re-dress, I pulled on my very unsexy pyjamas. Francesca wore one of my long baggy T-shirts over a pair of my cotton underwear with white tube socks pulled up her calves. I'd never seen anything sexier.

Neither of us had eaten much of Jane's party buffet, so we were famished. My stomach somersaulted as we worked alongside each other in the small kitchen. As the tea brewed, I buttered, and she jammed. Tea and toast felt fitting, given that was where it had all started.

"Catherine?" she said, her voice low and serious.

I turned, and after a beat, her face split into a grin, and she smeared a blob of strawberry jam on my nose. As I opened my mouth to protest, she leaned in and licked it off.

"It's no wild hedgerow, but it tastes good on you." She trailed the tip of her tongue down to my mouth.

Christ, she was going the right way about getting fucked again right here in the kitchen. And as if reading my thoughts, she levered herself up onto the counter and gripped me between her legs. Her fingers raked through my hair as she kissed me, all tongue and sex and jam.

Dad's key turned in the lock, and we sprang apart. Francesca hopped down from the counter.

"Alright, girls?" he said, ruddy-faced and glassy-eyed.

"Good thanks, Dad." I tried to steady my voice despite my racing heart. "Did you have a fun evening?"

"As good as can be. Why did you dash off?"

"I got my monthlies." Guilt pinched me at how easily the lie came.

"Better now?" he asked.

"Much." I smiled, my eyes flicking to Francesca.

"Do you mind if I stay over, Mr T.? I'd like to keep Catherine company if that's okay."

My chest fluttered as Dad shrugged. "It's no bother to me. Thanks for taking care of her earlier. I see she was in good hands."

Good hands alright. My cheeks flamed at the thought.

"Anytime." She gave him a sweet smile while at the same time squeezing my waist below his line of sight.

"Well, goodnight, girls." Dad nodded and ducked off to his bedroom, thankfully at the opposite end of the cottage with no adjoining walls. Not that Francesca and I hadn't already worn each other out.

I stacked some fresh logs on the fire, and we settled

under a blanket with our limbs entwined. The fire crackled as it took hold, and Francesca sat staring into the orange glow.

"Do you think Jeremy will be wondering where you are?"

I didn't want to ask her that, but at the same time I was curious about whether she was thinking about him.

"I think he can figure that much out for himself."

Her nonchalance made me relax, and my fingers traced lazy lines around her ankles until she leaned back into the cushions and closed her eyes. Soft shadows danced across her face in the firelight, and I'd never felt happier than in that moment.

I WOKE TO FRANCESCA PEELING BACK THE DUVET and climbing out of bed. I nestled into the warm space she'd left behind, watching as she stripped off my T-shirt and dressed in the thin light.

"Where are you going?" I said through a stretchy yawn.

"Oh, you're awake!" She spun around. "I need to get back; Jeremy has a trip planned for today."

The casual way she mentioned his name jolted me. I propped myself on my elbows, squinting without my glasses. "What, just the two of you?"

"I'd have thought so, yes." Francesca pulled off the cotton knickers I'd given her last night and glanced around as if she were trying to figure out where to put them. I reached my arm out from under the duvet, and she dropped them into my open hand.

"Don't you think that's going to give him the wrong idea?"

She tilted her head. "What idea?"

"That he has a chance with you."

"That's the wrong idea, is it?"

A heavy weight dropped in my gut. "But we... you and I. We..."

Her lips stretched into a disapproving grimace. "You're not going to get all jealous and make me feel guilty, are you?"

"I don't understand." I flopped back and covered my face with my hands to hide my threatening tears.

Francesca moved over to the bedside and pulled at my wrists, but my hands remained clamped firmly over my eyes, where those tears were making good on their threat.

Francesca's weight shifted onto the bed as she hitched up her dress and straddled me. With more force and greater leverage, she tugged at my forearms until I released. She stared down at me in bemusement, as if she were having to patiently deal with a massive overreaction.

"You do understand, Catherine." She cupped a hand around my cheek. "You and I have something precious and rare. But if we're to keep on doing this, sharing this special thing, it needs to remain just between us." She spoke in a slow, syrupy voice, pouring out words that should have sounded sweet to me — *precious, rare, special* — but they didn't.

I clenched my jaw until my teeth ached.

"So, what you're saying is, you want to keep us a secret. And you're going to date Jeremy too?"

Francesca rolled her eyes. "Let's not do this. Let's not ruin what was a magical night." She bent down to kiss me, and despite my better judgement, I let her. If I kissed her for long enough, if I could make her feel what I was feeling through this kiss, then she might not pop this perfect bubble.

When she pulled away, I tried to hold on to her even though it felt desperate and needy. She peeled back my fingers and climbed off me before tucking me in under the duvet.

"Why don't you get some rest? It was a big night."

"I don't want to share you with Jeremy," I blurted.

The muscle in Francesca's jaw twitched, and I knew I was pushing too hard.

She sharply inhaled. "Now you're making me feel bad. Come on, I don't want to think of you like this." She curled her lip as if repulsed by a bitter aftertaste.

I nodded, scared to say anything else because I didn't trust my brain to come up with the right combination of words, and even if it did, my voice would only say them all wrong. I wanted to rewind the tape of this morning, because now that it had unravelled, I wasn't sure I could fix it.

Her features softened, and she bent and kissed my forehead. "Stop worrying. I'll see you later, maybe?"

Then she was gone, leaving me alone in bed to sort through my tangled thoughts, like an impossible pile of laundry, separating light from dark.

15

TRUTH PINÃTA

PRESENT DAY

In the watery light of day, Catherine stripped down to her swimwear and wriggled her toes in the dewy grass. The cool morning air prickled her skin with goosebumps, and she wrapped her Dryrobe tighter around herself.

The Dryrobe had been another thoughtful gift from Penny, the woman who anticipated Catherine's needs before she'd even realised them herself.

Perhaps she shouldn't have given up on Penny so easily. But perhaps she'd never really had a choice; Penny had fallen in love with someone else, after all.

A small group of swimmers — three older women and a man — were already wading into the river, gasping as the fresh water lapped their bare skin. She used to watch these sorts of people with concern, wondering why anyone would want to swim in the river when there was a perfectly good swimming pool nearby, without the hazards of rocks, reeds, and any other unsanitary things that might be adrift in the British waterways.

However, after a while, her concern had turned to curiosity. She observed people emerging from the fresh water invigorated in a way she'd never seen at the local leisure centre — the only glow one got there came from irritated skin courtesy of the chlorinated water.

When she'd first suggested wild swimming to Penny, her friend had looked at her sideways. But within a fortnight, Penny had done some research, bought them both Dryrobes, and they hadn't looked back since. If too much time had passed, Catherine longed for the sharp gasp of air as the icy water jolted every nerve awake.

She closed her eyes and tipped her face to the pale-yellow sun streaking the sky with the pinky-promise of a nice day.

"Oi oi, Dryrobe wanker!" Penny panted up alongside her, breaking the moment's reverie.

"You're wearing yours, too." Catherine beamed at the sight of her dishevelled friend and leaned in to kiss her rosy cheeks.

"Sorry to have kept you waiting, babe. Lawrence got home last night, and—"

Catherine held up a hand. "Spare me the details."

"There are no details to spare; I just couldn't get back to sleep with all his snoring." Penny sat on the bench to pull off her yoga pants.

The two of them piled their belongings at the end of the picnic table and hobbled along the grassy bank to the water's edge.

"It's going to be freezing," said Penny, rubbing her arms.

"It's good for us; reminds us we're alive."

"What does that even mean?"

Catherine tilted her head at the question. "It's just something people say, isn't it? I suppose it's about mindfulness, remembering to be present and live in the moment. Like meditation, but wetter."

"Or perhaps it's that once you've felt how cold the water is, you know you couldn't possibly be dead?"

Catherine scoffed a laugh, and in a rush of affection for her cynical friend, she hugged her arm. "Think of all the endorphins; you'll be in a great mood after this. Maybe you'll even forgive Lawrence for snoring."

"Not likely, but he's taking me out to dinner tonight, so that might make up for it."

"Right, here goes." Catherine released Penny's arm and waded in. The cold gripped her ankles, but she pushed past the initial pain and took long strides into the river. The water squeezed around her middle, pushing the air to the top of her lungs until it caught in her throat. She slowly let the water support her weight until her shoulders were submerged, then she lightly kicked off from the riverbed. Once her breathing relaxed, the gentle flow of the river pulled the thoughts from her mind, and calm descended over her.

Blossom, bees, birdsong... and Penny thrashing through the water.

"Jesus H. Christ. I think my tits have frozen. They're like a couple of iced buns, look." Penny thrust her chest through the surface, exposing the taut fabric of her swim-suit over pebble-hard nipples. Catherine laughed and gave her a light splash.

"Loz says we're mad, by the way, and on this one isolated occasion, I think he might be right."

"It's lovely." Catherine sculled through the water, taking in the lush green surroundings. "Peaceful," she added. Penny seemed to take the hint, and for a blissful moment, soft silence rippled between them.

"Very mindful, very demure." Penny sucked in a deep breath and exhaled with a hum.

Catherine prised one eye open and looked at her peace-shattering friend, which Penny took as a cue to resume conversation.

"So, how's your hungry little pussy doing?"

Catherine shook her head and turned away to hide her grin. "My neighbour's cat," she pronounced each word slowly. "Juni—"

"Juni?" Penny's lips twisted in a teasing smile.

"Yes, short for Juniper. He's fine... he's a sweetheart, actually. I've rather enjoyed his company. You know we were talking about fresh starts the other day?"

Penny narrowed her eyes.

"Well, I've been thinking... maybe I should get myself a cat."

Penny vigorously shook her head.

"Why not?"

"Because it'll be another excuse for you to avoid putting yourself out there. You'll wither into one of those lonely old cat ladies."

"Pen! That's an awful thing to say. I just thought it might be nice to have another being to come home to in the evenings."

Catherine often recommended pet ownership to her clients. She'd even written a blog about it after reading up on the myriad health benefits of pets — lowering cortisol, increasing serotonin and dopamine, not to mention the joyful distraction... *from the yawning canyon of emptiness stretching out before me.*

Penny frowned.

"Juni makes these cute little chirping noises. It's very endearing."

"I think this freezing water is addling your brain."

Penny turned to swim for the bank, but Catherine stayed put, trailing her fingers through the water and trying not to think about how similar Penny's words had been to Francesca's.

Shrivelled old spinster.

Lonely old cat lady.

Was that really how people saw her? At fifty-six, she wasn't old. And she certainly wasn't withered, especially not here, in this cold water where she felt so alive with her blood pumping and endorphins soaring.

But the word *lonely* echoed in her mind, and she had to admit that loneliness had crept up on her when she hadn't been looking. At first, it had just stood quietly in the corner. Now, more often than not, it walked alongside her, weighing her down like a cold arm draped around her shoulder, corroding the shine off even the brightest of occasions. And now here she was considering companionship from a feline friend. Something steady, warm, and constant in her life, other than work. Was that really so dysfunctional?

No — dysfunctional is constructing your neighbour's flatpack furniture without being asked, just so you can hang out with their cat. Best not to mention that part to Penny.

"Are you staying in there all day?" Penny waved an arm in the air and jiggled about in her Dryrobe.

Catherine sighed and started swimming back towards the grassy bank.

"Can you swim a little faster? I'm starving and I have very cold boobies," Penny yelled.

Catherine had to giggle at her ridiculous friend and the shocked faces of the passing elderly couple walking a white Scottie dog.

With a forced smile, Penny turned to them and curtsied in her robe.

"It's okay," she said, "I'm a lawyer."

They eyed her up and down, shuffling away as fast as their withered legs would allow.

Dried and dressed, they wandered through the park, past the Royal Pump Rooms and over the bridge toward the restaurant they loved — the one with the terrace that overlooked the river.

Despite the chill in the air, they opted for a table outside and were shown to one of the few that were bathed in sunshine.

Catherine relaxed into the chair, relishing the sun warming her through to her bones, as Penny rummaged around in her oversized tote bag, muttering something about sunglasses. Overhead, a jet stream scored the sky with a white slash and conjured thoughts of the woman in red — the flight attendant, *ex-flight attendant*, whose name Catherine still hadn't learned despite their recent encounters around town.

"Ah-ha!"

Catherine opened one eye and observed Penny liberating a pair of tortoise-framed sunglasses from a tangle of headphones, which were also looped around a bunch of keys. She sometimes wondered how the two of them were friends — *former lovers* — when they were so categorically different, but she loved Penny because of who she was, not despite it. Maybe that was why their friendship worked as well as it did.

"What are you grinning at?" Penny slid the sunglasses over her eyes and sat back.

"Nothing. Just enjoying the sunshine, the sound of the river, and your company. This is lovely." Catherine angled her face back to the sun.

"What are your plans for the rest of the weekend?"

Penny's question was innocent enough, but like a pin, it popped the bubble. Because as lovely as this was, afterwards she'd go home alone, the rest of the weekend stretching out like an ocean to the horizon. She wouldn't admit it to Penny, but Juni really was the only bright spot, and he wasn't even her cat, which somehow made the whole thing seem sad and desperate.

"Oh, not much on. Just relaxing really," she mustered.

Their drinks order came, a bucket-sized cup of tea for Penny, and Catherine's oat milk latte served in a tall glass, which she wrapped her cold hands around.

"So, are you going to fill me in on all the latest with the deplorable Daltons?"

"Can I ask you something first?"

"Of course."

"I don't want you to think… to think I'm being weird."

"But you are weird. That's precisely why we're friends. We're two big weirdos together." Penny chuckled and sipped her tea.

"No, I mean, I don't want you to think I'm dredging things up that we've put behind us. You're so happy with Lawrence and I love him to bits. So, I don't want you to think for one moment that I'm not delighted for you. It's just that…" The words stuck in her throat.

"Oh, out with it, babe!"

Catherine sighed. "When you and I were… you know…"

"Fucking?"

Catherine's eyes widened, and she glanced around at the other diners, thankfully all enjoying their meals and paying them no heed whatsoever. She leaned in and spoke three times quieter than Penny had. "Yes, fucking." The word felt awkward in her mouth. "Well, did you ever want more? You know, like a proper relationship with me, more than just…"

"Being fuck-buddies?"

Catherine pressed her lips together and nodded.

At that moment, the waiter arrived from behind her with their food. There was zero possibility he hadn't just heard Penny, who was jiggling with laughter and hiding her mouth behind her mammoth mug of tea. Whilst the waiter set their plates down, Catherine's question hung over them like an ominous piñata, because now that she'd put it out there and handed Penny the stick, she wasn't sure she wanted it cracked open.

Penny picked up her cutlery and tucked into her poached eggs. She popped a loaded forkful into her mouth and released a satisfied groan. "Now, where were we? Oh yes, fuck-buddies."

Catherine shot her a disapproving look and made a start on her own meal — creamy avocado toast with sautéed mushrooms.

Penny smirked. "Babe, you were emotionally unavailable," she said matter-of-factly before crunching down on a piece of toast.

As Penny's response registered, Catherine's eyes grew round. "What on earth makes you say that?"

"Well, for one, you'd never let me stay at your place. You always insisted we went back to mine, even when yours was closer and it meant we'd have to get a taxi."

"I—"

"Don't deny it. You know it's true. But it wasn't just about your flat. You were never really prepared to let me in. I'm not the shrink here—"

"Psychotherapist."

"Sure." Penny grinned and took a long sip of tea. "I'm not the therapist, but if I were to take a wild stab, I'd say you closed yourself off after Francesca hurt you like she did all those years ago."

"That was literally decades ago."

"And it's been how long since you let yourself have a proper relationship?"

Catherine opened her mouth to respond.

"I'm not talking about flirting with internet weirdos or having fuck-buddies." Penny gestured with her fork.

"Fork-buddies?"

Penny narrowed her eyes. "I see you, Catherine Truscote."

As much as Catherine didn't want to believe that her emotional growth had been stunted by a love affair that expired over three decades ago, Penny's theory made sense. She'd spent her entire professional life helping other people fight their demons but had never raised the courage to confront her own. She'd turned her space into a fortress and wrapped her routine around herself like a thick layer of bubble wrap; nothing could penetrate it — not even joy.

Penny placed a warm hand over Catherine's cold one and peered into her face. "Love can only grow in the soil of vulnerability."

Catherine frowned. "Did you just quote Brené Brown at me?"

Penny gasped with mock offence. "How dare you! I made that up. But I do love Brené with all my heart. Maybe you need to see a therapist?"

"I am a therapist."

"All the more reason you of all people should know it'd be good to talk to someone qualified!"

"Who needs qualified?" Catherine grinned. "You've just sat there like Bargain Brené with your glossy-magazine psychology and managed to unpack over three decades of my bullshit in a single breath."

Penny shimmied her shoulders and fluttered her eyelashes. "Penny Weiss, lawyer and life-coach."

"Yeah, yeah. Don't get carried away."

Something shifted in the weighty pause that settled between them.

"Not that it changes anything now, but I tried, you know," said Penny.

"Tried what?"

"Tried to get you to open up when we were..."

"Fucking." Catherine finished the sentence quietly before Penny did.

"You're so sexy when you swear."

"I know," Catherine smirked.

"Things might've been different between us, is what I'm saying. But I needed more than you were able to give at the time... and then there was Lawrence."

"Lovely Lawrence."

"He is rather." Penny nodded in agreement.

"Well, at least it wasn't because I'm unlovable."

Penny leaned across and cupped Catherine's face in her hands. "Far from it. You're wonderful. And who knows what might come along if you open yourself up."

"Maybe, just maybe... it'll be a lovely little kitten who cracks open my withered old heart."

Penny smooshed Catherine's cheeks together, and laughter bounced between them.

16

BLACKMAIL

By rights, the conversation with Penny should have weighed heavily on Catherine — the biting revelation that she'd missed the chance of a real relationship with one of the best women she knew, all because she'd been too emotionally constipated. Yet Catherine had walked away feeling lighter.

Naming her loneliness seemed to have helped too, almost like she could dismiss it by acknowledging it was there. With her clients, identifying the root cause of their problems made it much easier to prescribe a course of treatment.

After all these years, Catherine had finally figured out what her problem was. She'd been getting in her own way. Now that she could see it, she wanted to step aside and help herself move forward. One step at a time.

On the walk home, she thought about looking into social groups and perhaps enlisting Penny's help to refresh her dating app profile. She'd struck gold once with Penny;

it could happen again, and this time she'd try not to hold herself back. And there was every chance she could bump into the woman in red again. Next time, she'd be brave and ask her name.

Scotch in hand, Catherine climbed the stairs. Juni greeted her at the door with meows and purrs, and whilst she was far from fluent in cat, it seemed like a warm welcome.

"Hello, little one. Let's get you some dinner."

She moved fluidly through the space now, switching on lights and navigating past the relative chaos of the flat's new inhabitants. She placed her glass on the kitchen counter and set about serving up Juni's dinner. He chirped, chatting away to her the whole while. When she leaned back against the counter watching him eat, she spotted the pink Post-it note next to the photograph on the fridge.

Catherine, there are chocolates by the kettle. Please help yourself, J x

Just "J" again. For a fleeting second, Catherine considered that maybe it was Juniper leaving notes for her. *Don't be ridiculous.* Her eyes drifted back to the photograph and the woman's strangely familiar smile. She took a long sip of her drink as she raked through her mind, trying to place those lips.

Juni softly headbutted her shin, which made her jump.

"Jesus, you have to stop doing that, or you'll give me a heart attack."

Juni arched his back and chirped as if proud of himself.

"Right, well, staring at this photo isn't going to get that furniture built. Will you be helping me this evening?" Catherine bent and ruffled her fingers over Juni's soft ears. "I've been informed that there's a chocolatey incentive over here; shall I have a look?"

By the kettle sat a decorative green box. Catherine picked it up and read the elaborate vintage typography out loud.

"Chocolate Amatller. Barcelona." *Fancy.* She opened the box and popped one of the dark chocolates in her mouth. In an instant, the rich cocoa melted on her tongue: earthy and ever-so-slightly fruity, but not bitter in the way dark chocolate could sometimes be.

"Mmm, your human has good taste," she said to Juni, who was watching through narrowed green eyes.

From the hall, Catherine opened the only closed door, which she assumed meant the room was out of bounds to Juni. Before she could stop him, he bounded in ahead of her and bounced across the neatly made bed, leaving deep footprints in the plush duvet.

"I'm not sure you're supposed to be in here." She felt much the same about being in someone else's bedroom — not that she hadn't been invited; J's note had strongly hinted that Catherine's help would be appreciated, but even so, it felt strange.

She flicked on the overhead light. The room was less cluttered with boxes than the hall and lounge, but Catherine's gaze was instantly drawn to the airer in the corner draped with an array of lacy pants and their matching bras. Once she'd taken a moment to recalibrate and stop comparing the obviously much younger woman's underwear to her own sensible Marks & Spencer cotton variety, which came in multi-packs of three sensible colours, she noted there was no men's underwear hanging out to dry. *No sign of a man in here at all, in fact.*

One silk robe hung on the back of the bedroom door.

One pair of women's slippers by the bed.

And only one of the bedside tables looked to have been used; the other housed a stack of small boxes, which Juni was now perched on top of.

Perhaps she'd got it wrong about a couple moving in here.

Perhaps it's Will's underwear drying on the airer, and he goes by Jocelyn at the weekends.

Or perhaps, up until now, the couple's relationship had been long-distance, and this was their first home together, which meant they'd be at it like Duracell bunnies right above her head.

She shuddered and berated herself for catastrophising, because *perhaps* she should just mind her own business and get on with what she'd come here to do.

The flatpack box was leaning against the wall. When Catherine went to move it, another pink Post-it note fluttered to the ground. She plucked it from the floor.

If you've made it this far, thank you so much!
Help yourself to more chocolates — don't be shy,
they're actually for you. Please don't let Juni chew

my bra straps (they're not as tasty as they look).
And shut him out of the bedroom when you leave.
Thank you again, lovely neighbour.
I owe you big time, J x

Catherine grinned at the note as if she were smiling at its author. Was this blackmail? Chocolates, IOUs, and feline company, in exchange for something she actually loved doing. Without really knowing why, she slipped the note into her pocket and got to work opening the box and setting the pieces out on the floor.

Juni moved closer to inspect the empty box before crawling inside until he was nothing but two glowing eyes in the shadowy depths. As per the instructions, Catherine constructed the four drawers first and placed them on the bed. Before she made a start on the frame, she went down-stairs and fetched herself another Scotch, speaking into the box before she went.

"I'll be back in five. No eating bras while I'm gone."

On her way back to the bedroom, she passed the kitchen and scoffed a couple more of those delicious Catalan chocolates. She'd always wanted to go to Barcelona. Tapas, city beaches, Gaudí — to name but three reasons — but she'd never got around to it. She had a sudden vision of herself in linen, sipping sangria by a sandy beachfront. *Yes, what a lovely idea!* Maybe booking a European trip would be a good way to start spicing up her life? And after that, she could book that trip to visit Mei — she'd always promised she'd visit.

As she got back to work, she hummed a tune, which

after a moment she realised was the Spice Girls, then before she knew it, she was scrolling in her music app and adding the *Spiceworld* album. She pressed play, turned up the volume and sang along, surprised to find that she knew most of the lyrics to most of the songs.

She didn't often listen to music; she found it too distracting, but listening now, she realised that was the point. It was distracting in a good way. Music filled the void that your mind would otherwise fill with chatter. She made a mental note of that for a new blog post.

Right here, in a stranger's flat with a stranger's cat, she felt more alive and hopeful than she had in a long time.

She stilled when she caught sight of herself in the large mirror propped on the floor beside the bed — her cheeks were flushed from dancing, her usually neat hair sticking up in every direction. And she was smiling — not just with her mouth but with her eyes too.

"I don't know what's got into you, but I love this for you."

The box started purring at the sound of her voice, as if Juni were echoing his agreement.

17

ADONIS

Catherine stirred to a persistent tapping.

She propped herself up on her elbows and turned her head, trying to place the noise.

Tap, tap, tap. It wasn't coming from above or outside. It was almost as if it were at her front door, *but surely not?*

The building's main entrance was wired up with two intercoms; one to each flat, so the person knocking must be her new neighbour. Unless of course they'd returned and left the main door open *again*, allowing someone else access to the building.

Another knock sounded, this one more urgent and slightly louder than the last. Catherine glanced at her phone. 7:26 a.m. on a Sunday. The one day of the week she allowed herself a sleep-in. She tutted as she pulled on her robe and padded along the hallway.

Tap, tap, tap.

"Alright, I'm coming," she said, an edge of irritation in her voice.

Without pausing to think about what she might look like, she unlocked the door — and did a double-take at the woman standing there.

Red hair. Red coat.

How? Why? Am I dreaming? Catherine's brain jammed with too many questions at once.

"Hi. I'm so sorry to wake you at this time." The words came out thick and fast in the woman's Scottish accent. "I just got back and... God," she clamped her hands around her cheeks, a look of wild panic flashing in her eyes. "I've looked everywhere, and I can't find Juni. I don't suppose he got out when you left."

Catherine stood there, probably looking as dumb as she felt.

"God — that was so rude of me. I'm Jules." She pointed up and smiled. "Your new neighbour."

And it all fell into place — 'J' for Jules, and the smile in the photo being so familiar because it belonged to this woman's face, and this woman's face belonged to—

"You're Bridie's daughter?"

Jules flashed a small, bashful smile. "The one and only."

"Wow! We've already met, but I had no idea it was you..." Catherine scrunched her eyes shut and shook her head. "I mean, that you were *you*."

"Yep, I'm me. I'd been planning to pop down and introduce myself properly, but things haven't really gone to plan with the move so far. It's all been a bit chaotic handing things over at work, so..." Jules's smile gave way to a grimace. "Look, I'm sorry again to disturb you, but

Juni, do you know if he…?" She subtly moved to peer around Catherine.

Instinctively, Catherine stepped aside, as if to prove there wasn't a cat hiding behind her.

"Er, no… I mean, he was still in the empty furniture box when I left. I moved it into your hallway before I headed back down here."

"Right, it's just that he's pretty sneaky. He's got out once or twice before. He can be very quick when you're not looking…"

"I'm think I would've noticed if he'd—" Before she'd even finished her sentence, Jules had moved inside. She stepped out of her court shoes, and Catherine gawked at the woman's back in disbelief, watching helplessly as she padded through to the lounge, clicking her tongue.

"Juni? I'm here, puss puss."

Catherine shut the door and followed on, peering around the doorjamb to see Jules on all fours, looking under her sofa.

"Hey, naughty boy, there you are!"

"Wait, what… he's actually under there?"

Jules lay on her stomach and stretched her arms under the sofa. "Gotcha!" She kicked her legs and tried to wriggle backwards. "Juni, stop it. Let go of that… fuck!"

Catherine craned her neck, surveying the scene from above. The slightly-dishevelled-but-exceptionally-hot woman on her lounge room floor rolled onto her back and met Catherine's wide-eyed gaze.

"I'm sorry, but he stuck his claws into something soft under your sofa, and… it's come unravelled."

Catherine stepped forward to look. A few of the jigsaw pieces had scattered out from the mat. "Oh, it's my puzzle mat. Don't worry."

Jules's lip quirked as if she were biting back a laugh at discovering Catherine's nerdy hobby, but she didn't pass comment. Catherine swallowed her mild mortification.

"I probably should've tried this first." Jules sat up, popping her eyes as she pulled a yellow pouch from her pocket.

"Dreamies," she said, answering the question Catherine hadn't asked. "They're like crack for cats."

Jules shook the packet; the contents rattled inside, and Juni darted out from under the sofa. She tipped a couple of the little pillow-shaped biscuits onto the floor, and Juni sat crunching them as she stroked his back.

Catherine shook her head. "I can't believe he's been under there all night and I had no idea!"

Jules chuckled and scooped up her cat. He purred as she cradled him in her arms like a baby.

"No harm done. I'm sorry again for the intrusion… and for the mess he made of your puzzle. I promise it won't happen again." Her eyes sparkled in a way that made Catherine wish she'd retract that promise, because even though she didn't recognise herself for thinking this, she'd enjoyed the audacious intrusion. In a heartbeat, she'd welcome more wake-up calls like this if they were on offer.

"Right, well… we better leave you in peace." Jules moved to the door, and Catherine trailed behind, words failing to come once again as her brain was still buffering.

She watched in silence as Jules pushed her feet back into her shoes and unlatched the door.

She turned and shot Catherine *that* smile.

"Oh, I will thank you properly, by the way. I mean, for everything you've done for me — what with Juni..." she smiled down at the floppy grey mass of cat now lolling in the crook of her arm, "...and the flatpack construction. I'm a bit hopeless when it comes to all that."

Catherine swallowed. "Anytime. Happy to help, I mean... it was my pleasure."

"Good to know." Jules's eyes sparkled again, then she turned and headed up the stairs.

CATHERINE PINCHED HER ARM TO MAKE SURE SHE hadn't just dreamt that.

Her new neighbour was the gorgeous mystery woman she kept bumping into around town. Her new neighbour was her lovely old neighbour's daughter. Now, here she was — living right above her. And she knew Catherine's name and had given her *that* smile.

Jules McPherson had just smiled at her, and it had made her knees go weak, so much so they still felt a little boneless.

Wait, she knows my name!

As far as Catherine was aware, Bridie and her daughter weren't close. The old woman seemed to bristle whenever Catherine asked her any personal questions, so she probed no more. Catherine was off the clock whenever they spent time together, so she eased into the woman's company like it was a comfy old armchair. She enjoyed Bridie's sense of humour, and they shared a taste for a *nice wee dram,* which they took turns to supply.

Now it was a surprise to learn that Bridie must have mentioned her, and Jules had remembered her name. Which maybe halfway explained why she had trusted Catherine with a key and her cat. And her underwear. *They're not as tasty as they look.*

Heat prickled Catherine's neck at the sudden, *very tasty* vision of Jules wearing the lacy underwear she'd seen strung out on the airer.

Oh, behave yourself! She pulled her thoughts out of the gutter and made a quick decision to walk off some of the weird energy thrumming through her. *Two quick laps around the park, you perv. And no Snoots for you today because you can't behave yourself.*

Catherine laughed out loud when she saw her reflection in the bathroom mirror; her hair was a wild mess. She'd answered the door looking like that. *Christ.*

She dressed quickly and made herself a coffee in her reusable mug before heading out. She noted with relief that Jules hadn't left the main door open this time, but she would make a point of mentioning it, particularly as Juni was a little escape artist. He wouldn't fare well on the main road outside their building.

Another sunny spring day met her outside — cloudless blue skies above and the sweet smell of blossom in the air. Catherine set a quick pace, trying to focus on the steps and stop her mind from wandering because every time it did, it ended at the same destination. *That smile.* How had she not equated the photo on the fridge with the woman in red?

On the one or two occasions she let her thoughts wander beyond *that smile*, she'd ended up ogling her imaginary projection of Jules modelling lacy underwear. An image that seemed to summon a silly grin, which she couldn't squash no matter how hard she tried. She forced herself to do a third lap of the park. She even considered a fourth as her thoughts were still spiralling, but her stomach growled so she headed home.

She tried her best not to imagine bumping into the other woman in their shared space and the future conversations they might have, but the task was impossible so she gave into it. By the time she'd reached the door and turned her key in the lock, she was so lost in conjured conversations that she didn't notice the man coming down the stairs until she face-planted into his chest, which felt like a solid wall of muscle.

Catherine stepped back, eyes trailing up the man's skinny jeans and tight black T-shirt until she reached his grinning bronzed face. He wore a black Yankees cap, had perfectly trimmed facial hair, and teeth so white the glare hurt her eyes.

Shit. She'd been so swept up in everything else, she'd forgotten about *him.*

She blinked, hoping to will him out of existence. But no, there he stood — a very real and solid Adonis of a man, who was no doubt very capable of putting together the flatpack furniture she'd spent two nights labouring over like an absolute mug. All the elation she'd felt at this morning's surreal turn of events slipped away, and she suddenly felt very foolish.

"Hiya," he said in a chirpy Northern accent, which irrationally made her dislike him even more. "Sorry about that, you seemed miles away. I hope I didn't startle you."

Yep, miles away thinking about your wife in her underwear, for goodness' sake.

"Well, you should look where you're going and not jump out at people like that."

"Alright," he laughed, a kind laugh that almost made her regret being awful to him. "I'm Will, by the way." He held out a paw-like hand.

"Yes, I know," she said and instantly wished she hadn't because she shouldn't know that, not yet. "Sorry. I had an unexpected early start, and I'm hungry now, so..." She gestured to her door, hoping he'd take the hint and move aside, but he didn't.

"Oh, I'm a right diva when I'm hungry, you know, like the Snickers ad? I get proper hangry. Anyway, I'm nipping down the shop, do you need anything?"

"No, thank you." She forced a small smile and pushed past him and his stupid white teeth and too-tight clothes. "And make sure you close the door after yourself. You people keep leaving it open," she called after his Dorito-shaped back.

She let herself into her flat and crumpled against the door, feeling completely winded.

After one liberating conversation with Francesca and one revealing conversation with Penny, she'd let herself get swept away in a delusional fantasy. *Not for the first time,* mocked the voice inside her head.

Maybe Penny was right; maybe she did need therapy. And clearly, she was by no means ready to start dating again when she'd so tragically misread Jules. Now she needed to bury any thoughts she'd had about that lucky bastard's gorgeous wife and scrub the image of Jules's flawless smile and ridiculous sparkling eyes from her head.

18

WHERE IS MY MIND?

1989

*I*n the stuffy train carriage, Jeremy flicked through a well-thumbed textbook, while Francesca rested her head on his shoulder, pretending to sleep — I could tell by the way her eyelids fluttered.

"Your mood's up and down like a bride's nightie, Trusty. Are you sure you're okay?" Jeremy's voice practically dripped with smugness, like the stupid grin that had spread itself over his thin lips ever since we'd boarded the train and Francesca had chosen the seat next to him. She hadn't breathed a word to me all morning, only dusted the occasional sultry look over me. It was a cruel, deliberate game, and the hollow ache of rejection throbbed in my chest.

I grunted a response and clenched my jaw, focusing on the barren grey landscape rolling by outside the misted windows.

Since the night we'd spent together, Francesca had shown up at the cottage again, but I buried myself under my duvet and ignored the muffled pleas and raps at the door until she gave up.

I spent the rest of the Christmas break alone in my room, filling my head with resolutions about what I would and wouldn't stand for. I hoped the distance I'd wedged between us over the last few days would give Francesca space to figure out what she really wanted.

Me or him. I wasn't prepared to let her have us both.

Winter clutched the start of term in its icy fist. The weather, in all its varying degrees of wet, descended like a grey curtain. From my dorm room window, I watched as Jeremy came calling for Francesca, collar turned up against the cold.

Pain twisted my gut as they left, huddled together against the bitter wind that howled across campus. I threw myself into my studies; that was what I was here for, after all. *This is good for me.* I stretched my neck and narrowed my mind to focus, devouring textbooks, scribbling notes until my hand ached, and seeking solace in statistics, as I tried to block out the image of them. But the phantom of her scent clung to my skin.

January unravelled with the same inevitability as my resolve, and by the second week of term, Francesca was tapping at my door and calling my name. I stood on the other side, my forehead pressed to the painted wood grain, determined to hold my ground and maintain the fragile peace I'd wrapped around myself. But there was something different in her voice — something that sounded a lot like remorse.

"I miss you," she said, and I caved.

I opened the door, my chest squeezing at the sight of her — sad eyes painted dark and dressed again in her gothy blacks and ripped denim. She looked so vulnerable, a raw contrast to the girl who had so recently chosen another over me.

"What do you want, Francesca?" I asked, my throat clenching around the words.

She looked up at me through her claggy eyelashes and, with one word, disarmed me.

"You," she said.

Mentally tearing up my resolutions, I swept aside my better judgement and pulled her into my room.

Francesca's minty tongue speared into my mouth, her fingers tangling in fistfuls of my hair as she pushed me back against the door and made my world spin.

"Nothing tastes as good as you do," she teased into my ear.

I arched, yielding to her persistent press as a flood of desire overtook me.

After that, we fell into a new pattern: one where Francesca wound up in my bed most nights. We'd have sex and fall asleep wrapped in each other. Sometimes I'd lie awake, watching the light change through the gap in the curtains and wondering how it was possible to feel so close, yet so distant to someone at the same time. Or how Francesca could make me feel like I meant everything and nothing all at once.

It was fine unless I tried to talk about feelings, or Jeremy, or anything she didn't want to talk about. Like the flip of a coin, Francesca's mood would change, darkness clouding her eyes as her temper flared.

"Isn't it obvious how I feel, Catherine?" she'd rage before pushing me onto the bed and showing me with her tongue, her body a tempest against mine.

"I think it's a *you* problem," she'd say with such confidence it had to be true.

"It's you I'm fucking, isn't it?" Her words dripped with disdain, but I found some small satisfaction in the implication that it was *only* me.

I loved the things we did together in the sanctuary of my room, the way her skin felt against mine, the way her body moved, and the secret language we shared, but every touch stoked a slow, painful hunger that left me emotionally malnourished.

"You're very clingy, Catherine. Perhaps it's because you lost your mother so young," she said without stopping to consider the harsh words. They stung like a slap, but I told myself not to be greedy, to be grateful for what was on offer and not take too much. I could only hope my restraint would be rewarded with abundance, so I continued to offer myself up to her as communion.

After a while, an anaesthetic-like numbness set in — even though her words still cut, I barely felt it anymore. I'd lap up every crumb of a compliment, then sit back, bloated and glowing, because *if she makes me feel this good, how can it possibly be bad?*

Francesca changed Jeremy and me in ways we had no words for. She seemed capable of carrying on as if our weird dynamic was perfectly normal. For a while, I let her drag me along to our old haunts. I spun like a third wheel as the two of them flirted, the whole time relishing the fact that it was me who'd fall asleep and wake up beside her.

Inevitably, a chasm formed between us. Time alone with Jeremy was out of the question; he talked endlessly about her, stirring an unpalatable cocktail of smug pride and sickly guilt inside me. I knew things he'd never know — the sweet taste of Francesca on my tongue, her whispered confessions in the dead of night, and the way she wrapped herself around me like I was hers. I wanted to tell him everything, but I didn't want to crush him with the weight of it. So I pulled away, making excuses to while away my time in the library and lose myself in the hushed rustle of pages.

And that's where the collision occurred.

Two over-caffeinated, bleary-eyed students crashing together in a shower of books and awkward apologies.

"I'm Mei," she giggled, peering at me through her long fringe as we swept up the fallen books from the floor.

"Catherine." I offered my hand, and she shook it with both of hers.

"Cat...e...reen," she repeated, her accent butchering my name in the most endearing way.

"Close enough." I laughed, and she did too.

"Some words can be difficult for me." She frowned, and

a deep line formed between her brows. "Maybe it's better for both of us if I can call you Cati?"

I nodded, already basking in the warmth of her energy as I shifted my heavy book bag back onto my shoulder.

The next day, we sat sipping coffee and exchanging the headlines of our two decades of existence, both of us fascinated by how our cultures merged and diverged.

Mei was unlike anyone I'd ever met. She jiggled with frenetic energy, as if her petite frame couldn't contain her spirit. Her laughter was contagious, and she had the most chaotic and colourful dress sense of anyone I'd ever seen.

Mei confessed to finding it difficult to make friends — the other foreign students arrived in their cliques, and the British students avoided her, perhaps assuming she spoke poor English. And so, she'd fallen through the social cracks.

For my part, Mei had arrived right when I needed a friend, so we became study-buddies and cappuccino-confidants. Unlike Jeremy and Francesca's company, Mei's was uncomplicated. She told me about Malaysia and how this was the farthest she'd ever been from home. Mei's parents saved hard to give her the chance they'd never had. She was their bright spark, their one big wish for the future. As a result, the heavy pressure weighed her down, as if their hopes were rocks in her pockets.

Something about her wide-eyed curiosity cracked me open. I told her about losing my mum, how my dad had curled into himself ever since, and how at times I felt so alone it was like my own thoughts echoed inside my head.

Weeks passed, and the connection deepened, until one

day I found the words I'd been burning to say taking slow shape in my mouth.

"Mei... would it change your opinion of me if I told you I was gay?"

I carefully watched her reaction, waiting for a recoil, a flinch, or for her to run from the Wimpy café we frequented in town — a place I knew Francesca would never step foot inside.

Mei slurped her strawberry milkshake through the straw and shrugged. "I already knew this about you, Cati."

"Oh!" I tilted my head, the echo of my words still ringing in my ears. "You, er, you don't mind?"

Mei giggled. "Why would I? It's who you are, and I like *you*."

I nudged my glasses back up my nose. "Right, yes. Okay. Good then."

Mei leaned forward. "You want to know something about me?"

My eyes snapped back to hers, which were sparkling with a secret.

"I've never liked anyone like *that*. Not a boy or a girl. Not one person, ever." She crossed her index fingers in an X.

"Maybe you just haven't met the right person."

Mei grinned. "What — like maybe you just haven't met the right boy?"

I opened my mouth to respond but closed it again because I'd already lost the point.

"See, I'm different. I know I'm different." Mei

shrugged. "I think that's why we're friends. We're both different."

A slow warmth spread through me. I felt seen and understood for the first time, like another layer had been peeled back and Mei hadn't been horrified by what lurked underneath.

The only thing I withheld from Mei was my relationship with Francesca. It was bigger than any words I had to explain it. Yet, what was there to tell? I couldn't find a label that would stick on that tin — a secret affair? A romantic tryst? Or was it just sex?

I wanted more, but settled for all Francesca was prepared to give. Besides, she'd made it clear she didn't want anyone else to know, which, coupled with her frequent coldness, made it feel like a dirty little secret that was best kept to myself.

OCCASIONALLY, FRANCESCA SURPRISED ME WITH unsolicited affection, a subtle brush of skin on skin or a small sway into me as we walked across campus together, our bodies connecting, and sparks jumping with the illicit thrill.

One daring day, she slipped her hand into my pocket and gripped mine. Hope rose inside me at the openness of her gesture, but the bubble burst when a shaven-headed student in a studded leather jacket yelled out to us from across the quad. Francesca yanked her hand back and sprung away from me.

I paused to look around at the small group of students gathered in a clearing between two trees where they'd strung up a handmade flag — three words painted underneath a large pink triangle: Gay Liberation Front.

"Hey girls!" Leather Jacket hollered again as she crossed the quad towards us.

Francesca tugged my arm. "Come on."

"Shall we see what she wants?" I asked, attempting a casual tone, though my heart pounded in my chest.

"No, we're not like them," Francesca hissed. "Stay away from them, or you'll get a name for yourself."

As Leather Jacket drew close, Francesca stormed off.

I turned and apologised to the warm-eyed girl now in front of me.

She smiled and handed me a flyer. "I just wanted to give you this. I thought you and your friend might be interested."

I looked down at the flyer, which said *Scrap Section 28* in a bold font over a pink triangle. Details of a protest march were printed underneath. Elation and mortification competed in a tug-of-war inside me because I'd been seen for who I was, Francesca too.

Leather Jacket gestured towards her group of friends. They were passing around a cigarette, laughter punctuating the words of their animated conversation. "We all need to stick together, you know. Those Tory bastards are taking away our rights."

I managed to squeak out a "Yeah."

"Anyway, I'd better get back. See you around, yeah?"

I nodded and watched her walk away with a confidence I wished I possessed.

I folded the flyer and tucked it into my pocket, in the space left by Francesca's hand.

ONE DRIZZLY AFTERNOON, I RETURNED FROM THE library to find Francesca brooding on my bed, Robert Smith's voice blaring through the headphones of my Walkman. I shook the water off my umbrella into the hallway and dropped it by the door. She must have heard me through the music, but she didn't look around.

"Hey," I said, loathing my face for lighting up at the sight of her.

She lay with her hands behind her head, her gaze fixed on the slow-growing damp spot on the ceiling; the same spot I often traced with my eyes, lying awake as she slept peacefully beside me. I stacked the library books on the desk.

The bedsprings creaked as I eased down next to her. She still hadn't moved, but the muscle in her jaw twitched. I reached over and pressed Stop on the Walkman, and silence padded the space between us.

"What's up?"

She didn't answer, so I softly placed my hand on her chest, hoping to calm the rapid breaths puffing in and out of her. I opened my mouth to speak again, but she turned her head and beat me to it.

"Where were you?"

I frowned. "I was at the library. I told you I—"

"Yes, but who were you with?"

My brain slowly caught up.

"Mei."

Francesca's lips puckered in a pout.

"She's my friend. We study together sometimes." I shrugged. "It's nice to have company other than you and Jeremy, especially because of how things are..." The last few words bristled out of me, but I didn't want to argue with her. I was tired and cold and needed a hug.

Francesca narrowed her gaze as if she were trying to peer through me.

I bulged my eyes. "What's the problem?"

"You haven't mentioned this Mei character before."

True. Instinct had prevented me from telling Francesca about my fledgling friendship, especially because of how it'd backfired the last time I'd let my two worlds collide.

"Haven't I?" My throat tightened around the words, and I tried to adjust my pitch. "I'm sure you don't tell me about all the people you chat to around campus."

Francesca scoffed. "You know I don't speak to anyone else. They're all morons."

I sighed and stood up, stripping off my damp sweatshirt. "Well, I am allowed to have other friends, Francesca. It's not like you and Jeremy don't make plans without me, is it?"

"Now you sound bitter. Are you doing this to spite me?" She sat up and swung her legs around. "I saw the way you two were looking at each other and laughing together like... giggling little girls."

"What are you on about?" I held up my palms. "We hang out, drink coffee and study. That's all."

"How do you think it made me feel seeing you with someone else?" Her voice cracked slightly, and the sound caught me off guard. I moved towards her, and in an instant the mood shifted. She linked her arms around my waist, and I held her head against me.

"I told you, it isn't like that. Mei's my friend."

I softly arched her head back and looked into her eyes, now swirling pools of insecurity.

Francesca's sudden fragility was a new foothold.

"It's you I'm fucking, isn't it?" I grinned, daring to echo her words.

The words seemed to stoke a fire. Francesca stood and gripped my wrists as she smothered my mouth with ravenous kisses. With frantic hands, we peeled away clothes until there was nothing between us but heat and breath.

19

EVER FALLEN IN LOVE

In the spirit of openness, I made a few half-hearted offers to introduce Francesca to Mei. She always declined with a curled lip, and quiet relief coursed through me. I imagined it would've been like introducing a cat to a mouse and hoping all would end well.

My friendship with Mei had given my confidence a boost, and in some small way it seemed to have redressed the power balance between Francesca and me. She complained about it, but having to compete for my attention made her thirstier for it, as if a bite of jealousy made her hungrier for me.

Once again, I returned from my lecture to find her ensconced in my room, mum's blanket draped around her shoulders, and my bunny slippers on her feet. She was munching biscuits on my bed and flicking through a copy of *NME*. As always, my heart squeezed at the sight of her, but I held my breath, waiting for the other boot to drop.

"I still don't know why you choose to hang out with that foreign student when you could be spending time with me," she said, not looking up.

I shucked off my coat and forced a levity I wasn't feeling into my voice. "Her name is Mei, and you're welcome to join us anytime."

She peered over her magazine. "And you'd introduce me as what — your *girlfriend*?"

"My neighbour...my friend," I said quickly. "You're my friend. And that's fine. I know you're not comfortable with people knowing about us... yet." I paused, letting the last word land, but she didn't react to it, which I took as promising. "I thought you had plans anyway?"

Francesca sighed and flipped the page. "Jeremy's working on his dissertation, or something equally dull. I didn't fancy spending the afternoon in the library watching you flirt with *her*, so I came back here."

I ignored the jab because it was better that way. "Don't you have an assignment due?"

"I got an extension."

I crawled up the bed, wriggling between her legs until I was able to duck my head under the magazine and peer up at her.

"What are you doing?" she huffed as if I were an unwelcome distraction.

"Giving you some attention." I jutted my bottom lip in a mock pout and said in a baby voice, "You obviously got lonely without me around. You're even wearing my bunnies that you so love to mock."

"Oh, shut up!" The corners of her mouth twitched with a grin.

A soft moment stretched between us. I rested my head on her chest, enjoying the warmth of her, and realising that I was actually too tired to start anything. She lazily stroked her fingers through my hair.

"Do you fancy catching the train into the city tomorrow? We could go shopping. Jeremy took me to this little Italian place by the canal; we could go there for lunch after. My treat."

I tried not to bristle at the mention of time she'd spent alone with Jeremy; it had been my choice to take a step back after all. They'd probably have included me otherwise. *Probably.*

"I can't tomorrow. I've got a lecture in the morning, then Mei and I are—"

"Seriously?" She stiffened underneath me. "You're choosing to spend your free time with *her*?"

The bedsprings creaked as I kneeled up between her knees. "You've only just suggested something. I'd already made plans."

"And you're choosing not to unmake them for me."

Tension spiked in the air between us.

"Fine," she said as if settling an internal debate. "Bring her along, too. You can introduce me as your *neighbour,* and the three of us will play nicely together. How does that sound?"

Awful. It sounded awful. I winced.

"I'm really sorry, but there's this rally. Mei wanted to

go, so I said I'd go with her. It's a demonstration of solidarity with the Chinese students in Tiananmen Square—"

"Why do you care about the students in China?" Francesca shrugged.

"It's about democracy and freedom of speech. You should care too."

"Forget it, then." She sat up, swung her legs around and left me alone with my thoughts, which quickly spiralled into regrets. Before long, the low bass of her music rumbled through the wall.

Francesca had never suggested an outing with just the two of us before. She was making an effort, and I'd brushed it aside. *I'm such an idiot!* Her dark mood would have set in like a storm, which I knew from experience was best to let rage and blow over.

I KNOCKED ON HER DOOR FIRST THING THE NEXT morning. No answer came, so I tried the handle. *Locked.*

"Shit!"

Crouching down, I tore a sheet of paper from my pad and scribbled a quick note. It was too late to change plans with Mei, so I suggested Francesca meet me at the union after the rally.

I signed it with a kiss and stuffed it under her door.

Only a handful of the professor's words filtered through my thoughts as I tried and failed to focus.

"Reduced prefrontal cortex activity..." *Francesca's eyes, as dark as a lake.*

"A highly active amygdala..." *The way her rage bubbled up and over.*

"Increased levels of cortisol... butterflies... racing heart rate..." *I'm in love with her.*

Of course, I'm in love with her.

The epiphany had me scooping up my books and skipping down the stairs of the lecture theatre.

"Sorry, so sorry," I said to the turned heads of my classmates.

"Is there somewhere more important you need to be, Miss Truscote?" The lecturer's pale face was pinched with derision.

"Sorry, I just need to..." *Find Francesca. I need to apologise for not putting her first.* I dashed out and down the hallway, to where, I wasn't sure.

To Jeremy's. Yes, he might know where to find her.

Somewhere between cortisol and cortex, a frantic determination took root. I had to tell her. She needed to know. And it was time Jeremy knew what was going on too — what he'd been foolishly getting in the way of.

I love her. I want to be with her, properly. And I think she wants that too.

With my head down, I sped across campus towards Jeremy's halls, charging through the icy rain that dotted my glasses. The biting cold stung my face and whipped strands of hair from my ponytail.

"Jeremy!" I shouted before I'd even reached the landing.

"Jeremy, have you seen Francesca?" I yelled to a row of closed doors. Even to my ears, my voice sounded overwrought. But this was important, no time for breath or composure. This couldn't wait. I needed to make a frizzy-haired declaration to the girl I loved.

Besides, love isn't perfectly groomed; love isn't pretending you're something you're not.

A door creaked open and Jeremy's head popped out, his ruddy cheeks even more flushed than usual. "Trusty? What are you doing here?"

I bounded towards him, but he retreated, pushing the door to and peering through the gap, but by then I'd already glimpsed his bare torso and tousled hair. A musky odour escaped his room as I drew closer.

"Oh!" I whispered, a smile cracking across my face. "You've got someone in there, haven't you?"

"Er, just give me a sec."

The door clicked to a close, and I leaned against the scuffed wall opposite, catching my breath. My heart felt too big as it bounced in my chest. *Okay, maybe love does need a little composure.*

The sound of muffled voices caught my ear. Jeremy shushed the other person. A moment later, he stepped into the hallway wearing a towel tied around his waist and a creased shirt, buttoned askew.

"I'm afraid you've caught me in a bit of a moment." He scratched his neck.

"It's okay." I smiled. "I'm just looking for Francesca. Have you seen her?"

"Er..." His eyes flicked around. He settled his gaze on the wall behind me.

"I see your mind is elsewhere." I laughed and knuckled

his shoulder. He looked down at the spot I'd touched as if I'd burnt him.

"Look, Trusty... there's something, I... well, I mean, we—"

"Wait..." A horrible sinking feeling took hold. "It's her in there, isn't it?"

Jeremy's nod was almost imperceptible.

Blood rushed in my ears. I swallowed and shoved past him, the door handle in my hand, twisting and opening. My vision blurring at the edges before settling on *her* in his bed, wearing nothing but his bedsheets.

"Good morning, Catherine." Her voice was cold and unapologetic, like I meant nothing to her and this should mean nothing to me. I was just a footnote in a bigger plot, an inconsequential comma in Francesca's story.

No, no, no, no, no.

Bile burned in my throat as I caught the sweet scent of her mixed with the sour odour I'd noticed before — the smell, I realised, of sex.

I turned to leave, but Jeremy's hands closed around my arms. His voice warped as he said, "Trusty, why don't you sit down for a minute?"

Her laughter hit me like a sucker punch, and I tore myself from his grip, stumbling out the door.

"Catherine, come back. Let's talk this over." His voice; maybe hers? I couldn't tell.

One foot falling over the other; tears streaming, blood rushing. Stairs, then air, finally air, but it was too much, too quick, and I was gulping in great big lungfuls until I was on my hands and knees vomiting the sludgy brown remnants of that morning's tea and toast into a hedge.

Laughter burst from a passing group of students.

"Christ, it's not even ten yet," one of them said, followed by another bright burst of laughter, the sound dropping like a stone of mortification inside me. I wanted to crawl under the hedge, but I found my way to my feet.

In the brief time I'd been inside, wet snow had settled into a slushy blanket on the ground. It splashed up my legs, the burning cold soaking into my Dunlops as I ran between the skeleton trees across campus towards my halls.

Faces stared, laughed and blurred. I heard my name called more than once, but I couldn't stop. My stomach ached with a sickening churn as bile clawed up my throat, threatening to escape and splatter a Jackson Pollock of puke over the fresh white canvas.

Brakes squealed, and someone shouted, "Look out!"

I whipped my head around, but it was too late.

Something blunt and hard slammed into my side, knocking the last of the wind from my lungs as it tipped me up, over and out.

PANIC!

PRESENT DAY

After the emotional whiplash of discovering the gorgeous woman in red was her new neighbour, Jules, then meeting her annoyingly handsome husband, Will, Catherine spent the rest of the day in a sour mood. It was a mercy she had no plans with anyone else; she was getting on her own nerves, which felt like a new personal low.

She considered returning to bed to sleep it off and reset, but she didn't indulge the notion for long. It seemed a lot like wallowing, and that was something she warned her clients against. Besides, she couldn't bear the possibility of hearing Jules and Will in the bedroom.

Catherine breathed through the squirming discomfort in her stomach, rolled out her jigsaw mat on the coffee table, and tried to immerse herself in the puzzle for a while. Progress was slow. She bristled at every bang and scrape from above.

Occasionally, muffled laughter travelled through the

walls, and she wondered whether they were laughing about her; the withered old woman downstairs, whom they'd tricked into looking after their cat and building their furniture. *What a mug!*

She didn't have to like them, but she needed to learn to live with a happy couple upstairs, serving as a constant reminder that she hadn't just missed the boat; she'd belly-flopped off the dock while trying to catch it. *Oh, stop being so melodramatic.*

After slotting an elusive piece into Sappho's face, Catherine stretched up off the floor and decided to reward herself with a drink. Her mood declined further when she discovered she'd finished the last of the Scotch yesterday evening. She'd been so involved with the flatpack she'd forgotten to make a mental note to get another bottle.

With a big sigh, she tugged on her long Puffa coat and set out on the familiar route, hunching against the chill that had crept in with dusk. A bell rang over the door when she entered the corner shop. She smiled at the usual man behind the counter and walked the aisles to the chilled section to contemplate the ready meals, none of which sounded appealing. She should've gone grocery shopping earlier, filled her fridge, and planned a nice evening for herself instead of fuming in her flat.

How on earth was she qualified to help other people when she couldn't even help herself? That was a question for another day. She settled on macaroni cheese and grabbed an extra-large bar of Dairy Milk on the way to the till, where she pointed to a bottle of Scotch from the limited range and paid, berating herself that she had forgotten her reusable bag (it wasn't the ten pence charge, it was the principle).

Thankfully, the main door was still locked when she returned, which meant she could postpone the difficult conversation, at least until it happened again. As she pushed inside, the smell of something delicious and savoury wafted out. Catherine stilled at the sight of Jules standing by her front door.

"Ah, that's why you're not answering." Jules spun around and beamed. She looked elegantly casual, wearing an oversized Oxford shirt and figure-hugging jeans. Jules was the sort of woman who'd look good in anything... or nothing at all.

Catherine tore her eyes away and glanced down at her carrier bag, the thin white plastic doing little to hide the sad contents it contained. *Microwave meal-for-one, comfort calories and sorrow-drowning booze. Christ.* "I nipped out for a few essentials."

"I popped down to give you this." Jules held up a gift bag. "It's just a little something to say thank you. And to apologise for all the noise we've made today."

"You shouldn't have. Really, it's fine." Catherine pursed her lips.

"Almost unpacked now though," Jules said through a breathy laugh. "It's starting to feel a bit like home."

Catherine flashed a flat smile and muttered her thanks as she took the proffered gift. She moved past Jules to unlock her door. The other woman stepped aside but didn't leave.

Hovering in her doorway, Catherine turned to look at

her again. Jules stood with a hand resting on the dark-wood newel post. "Um, if you're not busy this evening, you're welcome to join us for Chinese. Will's just plating up. He ordered way more than we can eat."

"Oh. Thanks, but I have dinner all sorted."

"Right, okay. Yeah, that's—" Jules scuffed a socked foot on the bottom stair, like she was wrestling with indecision about saying something else. "Would you like to come over for dinner next week? I can cook. I love cooking, so it'd be..."

Catherine frowned. "Have you got more flatpack you need building?"

Jules let out a laugh. "No, it's all done, thank you. I just thought it might be nice for us to get to know each other." Her hazel eyes looked so warm and inviting, Catherine relented; she really had no reason to be unkind.

"Okay, well, maybe when you and your husband are a bit more settled in, perhaps—"

"My what?"

"Your husband."

"I don't have a husband."

"Oh, I thought..."

"Oh my God!" Jules clapped her hand over her mouth to hold in her laughter. "You thought... me and Will were...?"

Heat burned in Catherine's cheeks.

"Will's my best friend. He's the one with the husband, not me."

"Oh, right!" Catherine laughed too as an irrational flood of relief coursed through her.

At that moment, the door upstairs cracked open, and Will yelled through the gap. "Dinner's getting cold and I'm bloody starving!"

"Keep your knickers on, Wilma, I'm on my way!" Jules rolled her eyes. "I mean, you actually met him earlier, right? He's camper than a row of diamond-encrusted tents."

"I don't like to make assumptions about people." Catherine chewed her lip because all she'd done so far was make assumptions, and how wrong she'd been. She really should know better.

Jules tilted her head. "Are you sure you don't want to join us?"

"You're kind, but really, I'm all set." Catherine's chest clenched. She needed to compose herself, but in the moment, Penny's words about bravery bounced through her mind, so she took a leap. "If the invitation's still open, I could come over for dinner next week. How about Friday?"

Jules grinned. "It's a date."

Catherine lingered in her doorway watching as Jules climbed the stairs, but just before she was out of sight, she leaned over the banister.

"Oh, and just to put the record straight... I'm not."

Catherine angled her head. "You're not what?"

"Straight." Jules winked and disappeared.

In the kitchen, Catherine was still smiling like an idiot as she unpacked her 'essentials' and popped the macaroni cheese in the oven. After staring at it for a long moment, she opened the gift bag from Jules and pulled out a cylindrical tube wrapped in tissue paper. Her eyebrows shot up as she peeled back the paper to reveal an eighteen-year-old bottle of Scotch.

The woman's timing was terrible, but this was the perfect gift. It was almost like Jules knew her, and perhaps she did. *Bridie must have been more in touch with her daughter than she'd let on because otherwise how could Jules have known? Whisky isn't for everyone. But then again, she's Scottish — it's in their blood.*

Catherine poured herself a measure of the less fancy Scotch she'd just bought. The eighteen-year-old deserved an occasion. Perhaps she'd crack it open with Jules.

Her day had started brilliantly, gone terribly downhill, and now here she was standing in her kitchen, elated because she had a date. *A date!*

CATHERINE FELL ASLEEP WITH A SILLY GRIN plastered across her lips, but woke in the thick of night with cold sweat prickling her skin. She threw off the duvet and gulped down some water, then lay awake blinking in the swirling blackness of her bedroom, willing sleep to return but doing nothing to slow her runaway thoughts.

The relentless self-doubt that plagued her seemed to be amplified in the small hours; her chaotic mind swung from the mundane to the catastrophic in a matter of seconds. Just because she was a mental health professional, people assumed her own mental state was in tip-top condition. If they could actually see the jumble of thoughts that tumbled around inside her head on a daily basis, she was sure she'd be struck off.

Date panic set in... what to wear, what to bring, what to talk about. There were so many things to consider. Should she buy new underwear? Should she shave her armpits? Her legs? Her nether regions? The thought of being unprepared for anything, even the most basic of intimate encounters, sent a fresh wave of anxiety crashing over her.

She imagined Jules, the object of her current, slightly obsessive affections, and a knot of apprehension tightened in her stomach. What if they had nothing in common? What if they had too much in common? What if it all went horribly wrong and then they were stuck living in this proximity? Jules would move on and date other women. Younger, more attractive women, who, with effortless elegance, would sport lacy lingerie like the ones she'd seen draped over the airer in Jules's bedroom. Then she'd have to lie here listening to them having noisy sex right above her bed. She'd be even lonelier than before, and she'd have to move out and leave her lovely home...

What had she been thinking? *A dinner date with Jules is a truly terrible idea.*

The sane voice of Penny crept in with words she hadn't yet said, but no doubt would when Catherine put all this to her. *But what if it all works out?*

She took a slow, calming breath, and then another and another until sleep found her again and she woke to the chiming of her alarm clock.

With a swift lap around the park, Catherine shook the

lethargy from her legs before returning home to refuel with muesli and a refreshing shower.

While waiting in line for coffee at Snoots — a Monday treat — she checked her schedule. Another jam-packed day where Stephanie had left barely any time between sessions. Catherine sighed, a familiar frustration bubbling up. She really must speak to the agency about sending a different assistant. And she must catch up with Jeremy and ask about Francesca.

Coffee in hand and scrolling her phone, she almost bumped into the person heading into the café.

"Sorry," she mumbled with a quick glance up and did a double-take. "Oh, hi," Catherine said with a breathy laugh as her pulse peaked. "Hi."

Jules stood in front of her, smiling. Her red curls were swept up into a messy bun, and her makeup-free face was glowing in the fresh morning air.

"I'm not stalking you, honest! Will sent me out for pastries, and I thought I should oblige, seeing as I had him lugging boxes until the wee hours."

"I guess I better get used to seeing you around, and this really is the best place for pastries."

"Oh, and I meant to ask if you've any allergies or anything."

Catherine blinked. "Sorry?"

"For Friday, I'm cooking you dinner... that's if you..." Jules reached up and touched the back of her neck. The movement didn't escape Catherine. It was hard to imagine, but was Jules anxious about their date too?

"Of course. Friday. I'm looking forward to it. No allergies, but I'm vegetarian."

"Great, you're easy." Jules's eyes bulged. "I mean, *that's* easy, you're a veggie. Vegetarian. Yes. I can do you." Her eyes grew wider still. "That, I mean, I can cook that." Colour crept up her neck and into her cheeks. The bashful display went a long way to settling Catherine's nerves. She smiled and touched Jules's arm. *We're in this together.*

"Please don't go to too much trouble; I'm not a fussy eater."

"Okay, good. Well, I'll see you Friday, and probably a hundred times before then, too." Jules's laughter carried like blossom on the breeze.

In a rush of endorphins, Catherine practically skipped to work, the fragrant morning air thick with hope and pollen. She keyed in the code to let herself into the office and was greeted by the sounds of clattering crockery and muttered curses as Stephanie rattled around in the kitchenette. Catherine paused in Reception to open the blinds and window, bathing the small room with light and air — another small thing Alice had done instinctively, which Catherine had taken for granted.

"Morning, Stephanie," she called out as she passed. Stephanie squeaked a surprised response.

As the lights of her office flickered on overhead, Catherine pulled off her light jacket and sank down into her desk chair, affording herself a grounding moment to sit still and sip her coffee before her busy day began. A soft rap at her door interrupted, and Jeremy's face peered into the room. He looked much brighter than he had last week;

tired eyes, but at least groomed and with some colour back in his cheeks.

"Oh, I didn't realise you'd be in today."

Jeremy pulled his thin lips into a smile. "I have things to do, and I feel a little useless rattling around at home." With three bouncy strides into the room, he perched on the chair opposite Catherine.

"How's Francesca doing?" Catherine's mind flashed back to the hotel room and the unravelled state she'd found her in.

"She's home, thankfully. I think your visit did some good." He frowned. "I know she can be... difficult."

Catherine steadied her voice and shifted in her seat a little. "Look, this might be hard for you to hear, but Francesca's behaviours are—"

"Awful, I know."

"No, I was going to say... consistent with narcissistic personality traits." Catherine swallowed. "I really think she needs a formal diagnosis and some proper support. Not just for her sake, but—"

"Yes, yes. I agree."

Catherine's eyebrows lifted. "You do?"

"Honestly, I've known for longer than I care to admit. As you say, all the traits tally." Jeremy stared intently at his clenched hands. "This isn't the first time she's taken things badly after a... break-up."

"Right." Catherine swallowed again.

Jeremy drew a sharp breath. "But this time I was brave and broached the subject with her."

"You did?"

"It's early days, but she's receptive to the idea of therapy. And I suppose if it is NPD they might prescribe mood-stabilisers. But she's open to it. That's something."

"That's great, Jeremy." Catherine refrained from adding the words perched on the end of her tongue... *and long overdue.*

"Quite. Yes." He slowly nodded. "I'd like to do something to thank you... you know, for coming to our aid in a time of need and helping things along like you have."

Catherine held up her hands. "There's no need."

"Lunch! Can I take you to lunch this week? Somewhere nice."

"Really, it's fine and besides my diary is—"

"Please, Catherine, for me. It's important." He hit her with that pleading look she couldn't resist.

"Okay, alright. Just not today. I'm off to the University Hospital to see a patient — the final hangover from all the Alice business."

Jeremy winced.

"And not Friday," she added quickly. "I can't do Friday."

Jeremy bobbed his head. "Got it. Not Friday."

Friday was reserved for Jules and mentally preparing for their date. Catherine gripped her fingers around her reusable cup because a rogue wave of panic surged again at the thought.

FOR THE SECOND NIGHT IN A ROW, CATHERINE LAY awake, staring into the dark. For a while she thought about Jules lying in the room above her. *Is she restless too? Or does she sleep like the dead?*

There was so much to learn about a new person in your life, but wasn't that supposed to be the fun part? The thrill of discovery, the slow unveiling of personality, the shared laughter and quiet confidences — these were the things Catherine craved. Perhaps she wouldn't like what she found out. Or worse, Jules wouldn't like what she discovered as she peeled back Catherine's layers to find her shrivelled, old core.

Enough with the old — you're fifty-six, not a nonagenarian.

Her mind drifted to Jeremy and the curious lunch he was planning. A mixture of anticipation and dread swirled in her stomach. Despite her reluctance, she was a little intrigued. She'd sensed there was more he wanted to get off his chest.

Resigned to wakefulness, Catherine swung her legs out of bed and padded to the kitchen. As she waited for the kettle to boil, the image of the man she'd earlier visited in hospital flashed into her tired mind — Alice's friend, George — a chronic insomniac, suffering from grief-induced episodic memory loss. There was something about the hunch of George's broad shoulders that reminded her of her father — the way his weary face crumpled when he spoke of his loss. That was why she'd picked this career path, after all — and really why Jeremy had, too.

A memory stirred as she steeped a Chamomile Teapig, adding a squirt of honey to take away the bitterness.

* * *

THEY SAT IN THE OLD STABLES, LEGS DANGLING from the mezzanine floor as Jeremy popped the cork on a bottle of vintage Champagne he'd swiped from his parents' wine cellar.

"Are you sure they won't mind?" Catherine scanned the bottle's dusty label. It was older than her, and probably worth more than her dad earned in a month.

Jeremy shrugged. "School's out. We're celebrating!"

She took a tentative sip and giggled when the bubbles fizzed up her nose.

"Have you decided what you want to do at uni yet?" he asked.

"Yeah, I've been thinking about it, and I want to help people somehow. I wondered about training to be a psychologist or something?"

"Right, yeah. Psychology," he said and swigged another mouthful before passing the bottle back to her.

"My dad needed help after my mum..." She took another sip from the bottle and left the end of the sentence hanging because still the word was too hard to say.

"Do you reckon psychology would help me understand girls any better?"

Catherine spluttered. "Yeah, maybe."

"Right, well that's settled then. I'll do psychology, too."

She laughed, but Jeremy didn't, so she turned and took in his earnest expression.

"You're serious?"

"Of course!"

CATHERINE CARRIED HER STEAMING MUG THROUGH to the lounge and flicked on the lamp. She'd allow herself a little time with the Sappho jigsaw while her tea cooled, and maybe after that sleep would claim her again. But she lost herself in the puzzle until the thin dawn light strained through the blinds.

Bedtime isn't just sleep — it's a gentle seduction into calm.

Dim the lights. Let shadows soften the edges of your day and wrap around you like an embrace.

Savour the stillness, the hush, the warmth, the weight of rest waiting for you.

Breathe slowly. Let the rhythm from each exhale melt the tension from your body.

Let sleep unfurl, unhurried and effortless; imagine it like silk slipping through your fingers.

Catherine posted her latest blog and sat back, watching as a flurry of likes and comments tallied on her screen. She removed her glasses and rubbed her tired eyes. The *ding* of a new message hitting her inbox reclaimed her attention. Her heart fluttered at the name: *Betty,* whom she hadn't heard from in months. Not since the grief blog, in fact.

BETTY77:

Once again, your timing is impeccable.
I've been struggling with sleep lately.

Catherine scrambled to fire a quick message back, exhaustion momentarily forgotten in her desire to keep the thread alive.

DR.T:

Hey!

Nice to hear from you; it's been ages.
How are you?

BETTY77:

Life has been wild, endlessly busy! But, Dr Mindful, you'll be pleased to hear I've made some positive changes. Things are looking up.

And I'm mostly remembering to breathe, thanks to you! x

DRT:

That's great! And yes, keep remembering to breathe (note to self, also)! x

It was always a boost to hear she'd made a difference to someone's life, even in a small way. That was all any professional wanted to hear, wasn't it?

Yes, but Catherine couldn't deny she also inexplicably yearned for more from this interaction. She'd missed it, and even after the time that had passed, she still felt an undeniable pull to this internet stranger, which definitely said more about her than them. She reread Betty's message, overanalysing the words and taking small delight in the flirty nickname, the compliment, and the kiss.

"Oh, to hell with it," she said aloud. Then, surrendering to impulse, she typed another message.

DR.T:

> A while ago you suggested we meet for a meal. I'd like that if, of course, you're still interested?

Her fingers hovered nervously over the Enter key; before she could overthink it, she pressed send. A message instantly dinged back. A tremor of excitement surged through her — quickly replaced by confusion.

POSTMASTER:

> Your message to Betty77 could not be delivered. The user you attempted to reach is unavailable or does not exist. Please check the username and try again.

"Wait... what?"

Catherine tried again.

Another unwelcome automated intervention pinged through, and she scowled at the screen.

"Stupid thing. I don't understand. She was right there a few minutes ago."

Her chest heaved with a resigned sigh, and she snapped her laptop shut.

"Well, that's that then."

21

TAINTED LOVE

1989

"Cati? Cati?"

My mind gripped the far-off sound of Mei's voice like a rope pulling me back to consciousness. My eyes flickered open, my vision straining against the brightness. Mei's concerned face came into view. Snow flecked her black hair, tied in bunches with neon-coloured scrunchies.

"Where am I?" I rasped.

"You're awake! Good, that's good." She disappeared from my field of vision.

I tried to sit up, but a sharp pain speared my side. I rolled back, turning my head to follow Mei's voice.

"Oi, you!" Hands in the air, Mei charged after a dishevelled man wheeling a bicycle. "Where are you going? You need to apologise."

The man turned and scowled. "Look what she's done to my bloody bike. Not to mention my jacket. She owes me an apology." He held up a shredded sleeve. "It's ruined."

"You can't just run someone over and walk away."

"The mad cow ran out in front of me on the bicycle path."

Mei looked around with narrowed eyes. "Where is this bike path?"

The man pushed thick-rimmed glasses up his nose and huffed. "Granted, you can't see it now because of the snow, but she should bloody look where she's going in the future." He strode off, the wheel of his buckled bicycle squeaking as he went.

Mei paced back to me, tutting and shaking her head. "What a tosser! Come on, my friend. We don't need that bastard, anyway. Can you stand?"

"I... I don't know. I'll try." Breathing through the agony, I tentatively sat up, hissing as pain snagged in my side.

Mei planted her feet and thrust her hands down to me. "One, two, three."

I squeezed my eyes shut as she heaved me onto my feet. I appraised my injuries. I was able to stand, so my legs were okay. My arms were grazed, but fine. Aside from a splintering headache, the pain was local to my left-hand side.

"Okay, you're freezing. We need to get you home."

Mei wove an arm around my back and helped bear my weight as I limped alongside her, flinching with every step.

"So, how come you skipped your lecture, huh?"

The cold had numbed my extremities, and the shock of the bicycle crash had temporarily numbed my senses, but as we moved across the green — now white — it all came crashing back.

Francesca, naked in Jeremy's bed.

My stomach lurched, and I doubled over, losing my grip on Mei and expelling a mouthful of bile into the pristine snow.

"Oh, I guess that answers the lecture question," Mei said.

A chorus of disgust erupted from a huddle of passing girls. Mei brandished a one-finger salute at their departing backs.

I wiped my mouth with my hand, and we resumed our slow hobble.

In my room, I got out of my wet clothes while Mei went to make tea. I lifted my T-shirt, fingering the tender flesh over my ribs. A colourful bruise was already blooming. Gooseflesh prickled my skin, so I pulled on my pyjamas and eased myself into bed, nestling under my duvet but still shivering, my body clenching every time I convulsed.

Mei softly called through the door before entering, "You decent, Cati?"

"Yeah," I said.

She pushed into the room with a steaming mug in one hand, a glass of water in the other and half a packet of cream crackers tucked under her elbow.

"They're not mine," I said.

Mei shrugged. "You need something in your stomach. Drink some water first."

Red-hot pain seared in my ribs as I tried to sit up, so I rolled onto my good side instead and sipped the water. The wetness softened the parched edges of my mouth, and it felt so good I gulped some more.

"Whoa, not too much, too quick. You'll be sick again!"

"Sorry," I said.

"Oh, I found some ibuprofen, but you need to eat some crackers too." Mei rolled two tablets into my open hand. "Should I call a doctor, or a hospital? Or your dad?"

"I'll be okay. No need to worry my dad."

"I could send for your friend, Jeremy."

"No," I said a bit too loudly. "No, please don't do that. I'm fine."

Mei blinked, crossing her legs as she lowered herself onto the floor. "Okay, I'll stay for a while."

"You'll miss the rally."

Mei shrugged. "It's fine. Now eat!"

THE NEXT TIME I OPENED MY EYES, IT WASN'T TO Mei's kind face, but to Francesca glowering at me from the doorway. She cut an eerie figure against the stark hallway light behind her.

"Oh, you're finally awake." She stepped into my room and closed the door. She wasn't wearing her usual ripped goth-girl getup, but clothes akin to those she'd worn to meet the Daltons last Christmas. She wore softer makeup and even had a different scent. *Is this who she is for him?*

Get out — I wanted to scream at her — *of my room, of my head, of my life.* I swallowed the little saliva left in my sour-tasting mouth, but the words wouldn't come.

Francesca shifted onto the edge of the bed, and the

movement sent pain coiling through me. I gasped and clutched at my side.

"That's right, your little friend said you'd gone and hurt yourself."

"I didn't hurt myself. Some lunatic on a bike knocked me over."

Francesca shook her head as if disputing the fact.

"Where is Mei?" I asked.

"I knew that's who you'd go running to."

"What? No, don't try to twist this around," I hissed. "I hope you weren't awful to her, Francesca."

She shrugged.

"How long have you been sleeping with Jeremy? He already knows about you and me, doesn't he?"

A smirk played on Francesca's lips, and I wanted to smack it off her face, but it hurt too much even to sit up properly, let alone to inflict a wound on someone else.

"It must have been a shock for you earlier."

Tears prickled my eyes. "A shock? You've been sleeping with both of us!"

"I never said that you and I were exclusive, did I?"

Her question landed on me like a bucket of ice water.

"I, I thought you... you said that... it was me..." I frowned because I couldn't grip hold of the evidence I was looking for.

No, she'd never said we were exclusive. I couldn't fight my corner, because I was already on the floor, her boot pressing into my back whilst the referee held up her arm and declared her victorious.

How on earth had I lost this fight when I'd had the

upper hand? Pain throbbed in my head, and it became harder to pull air into my lungs as my chest tightened. Francesca cupped a cool hand around my burning face and swiped her thumb across my cheekbone. Anyone else might have mistaken the look on her face for concern, but it was a thin mask. I could see right through it now, because I'd read about people like Francesca.

"You look terrible," she said. "You should get some rest."

I nodded, blinking away stinging tears as she pushed the damp hair back from my forehead and kissed it.

"I'll come by to check on you later. Maybe then we can smooth things over properly."

I watched as she left, clicking the door closed behind her.

I might be a heaped, broken mess, and she might have won this round, but I wasn't going to lose myself to her. *No, she'd never said we were exclusive, but that doesn't make it right.*

I listened until the shuffling stopped next door, and Francesca left her room. I waited until I heard the door along the hallway creak to a close. I cursed through the effort of sitting up, my breathing rapid and shallow because it hurt to breathe too deeply. Blood rushed from my head and the room tipped sideways. I gripped the edge of the bed and pushed myself to my feet. In my current state, I could hardly achieve stealth mode, but I needed to hurry before she returned.

The next time I faced Francesca, it would be on my terms.

I STOOD UNDER A HOT SHOWER, BLINKING THROUGH fresh tears and gulping around the smarting lump in my throat. The water stung the grazes on my hands, but I relished the steam and finally felt warm again. I wished I could rinse Francesca away with the soapsuds, but she wouldn't wash off that easily.

Before pulling on fresh pyjamas, I carefully assessed the crimson bruise on my ribs, exploring the tender area with my fingertips and hissing at the touch. *There isn't much they can do for bruised ribs anyway.*

I rooted around in the bathroom cabinet and found a packet of ibuprofen. I cupped cold water in my palms and swallowed a couple of tablets, pocketing the rest for later. I would replace them, and anything else I'd borrowed, but first I needed to rest.

Now that the nausea had passed, my empty stomach growled for food. I made a mug of tea to accompany some buttery toast — my favourite comfort food. But even that didn't fill the hollow inside me now that the bubble had been burst.

When I returned to my room, I did something I hadn't done in months: I locked my door.

I'd taken to leaving it unlocked because I enjoyed finding Francesca in my space, even though she usually left a mess in her wake. But right now, I needed to keep her out.

The rapid rattling of the door handle startled me awake. Hours must have passed as my room was dark aside from the soft glow from the lamps in the quad, four floors down.

"Are you in there?" Indignation wrestled with the concern in Francesca's voice. Her knuckles rapped on the wood, and the handle rattled again. "Why is your door locked?"

I drew a breath and mustered my strength. "I don't want to see you."

"Oh, for goodness' sake, Catherine. Stop fooling around and let me in."

"I'm not the one who's been fooling around, Francesca." I sounded as bitter as I felt.

"It's not my fault you made assumptions about how things were…"

I blinked in disbelief. I'd been so stupid. Why did I let myself trust her after what had happened at Christmas?

Francesca lowered her voice. "As I said before, I never denied that Jeremy and I were… look, this is complicated. I don't really want to stand in the corridor airing our dirty laundry."

"Maybe you should've thought about that before you fucked my best friend," I screamed. *So much for staying calm and keeping my power.*

Seconds later, Francesca's door slammed and the bass of her music pulsed through the thin wall between us. *Oh, the irony of her listening to The Cure right now* — it couldn't be further from an antidote. She'd ripped my heart out, and now she was trying to perforate my eardrums.

I pounded my fist on the wall. It was a pathetic counter-rhythm, but momentary relief came as the sound muted. Then Francesca's muffled voice retorted, "I'll turn it down when you stop sulking and let me in. I don't know why you're being like this."

The music resumed, and I swear she turned it up another notch as the rhythmic thumping intensified, a deep, guttural thrum that resonated in my bones. I snatched my pillow up around my head, muffling the sound slightly, but the vibrations continued to pulse through me.

I squeezed my eyes shut. I wanted to banish her from my thoughts, but the music conjured mental pictures of her throwing her head back and twirling around in abandon, or lying on her bed, her dark eyes stormy. Hot, silent tears tracked a path down my temples.

THE HALLS WERE BLISSFULLY QUIET WHEN I WOKE in the thin dawn light of a new day.

For a moment I imagined it had all been a bad dream. But Francesca wasn't curled around me in my bed, my door was locked, and I felt like I'd been run over — both emotionally and physically — which of course I had.

I dressed, wincing as I pulled clothes over my ribs, and made a hasty exit, careful to close my door quietly behind me. Outside, the world was a washed-out watercolour of greys and blues. My breath misted in the freezing air as I speed-walked across the frosty campus towards the library, hoping to catch Mei before her lectures started.

The early-morning hush of campus was broken only by

the crunch of footsteps on the frozen ground and the occasional distant shout. I stopped at the café to grab a cup of coffee. Mei wasn't in our usual library nook, so I waited on the bench outside, jiggling my legs to keep warm. The wind whipped at my hair, and I pulled my scarf tighter, burrowing into the thin layer of fabric.

With her neon pink bobble hat, Mei wasn't hard to spot. Her colourful clothes looked particularly striking against the frozen backdrop. As she drew closer, I saw that her face was rumpled in a frown, which didn't lift when she looked up and spotted me.

"Morning," I said, my stomach twisting with a fresh wave of anxiety.

"Hey," said Mei with a flat smile. She avoided eye contact and moved past me up the steps to the library door.

"Mei, wait! Can I speak to you?"

She didn't turn around, just pulled the door open. I dived in her way, gasping and pressing a hand to my side as the sudden movement sent sharp pain coursing through me.

Mei looked at me, her eyes softening. "Cati, you're still in pain?"

"Yeah, my ribs are sore." I widened my eyes. "You should see the bruise! You love colourful things, so..."

Mei grimaced and looked down at her technicolour high-tops.

"I'm sorry about Francesca. I don't know what she said to you, but I doubt she was kind."

Mei clamped her lips together and shook her head.

"She's my... well, I mean, we've been... but it's over now because she's—"

"Watch out!" Mei pulled me out of the way as a student burdened with books pushed through the library doors behind me.

"Sorry, so sorry," he said. We watched as he skipped down the icy steps, and with an impressive contortion of limbs he somehow avoided spilling his books and himself.

Mei looked back at me, her rich brown eyes full of concern. "She isn't a good person, Cati. I'm so surprised you—"

"No, I know. She's awful. I never should've got involved with her." I raked my fingers through my hair. "It's hard to explain, but she has this pull. She can be so... I don't know, she's intoxicating—"

"I think what you mean to say is that she's toxic?" Mei sniffed.

I winced and gave a short nod. Hearing it so plainly from someone else hurt more than I thought it would. Mei was right though. *Francesca is toxic.* Why had I been so blinkered?

"She warned me to stay away from you, Cati. She said I'd been a bad influence and changed you for the worse. She said this was all my fault—"

"What? No! That's not... ugh!" I clenched my fists. "Look, just ignore whatever she said to you; she twists things."

"She's scary! I don't want to be unkind, but she's a bit — I don't know the right word in English." Mei twisted two fingers at her temple, her eyes wide and unblinking.

I swallowed. "Yeah, I know. I'm sorry you had to face her alone, and I promise it's over. I'm staying clear of her, well, as much as I can when I..." I gulped, and sudden tears threatened. "I need a friend right now, Mei. Please—"

Mei touched my arm; her hand was surprisingly warm against the morning chill. "Of course, Cati, whatever you need, but..." Her doll-like face suddenly looked so serious. "Can we go inside now, please? I'm freezing."

My laugh escaped in a puffy cloud. I pulled open the heavy oak door, and we bustled into the foyer, the familiar scent of old books and polished wood filling my lungs.

Comforted by the quiet hum, I stayed long after Mei left for her lecture, and well into the afternoon. But I was tired and uncomfortable, and after a while, I gave in to the call of my warm bed and pyjamas. Francesca would probably be out with Jeremy, anyway. A pang of resentment twisted in my gut, but I shook away the thought of the two of them together.

He's welcome to her. They can have each other. I just wanted to sleep.

Head down, I braced myself against the bitter wind, which felt like it was blowing straight off the Arctic. The ironclad sky threatened more snow. As I approached the halls, I saw a scattering of things in the quad, before realising they were my belongings cast from my window above — my mum's blanket snagged in the bushes, my books, uni work, photographs, and cassette tapes, soaked and drowning in a slushy puddle. *No, no, no.*

Hot tears sprang as I frantically gathered up my things, ignoring the passing gaggle of girls I recognised from the floor below ours. They pointed and whispered, their giggles carrying in the biting air.

Wild rage burned in my stomach as I charged up the stairs, my sorry possessions bundled in my arms, the wet blanket clinging to my chest. I dumped the sopping pile at my door and hammered on hers.

"What the fuck, Francesca?" I pounded my fists so hard the door rattled in its frame.

"It's open," she called casually from inside.

I clenched my teeth and charged into her room. Francesca lay on her stomach, feet swinging in the air as she flipped through a magazine, the scent of her new perfume — a sickeningly sweet citrus smell — cloying in the air.

I stormed over, ripped the magazine away from her and flung it across the room. It landed with a soft thud against the wall.

Francesca smirked and twisted around. "It seems I finally have your attention."

I wanted to launch myself at her. I'd never wanted to hurt someone as much as I wanted to hurt her in that moment, but my anger bubbled over into tears. I clenched and unclenched my fists, struggling to control the tremors that wracked my body.

"Look, why don't you sit and take a moment to calm down?" she said. "I'll go make us both a nice cup of tea, and we can—"

I turned and left her room, letting the door bang behind me. Within seconds, the door was flung open again. She leaned on the doorjamb watching as I struggled to pick up my things, the wet blanket dripping onto the floor.

"You're being unreasonable, Catherine. I'm trying to—"

I stood, letting everything fall from my arms.

Then I was in her face, inches from her. The last time I'd been this close to her, very different emotions had been sparking between us.

Francesca didn't pull back; she stared me down. I could feel the rage contorting my features; if there'd been a mirror, I wouldn't have recognised myself.

"Leave. Me. Alone." Each word came out in a low growl, a guttural sound laced with a venom I hadn't known I possessed.

"That's not what you really want, though." Her voice was a soft caress, and she traced her fingers up my arms, the touch feather-light at first, then tightening into a possessive grip around my biceps. "I know you, Catherine. I know you better than anyone ever has or ever will."

I looked into her eyes, flickering with a disturbing mix of darkness and desire, and it sent a shiver of revulsion through me. The desire — that was the dangerous part, the siren song that had lured me in for so long. Now, looking at her, all I felt was the bitter sting of regret.

"I was stupid to think I was in love with you." The words escaped before I had a chance to stop them. She flinched as they landed on her harder than a physical blow.

I lifted my palms to her chest and pushed her. She

stumbled backwards, her mask slipping as genuine shock registered on her face.

"You're completely deranged. I meant what I said. Stay away from me, Francesca."

I gathered my things into my room and bolted the door shut. The small space felt suffocating, but finally alone, the tension broke, and I slid to the floor, wincing.

I couldn't live like this. In the morning, I would go to Student Services and request an urgent transfer to different accommodation.

But in the morning, I didn't have to.

Francesca had already gone.

2 2

EVEN AFTER EVERYTHING

PRESENT DAY

By the time Thursday rolled around, exhaustion had seeped into Catherine's bones. Spiralling thoughts and anxieties had triggered a bad bout of insomnia, which meant instead of sleeping she'd sat up sipping chamomile and doing the Sappho puzzle.

With a satisfying click, she'd slotted the last piece into place at around 5 a.m. She snapped a photo and texted it to Penny, who replied with an aubergine emoji and said,

PENNY:

Marvellous, but you really need to get laid, babe x

As Catherine chuckled at the message and rolled Sappho away, the ceiling creaked, bringing her back to the present. Despite sharing an entranceway and assuming they'd bump into each other all the time, she hadn't seen Jules since the other morning at Snoots.

Now, she smiled and cocked her head to listen out for

the soft, padded sounds of her new neighbour moving around above her. *Penny's right; you really do need to get laid.*

Catherine mentally berated herself for being a creep and committed to an extra lap of the park as penance, although her morning walk was hardly a punishment. The clear sky beyond the puffy cloud breaks hinted at a bright day ahead, but the air was dewy and still cool, so she set off at a quick pace to get her blood pumping. She mindfully focused on the chirps and whistles of birdsong, a big dog's deep bark, followed by an answering yap from a smaller breed.

Heavy-breathing runners sped past, Lycra shuffling and stretching across rippling muscles. Further along the path, a flock of women power-walked in a synchronised sashay, their matching pink jackets identifying them as the Stroll Sisters. Catherine gave a small nod as they passed. She'd once contemplated signing up, but pink really wasn't her colour, and she enjoyed the solitude of her morning walks — this was always the calm before the storm of a day ahead, full of complex people and their complex problems.

On the way home, she couldn't resist the draw of Snoots. Admittedly, it wasn't just the coffee pulling her in, but the hope that she might bump into Jules again.

Tomorrow. You have a date with her tomorrow. Christ — tomorrow!

She knocked back a double espresso and braced herself for her busy day.

First up, a long-term client with bipolar disorder.

Catherine listened as the emotionally fraught woman listed off her worsening symptoms, and she recommended an adjustment to the dosage of her medication. Then, she called through a quick coffee order to Stephanie before her telephone consultation with Doctor Harding at The Milverton Clinic. They discussed their shared patient's recent behavioural changes, which had led to hospitalisation, and they agreed on a course of treatment. Next up, evaluation of a new patient referred for possible ADHD. After only five minutes in the young woman's company, Catherine was ready for a nap and in no doubt that the woman had ADHD, but she ordered some further diagnostic tests just to be sure.

She got up to make another coffee and stretch her legs before facing her final clients of the day — the couple she privately referred to as The Grudgewells. It would be unprofessional to tell Nigel and Carol Dudwell that they really needed to give up the ghost of their dead marriage. And besides, it was an easy — if not awkward — fortnightly session, where she usually wrote out her grocery list as they sat seething in silence, refusing to answer any of her questions or address each other at all. Inexplicably, they always left holding hands. Despite Catherine's years of experience, some things were quite simply beyond her.

By midday she was dreading lunch with Jeremy. *Really dreading it.* For the first time, she'd sat through The Grudgewells' session willing the time to tick slower.

She'd been pleased to hear Francesca was doing better, but she didn't need to dissect it all over a meal with the woman's husband, even if he was her oldest friend.

Why did I agree to this? It was a good question, but she'd never denied him anything he'd asked of her. She'd enabled him, just as much as he enabled Francesca.

She pulled on her jacket and called out to Stephanie as she left the office.

JEREMY WAVED FROM A TABLE ON THE TERRACE AND got up to greet her when she arrived, kissing both cheeks like he used to. Warm after the ten-minute walk, Catherine slipped off her jacket and sat.

He passed her the menu and poured water into her glass.

"Glorious weather, isn't it?" He relaxed back into his chair, the collar turned up on his polo shirt, and sunglasses perched atop his head.

"Mmm," she agreed with a flat smile, a little unnerved that he seemed too relaxed, too pleased to see her. This whole thing was starting to smell like another favour.

She scanned the menu and, without overthinking, settled on a pine nut pesto ravioli. And she'd have a small glass of the Pecorino to take the edge off whatever this was. As soon as she closed the menu, the waiter hovered over them, ready with his pad. After he'd bustled off, she and Jeremy were left to *enjoy* each other's company.

"So..." she said, reaching for something to say. "Is Francesca still doing well?"

Jeremy bobbed his head enthusiastically as he swallowed a mouthful of water. "Yes, yes. She's doing great, in fact! I'm really hopeful that we've turned a corner with everything."

"Good, I'm pleased."

Jeremy tipped his head and cocked his lips in a wry smile.

"No, really, I am," she said. "It wasn't very nice to see her like that."

"Right, of course. No, it wasn't. And thank you again for going to her. You understand now, at least, why I was so worried."

Catherine nodded. After a beat, Jeremy frowned and drew a breath.

"You were right — all those years ago, what you said about her. Even though I didn't want you to be right..." He held up his hands. "Actually, if I'm really honest, I hated that you knew her better than I did."

As much as Catherine enjoyed him saying it, it was uncomfortable watching him do so. She diverted her eyes to the river bubbling by below them. *Water under the bridge.* Or at least that's what she'd thought until recently. But to paraphrase the walking man-mullet, Rod Stewart, *the first cut was the deepest...* and so it seemed; she'd never truly healed.

"I was always jealous of what you had with her. I could never compete," Jeremy continued.

Catherine surprised herself by scoffing. "She married you. You won." She wasn't bitter, not anymore. Decades had passed — yes, she was still tied to Jeremy, but she'd moved on from all of that. She'd had other lovers and a whole lifetime of experiences since.

She closed her eyes, hoping he might've disappeared when she opened them again. *No such luck.* "Look, why are you dredging all of this up now?"

"Well, even after everything, I still love her." He fiddled with the napkin folded under the cutlery. "Deep down, I think she loves me too... for more than my money."

Catherine opened her mouth to protest, but when she looked back at his face, his earnest expression stamped out her words. Perhaps, as with The Grudgewells, there was a marital bond she couldn't comprehend, something transcending common sense.

If she were a contrary woman, she'd tell him that Francesca only loved his wallet, just as she'd tell Nigel and Carol Dudwell that no company is better than the wrong company. But who was she to argue on this point?

A shrivelled old spinster. Francesca's words echoed again.

Their drinks arrived, thankfully interrupting her need to respond.

"We're going to Italy," he announced, raising his glass of white wine in celebration.

"Ah, good. A vacation will do you—"

"No, not on vacation." He glanced up, letting the pause linger for dramatic effect. "We're going to live there. I've bought a place in Tuscany. My offer was accepted this morning, so, all being well, we'll..."

"Hold on... did you just say that you're moving to Italy? I mean, shouldn't we have discussed this first?"

Jeremy's lips drew together in an infuriating half-formed question, which she wasn't prepared to let him finish.

"Don't you dare say 'why'... I'm your bloody business partner. Your decisions impact me too. What about the practice?"

"Yes, I was about to get to that—"

"I can't afford to buy you out." The words rushed out of her in a sudden surge of panic.

Jeremy held up his hands. "Good, because I'm not selling."

"So what, you expect me to keep running things, while you're off living your best life in the bloody Italian Riviera?"

Jeremy chuckled, and she had to fight the urge to lunge across the table at him, or douse him with the jug of water, ice cubes and all. He must have sensed her irritation as he held up his hands and squashed the laughter in his voice when he spoke.

"I'm signing my half of the business over to you. It'll be all yours, so do with it what you will. Run it alone. Bring in another partner. Or sell it if you want..." the words floated between them like dust motes in the afternoon sun, "Go live out your days in a queer hippy commune, foraging wild berries and teaching conflict resolution with crocheted sock puppets." He pincered his fingers in a goofy demonstration. "I won't hold you back."

He poured himself another glass of water from the jug that she somehow hadn't emptied over his head.

This was a lot. This was too much. Her noisy thoughts swirled along with the rush of the river, the chatter from the other tables, and car horns honking at the intersection. Their food arrived before she said another word, and Jeremy sat, waiting patiently. Slow, strong and ever-present, like he'd always been.

"It doesn't seem fair," she eventually said.

"It's more than fair... after everything, you deserve it. Ma and Pa will be delighted!" He gestured to her with a forkful of salad leaves. "They think the world of you, you know?"

And truly, she thought the world of the eccentric pair too. They may not have been blood relatives, but they'd treated her like one of their own from the day they'd met her. Their generosity had seen her through university and established her career. She owed Jane and Jasper a lot.

"Anyway, it's settled. The paperwork is with the lawyers. We'll work everything through together, of course, but this is what I want—"

"You can walk away from it all, just like that?"

"There's only so many years a chap can sit listening to other people's problems whilst not dealing with his own." His mouth stretched into a sardonic grin.

Catherine sipped her wine, trying to hide the *you said it* look no doubt written all over her face.

"The fact is, Francesca needs this. We both need this. I've spent my entire career prescribing remedies to other people, and it's time I wrote my own script — it could be worse than retirement in a Tuscan villa."

Catherine popped a ravioli parcel into her mouth and considered him as she chewed. Yes, this was a snap decision, but instinct was telling her it was the right one — for him and for herself. Like Penny had said a few days ago — *don't you think it's time you broke away from the Daltons and all their nonsense?* This was her out.

"You know I think the world of you too, Trusty. I heard what you said about not dredging up the past, but I'm still truly sorry for what happened back then. I wish it hadn't been like that and things had been easier for us. We always had fun, didn't we? I mean, at least we did before..."

Before Francesca. Catherine sighed and prodded her tongue at a stray piece of pine nut caught in her teeth.

"Once we're settled, do you think you'd consider paying us a visit? You might make sure she hasn't finished me off and stuffed my corpse in a closet, whilst she carries on with the pool girl."

Catherine snorted out her wine. "Not a chance."

"That she'll be carrying on with the pool girl?"

"No, that I'll ever visit you."

Jeremy pressed his lips together, but he couldn't hide the smile in his eyes.

Catherine picked up her wine glass and clinked it to his.

"Cheers, it is then. To you and your fresh start."

23

KARMA CHAMELEON

1989

*J*eremy had tried to reach out to me. I left countless calls hanging in the hall, his tinny voice calling my name through the receiver. I blanked him outside lecture theatres, in the canteen, and in the café. And I binned all the notes he'd pushed under my door, stating meeting times and places that I ignored. But I couldn't avoid him forever, so as per the instructions on his last note, I sat waiting on a bench outside the library. I tilted my face to the sun as it warmed my skin and thawed the deep chill in my bones. The first nice day of the year; all buds and birdsong stirring the campus from its bleak sleep.

Six weeks had passed since Francesca's departure. In her wake, she'd left an unbearable hollow, a cold side of the bed, and a constant ache in the pit of my stomach. But the time and distance had helped me realise that the version of her I was grieving wasn't real. I'd been in love with a false persona, duped by desire — the real Francesca was despicable, and she could go to hell. *How thin the line was between love and hate.*

There'd been no word from her, not that I wasn't glad. A few days after she'd gone, a couple of people from Student Services came by to clear out her room. When I passed, I peered through the propped door and watched Robert Smith being carelessly torn from the wall. The sleeve of Francesca's black hoodie hung from a bin bag dumped in the hallway. I rifled through it, searching for my bunny slippers, but there was no sign of them. I resisted the urge to squirrel away her hoodie; nothing good could come from pressing it to my face and inhaling her sweet scent. *God, I miss her.*

"Trusty! You came!"

I shielded my eyes, squinting in the direction of Jeremy's voice. He stood taller and walked with more confidence. He'd grown a moustache and wore an Oxford shirt rolled to his forearms, unbuttoned at the neck. The audacious bastard looked happy.

"I'm so pleased to see you." He sat and moved to pull me in for a half-hug, but thought better of it, his hand hovering for a moment before landing awkwardly on my shoulder. "How have you been?"

"How do you think?" I scoffed.

"God, yeah." He combed a hand through his hair. "I'm sorry about how everything turned out."

"No, you're not," I said, unable to strain the bitterness from my voice.

He hit me with a wounded look, and for a moment I glimpsed the gangly, goofy guy I'd grown up with. This wasn't his fault. He was as much a victim of Francesca as I was.

Jeremy leaned in and lowered his voice. "I know it must have been hard seeing Francesca with me like that. I wanted to tell you right from the off, but—"

"When did you start sleeping together?"

Red blotches flushed up his neck and into his cheeks. "Trusty, that's a bit—"

"When?"

"January."

Fuck. I couldn't compose my face, so I covered it with my hands.

"Francesca said we needed to tread carefully with you. She told me that, well... she thought you had a bit of a crush on her and she didn't want to upset you."

I dropped my hands, my limbs heavy with indignation, which Jeremy immediately misread.

"Don't worry, your secret's safe with me. Uni is the time to experiment, you know, when we're all young, dumb and full of..."

My stomach curdled. "Please don't finish that sentence."

"All I'm saying is that it's cool with me. Hell, if it makes you feel any better, I snogged my mate Barnaby Blake when we were in Upper Sixth — tongues and every-thing!" He grimaced. "It was very bristly. I don't know how you girls can enjoy it."

"Jeremy, I'm gay."

"You're young; there's still plenty of time to figure all that out."

"There's no *figuring out* to do. I'm a lesbian. A dyke... whatever."

Jeremy raised his eyebrows. "Well, good for you, but—"

"Francesca and I started sleeping together last year."

He looked at me with a blank expression.

"We were having sex, Jeremy."

He blinked rapidly, as if his eyelids were trying to power up his brain.

"Say something."

He slowly nodded his head as if rocking his jammed gears back into motion. The next words that came out of his mouth were not the ones I was expecting.

"I'm taking a gap year." His Adam's apple bobbed.

"I'm sorry, what?"

"At the end of term. I'm taking some time out. Francesca and I are going interrailing. We'll start in Europe, but who knows where we'll end up." He ducked his head, his strawberry-blonde hair aglow in the sunlight. "I wish you were coming too, Trusty, but I see how that might be awkward now..."

A fresh wave of jealousy threatened to throw me off balance, but I pushed through it. "What about your degree?" *Of all the bloody things to ask him.* I imagined Francesca rolling her eyes.

"I'm deferring for a year and Francesca has dropped out; she's... rethinking her options."

Silence lingered in the wake of our bombshells.

"And you still want to go away with her after what you've just found out?"

Jeremy pushed his lips together as he weighed the question. "Did you ever imagine that someone like me would even get close to someone like her?"

I sighed. "I don't think she's who you think she is. I've learnt that the hard way."

He puffed out his lips. "Okay, well obviously I still have a lot to learn about her, but I'll have plenty of time to do that while we're larking around Europe. She's different when it's just the two of us. I don't know how to explain it."

"I do…" I said, as it clicked into place. "She's a chameleon."

Jeremy frowned. "Come again?"

"Do you remember covering social chameleons in the Abnormal Psych module?"

"What are you getting at?"

"You've seen the way she changes, like how she was at Christmas with your parents. We'd never seen that side of her before—"

"I think she was just trying to impress them. And it worked, they love her." Jeremy chuckled.

"Exactly. She adapted who she was to impress them. But she does it with us too." I angled around to face him. "She's this vampy goth girl around me and a refined version of herself for you. And there's the way she manipulates and twists things. She dials up the charm, but I've seen the mask slip too. Underneath, she can be so callous and cold."

The disturbing revelation fell into place. Francesca had the ability to shape-shift, to become whatever she needed to be to get what she wanted. I was certain I was right and hoped I'd put forward the case well enough for Jeremy to see it too.

Jeremy frowned. "So... sorry, what? You think she's a psychopath?"

"Yeah." I released a slow breath and nodded. "Yeah... maybe. I don't know if it's exactly that, but there are definitely characteristics of the dark triad—"

Jeremy spluttered a laugh. "Seriously, *the dark triad?* You sit through a couple of lectures on personality disorders and now you're trying to diagnose the girl who bruised your feelings?"

I narrowed my eyes. "What? Wait... no, that's—"

"I understand it must be difficult for you that things have swung in my favour, but—"

"She's messed us both around. She lied to both of us, played us off against each other, and spent weeks jumping between our beds."

He held up his hands. "Okay, yeah. I admit I've been a little taken aback by that revelation, but I'm not about to ruin a good thing with her by taking the moral high ground."

I puffed out a frustrated breath.

His brow furrowed. "She obviously wanted to blow off a little steam and needed more than one outlet—"

"Wow. I'm not talking about Francesca's *needs;* I'm talking about her *nature.* She has... issues."

Jeremy laughed. "Don't we all!"

"Clearly! But I'm worried for you. I'm telling you to be careful."

"And I'm telling you, this isn't good form, Trusty." He patted my knee and jutted out his bottom lip as he stood up. "Try to be happy for us, eh?"

24

M&S S.O.S

PRESENT DAY

This is an S.O.S from M&S!

Come quickly.

Please x

Catherine fired the texts to Penny and dropped her phone back in her bag before resuming her panicked sweep of the Marks & Spencer lingerie department.

Far too frilly.

Far too pink.

Far too... big! Bloody hell, I could use that as a hammock.

What the hell am I doing? She drew a breath and avoided eye contact with the young sales assistant, who now seemed to be making a beeline for her. *Shit.*

"Need any help with anything?" The sales assistant

slapped out the words through her over-inflated baby-pink lips.

"Er, no. Thank you, just browsing."

The sales assistant batted her thick fake lashes and openly gawped at Catherine's chest.

"C cup, I reckon, but I can squeeze you in for a fitting if you like."

Catherine resisted the urge to cover her boobs, as if the assistant could see right through her top.

"No, really. I'm fine. I'm waiting for a friend."

"Suit yourself," the assistant said to her chest with a smirk. "I'll be over by the fitting room if you change your mind." She looked Catherine up and down and strutted off.

"Christ!" Catherine muttered. *I'm old enough to be her mother.* She quickly vacated the area and headed for the café, which seemed like the safest place to wait for Penny with a cup of tea and a slice of something sweet for the shock.

As Catherine poured a second cup from the teapot, Penny barrelled up in a bluster of expletives that had a wave of purple-rinsed heads turning to look at her. She held up her hand in apology and leaned in to brush a kiss on Catherine's cheek.

"Sorry I'm so late, babe. I've had a right fucking day of it." She fanned herself with a menu as she slumped in the seat opposite. "They've moved that tribunal date forward, so we've all been buzzing around like flies at a barbecue. I'm supposed to be packing for the fucking Lake District.

Loz wanted to set out at midday, but bloody Dixon called me in at sparrow's fart, so..."

"Oh, Pen. You should've said if you were too busy. This is silly. I'm being ridiculous..." Catherine dropped her gaze.

Penny reached across the table and covered Catherine's hand with her own. "No, you're not." She ducked her head until she met Catherine's eyes. "Besides, it's fine. Everything's in hand now at work. I just need to get home, bung a few bits in a bag and we'll be off. So, what's happening?"

Catherine groaned. "I have my date with Jules tonight... I've been trying to think of a way out of it all week."

"Why on earth would you want to do that?"

"Because it's stirred up feelings I'm not even sure I should be feeling at my age. I'm too old for all this."

"Firstly, there's no such thing as too old — unless you're a banana. And secondly, feelings are good. So what — you're nervous? That means you actually like her, and this could be something. But if it isn't, chalk it up to experience and move on. The point is, you're finally ready to put yourself out there. Just relax and have fun."

"But what about underwear?"

Penny blinked. "Sorry, what?"

"Should I get something sexier than the plain ones I have?"

Penny glanced around before looking back at her with a half-cocked grin. "Babe, you're in entirely the wrong shop if you want to buy sexy underwear."

"Well, yes. I've gathered that, although I'm pretty sure the sales assistant was just hitting on me."

Penny's eyes lit up. "Really?"

Catherine nodded with a grim smile and took a sip of tea.

Penny leaned in and whispered, "You know, I once had sex in an M&S fitting room?"

Catherine spluttered her mouthful, laughing as she mopped the mess with a napkin. "What?"

"You heard me." She sat back, looking pleased with herself.

"I mean, how? When?... no, why?"

"Oh, years ago." Penny waved the questions away. "And we're not here to talk about that. Why are you suddenly so worried about underwear? Were you this bothered when you were seeing me?"

"Well, no. I suppose I hadn't really thought about it."

"So, why are you thinking about it now, you slutty little minx?"

Catherine mock-gasped. "It isn't like that. It's just that I've seen her underwear, and I don't want to be a disappointment... besides, you're a fine one to call me slutty, Miss-Have-A-Shag-in-Sparks!"

Penny cackled. "Wait! When did you see her underwear?"

"Oh, it was hanging out on an airer when I went in to feed the cat."

"Look, babe, you're overthinking. Try to relax. If things progress to the bedroom and she's got her priorities straight, she'll be more interested in what's underneath your underwear, right?"

Catherine nodded. Penny was right. Penny was always right. But still, this didn't make her feel any better.

"You'll text me, won't you? Let me know you're okay? Unless you're having too much fun, of course." Penny winked.

Catherine resisted the urge to give her annoying friend a dead arm. She wouldn't be having any fun because she'd be too worried about her knickers to think about anything else.

CATHERINE ROLLED UP THE SLEEVES OF HER WHITE linen shirt, which she'd paired with some slim-fitting herringbone checked trousers. She exhaled a shaky breath and scrunched her fingers in her hair; she'd gone for a slightly ruffled look — effortless-looking effort. She applied a generous swipe of concealer around her tired eyes and a liberal spritz of her favourite perfume, hoping that Jules might appreciate the warm, woody fragrance.

Okay, shoes or no shoes? She quickly settled on her suede mules, which she reserved for around the house, but they were trendy enough to look good with the rest of her outfit. And she wasn't really leaving the house, after all.

Once again she wriggled her hips to adjust the unfamiliar underwear which was riding up ever-so-slightly and making her way too aware of everything down there.

Nothing like a pair of uncomfortable knickers to kick-start your libido.

After parting ways with Penny earlier, Catherine grabbed the first sort-of-sexy matching set of underwear she'd spotted in her size, not wanting to linger for too long and risk being ogled by the sales assistant again. She scurried to the till downstairs and waited in line, only to be called up by a dough-faced woman whose thin eyebrows disappeared into her hairline as she scanned the lingerie.

"Do you need a bag?" She held up the offending items and may as well have announced over the tannoy that she, Catherine Truscote, was buying sex knickers.

"No, they're for a friend," Catherine said in a panicked yelp. *Oh God! Why did I say that?*

The assistant tilted her head.

"Sorry, I mean, no. Thank you. I have a bag." She patted the tote under her arm. She paid and left the store, never to return.

And while the label sounded exotic — *Brazilian Lace Trim* — almost like something one might eat rather than wear, there was nothing at all sexy about pulling said lace out of one's arse crack. Why had she even worn new underwear anyway, for goodness' sake? It's not as if anything like *that* was going to happen on the first date. Or ever, if she continued being this uptight and neurotic.

One last check in the mirror. She looked good and even felt good, despite the nerves zipping around inside her.

"Don't overthink. Try to relax," she repeated Penny's advice aloud and took a few controlled breaths. *It's dinner with a new friend, that's all.*

Dinner with a hot new friend.

Her hormones raged like those of a teenager. *I'm fifty-six for fuck's sake. What is this, cougar puberty?*

Catherine grabbed the wine she'd bought for the occasion, nice bottles of both red and white, and she pocketed the treats she'd picked up for Juniper. She'd missed his company over the last few days and was excited about seeing him again. Although not as excited as she was about seeing Jules. She'd considered buying flowers but had over-thought it until she walked away from the florist empty-handed. *Next time.* She'd definitely bring flowers next time.

In the entranceway, the quiet thrum of music drifted from upstairs with the faint sound of Jules singing along to a song Catherine didn't know. The last time she'd climbed these stairs was to build flatpack furniture and feed the cat.

She knocked. No answer, but through the door came the wail of Jules singing off-key to the outro of the song. Catherine chuckled and knocked a little louder.

"Come in," Jules's voice beckoned.

As Catherine entered, Juniper padded along the hallway towards her, his tail held high and swishing like a furry antenna.

"Hello, you," she said, bending to pet him.

He responded with a little meow and nuzzled into her shins.

"Oh, he's such a flirt."

Catherine's head whipped up at Jules's voice as she peered around the kitchen doorframe, red hair piled up in a messy bun, cheeks flushed, and an apron tied around her neck.

"Something smells delicious."

"Come on through. Sorry, I need to stir; it's risotto! You like mushrooms, right?"

"I love mushrooms."

"Lucky guess." Jules shot her a smouldering smile before disappearing back into the kitchen.

"Come on, you," Catherine said to Juni while rubbing his ear. "Let's do this." She drew in a deep breath and followed the mouth-watering aroma.

Half-expecting to see chaos unfolding, Catherine's eyebrows raised at the relatively tidy space considering Jules was mid-meal-prep. Music played from a retro-looking speaker on the windowsill, and Jules bopped her hips as she stirred a wooden spoon in a large flat pan on the hob.

"Welcome to *mi casa*." Jules beamed and reached over to lower the volume. "Not that you haven't been welcomed in by Juni several times already."

Catherine smiled and nodded to the radio. "No Spice Girls tonight, then?"

"Ha! No, just a bit of Florence and the Machine. But you've clearly overheard my guilty pleasure."

"I think the Spice Girls might be my guilty pleasure too," Catherine said instead of admitting she had no idea who Florence's Machine were. She still wasn't cool enough to know what music normal people listened to.

"That and jigsaw puzzles, eh?"

"Oh, I don't feel any guilt about the jigsaws. I'm not

ashamed to say I love them; they help me unwind. Some people have books, but reading doesn't help to hush my noisy thoughts, so I self-prescribed puzzles years ago..."

Catherine tailed off, suddenly aware of her inner Penny telling her to enthuse a little less about niche interests if she ever wanted to get laid again. Heat bloomed in her cheeks at that unhelpful thought, but Jules turned and fixed her with a kind smile.

"I, er, brought wine." Catherine held up the two bottles. "I didn't know what you liked or what you were cooking, so..."

"Ah, lovely. Thank you! I know it's usually white with risotto, but do you fancy cracking the red?"

"Yeah, actually. Red would be..."

"Glasses are in there." Jules gestured her wooden spoon at the cabinet next to the fridge. "Sorry, need to keep stirring, are you okay to—"

"Sure, no problem. I'll pop the white in the fridge." Catherine released a soft laugh at the sight of the photo. In hindsight, the woman was obviously Jules — with that unmistakable smile stretching across her face. And Will was clearly gay — no straight man she'd ever met was as well groomed. She didn't know how she'd missed it before.

"Oh, and I brought some treats for Juniper, too. Does he like..." Catherine glanced at the packet, and read the name aloud, "Lick-e-Lix?"

"I don't know about him, but I do."

Confusion stalled Catherine for a moment. "You like cat treats?"

Jules threw her head back and laughed. "Sorry, I was being smutty."

"Oh, right," she said, turning the words over in her head until the penny dropped. *Oh God!* Laughter tittered from her too; partly through mortification, partly because Jules's whooping belly-laughs were contagious.

Jules battled to catch her breath and swiped a tear from her cheek. "I'm so sorry, that was..." She waved a hand in apology, before clutching it around her middle. "Sorry, it's Will... he's a bad influence. He has my mind as filthy as his."

"I'll never look at cat food the same way again."

"Juni loves Lick-e-Lix. You can give him some now if you want, his bowls are in the—"

"I know." Catherine smiled and took a small dish from the cupboard. She squeezed out the creamy pink paste and popped it down for Juni, who sat by her feet chirping in anticipation.

"Yep, I was right." Jules glanced over and giggled.

"What's that?"

"I always suspected the traitorous little bastard would give me up in a heartbeat if food was involved."

Catherine uncorked the wine and poured two generous glasses. She passed one to Jules and clinked it with her own before taking a sip.

Mmm, she'd chosen well.

"Can I help with anything else?"

"No, no. It's nearly done. Why don't you go through to the lounge and make yourself at home? I won't be much longer."

CATHERINE DOUBLE-BLINKED WHEN SHE ENTERED the lounge. The chaos she'd seen a few days before had been composed, and with Jules's possessions in place, the room had taken on a whole new personality — not a doily or knick-knack in sight.

Statement rugs cleverly zoned the space, and two large colourful canvases adorned the walls. Scatter cushions and a plush throw dressed the sofa, and an oversized three-wick candle flickered on the coffee table, perfuming the air with a pleasant zesty scent.

The bookcase she'd built now sat flush against the wall, the shelves lined with books. By the window, a small round dining table had been set for two and, judging by the statement tableware, Jules was used to entertaining. Still, Catherine's chest squeezed at the effort Jules had gone to *for her.*

The only sign of Juniper's existence was a tall, well-worn scratching post tucked in the corner with a bunch of sisal threads pulled loose.

Catherine eyed the doorway before reaching around to liberate the lace underwear from between her bum cheeks, where it seemed intent on riding. She sipped her wine as she scanned the books on the shelves — chunky spines bore names of authors she didn't recognise, shouldering up to the few she actually knew. And there was an entire row of travel guides. She tilted her head and eyed the names of cities she'd never even heard of before.

Where the hell is Tbilisi? Were these all the places Jules had already visited, or the places she dreamed of visiting? Either way, Catherine suddenly felt small and humbled by Jules's worldliness. By comparison, her own life seemed like a tapestry woven from mundane threads. She'd never really lived beyond this small town, where the decades had been swallowed helping other people to mend their broken lives and move on. But she'd never really moved on herself, *had she?*

Christ, I'm being triggered by a bookcase.

She shook the negative thoughts from her head and turned to the glorious sight of Jules carrying two steaming dishes into the room. She'd taken off her apron, revealing a grey sweatshirt and form-fitting jeans.

"Grab a seat," she said.

Jules set a dish in front of her, and Catherine's mouth watered at the sight of the seared king oyster mushroom atop a bed of risotto and garnished with a pretty purple flower.

"I'll just fetch my wine. And it looks like you need a top-up."

Catherine glanced at her empty glass; in the midst of her bookshelf crisis, she'd gulped her wine too quickly. When Jules reappeared, Juniper wove between her elegant bare feet as she crossed the room.

"Wow, this looks incredible. Thank you."

Jules beamed. "I love to cook, so it's my pleasure." She filled Catherine's glass and topped up her own before setting the wine down between them. "Besides, I owe you."

Catherine batted away the words and mirrored Jules as

she unravelled the cutlery from the napkin and laid it out on her lap.

"Bon profit." Jules's smile accentuated the crinkles at the corners of her warm eyes.

"Mmm," Catherine moaned. "This is delicious."

The rich, meaty mushroom paired perfectly with the creamy risotto. It looked and tasted like fancy restaurant-quality food, and not something Catherine would ever be capable of producing herself. Not that she'd tried — going to all this effort for one carried little appeal, so over the years she'd slumped into an easy routine of simple dishes and microwave meals.

Silence stretched awkwardly between them as they ate. Catherine grappled for something to say before landing on, "It's been quite the transformation in here since my last visit. I thought I'd taken a wrong turn when I walked into the room."

"Hmm." Jules finished her mouthful. "Yeah, it was a big help to have Will here for a couple of days. He has a flair for interior design! Although he wouldn't know how to build flatpack, even if the instructions slapped him around the face."

Catherine laughed.

"Thank goodness you showed yourself to be more than capable; otherwise, my books would still be in boxes." Jules picked up her glass and tipped it Catherine's way before taking a long sip.

"I was looking at your books, actually. Your travel guides, are they all places you've been, or...?"

"And with one brief look around, she uncovers another

of my guilty pleasures — buying travel guides!" Jules laughed. "No, outside of the airports, I haven't been to even half of those places. But I always made a point of picking up a guide for the cities I liked the sound of, I guess as a prompt to go back one day and explore."

"Sounds like a lovely idea. And I suppose even more appealing now that you're not flying here, there, and everywhere for work."

Jules licked her tongue around her teeth. "Exactly."

"And that makes me feel a *little* less unworldly, too."

"I'm sure you're worldly in other ways." A small grin lifted Jules's red lips, and Catherine had to look away as it would be indecent to stare at her mouth for much longer than she already had. It was a very lovely mouth.

"So... I have a confession to make." Jules left the intriguing statement hanging as she chased another forkful of food with a sip of wine.

Catherine swallowed, taking the bait. "Go on."

"I knew who you were."

"Sorry?"

"I thought it was you when I saw you at the tapas place. Then when I checked, I realised I was right; it was *you*." Jules took a breath and continued. "It's why I was a bit tongue-tied when I bumped into you at Snoots. I wanted to say something, but I realised I didn't really know how to explain myself without sounding like a complete weirdo."

Catherine's mouth settled into an unsure half-smile as she tried, and failed, to gather the pieces. Jules sat back and wiped her mouth with her napkin.

"Even when we weren't on the best terms, I still called my mum every week. She talked about you *a lot*."

"Me?"

"Yeah, assuming you're the nice young woman from downstairs?" Jules affected a high-pitched trill, which was a near-perfect impression of Bridie. "Lovely wee lass. Her name's Catherine. She's a doctor, you know."

Catherine puffed out a laugh, but her brain was still struggling to pick up the thread.

"At first, I thought, ah, here we go, she's trying to guilt me again for leaving. She's rubbing it in that someone else is popping by to spend time with her, when her only child has wedged whole countries' worth of distance in the way." Jules rolled her eyes.

"She was a lovely lady. We spent many an evening together during the lockdowns; I figured we counted as one household and we both needed the company." Catherine stared into the middle distance as the pandemic came back to her like a weird dream she'd just remembered. "What a strange time that was."

"Mmm." Jules shifted in her seat. She picked up her wine, eyeing Catherine over the glass as she drew a slow sip. Under Jules's gaze, Catherine's mouth went dry, so she mirrored her and drank.

"Well, I think you helped to change her mind."

Catherine cocked her head. "How so?"

Jules let out a soft laugh. "Can you imagine her disappointment when she found out I didn't like whisky? Well, double that when she found out I didn't like men."

Catherine mock-gasped. "You don't like whisky?"

"Ach, no!" Jules smiled, but something sad lingered beneath it. "I'm more of a gin lass."

Catherine frowned. "I'm sorry. I didn't realise Bridie had a problem with... I mean, she mentioned you, of course, and I knew the two of you had drifted apart, but she never told me why. She never mentioned you were—"

"Gay? No, she was mortified by it. But you won her over."

"I don't see what I did."

"She got to know you and realised that we lesbians aren't as awful as she'd once assumed." Jules shrugged and drained the wine in her glass.

"It must have been difficult for you. I can understand why you kept your distance."

Jules refilled her glass and emptied the rest of the bottle into Catherine's.

"You didn't explain how you knew who I was."

"Ah! Yeah... that." Jules grimaced. "All of Mum's mentionitis about her lovely wee doctor friend sparked my curiosity." She drew in a breath and exhaled her next words in a rush, like she was trying to breathe them out of the room. "So, I got to researching you a bit."

Catherine laughed. "You did what?"

"I just wanted to make sure you weren't doing a number on her and swindling me out of my inheritance. I found your Facebook profile, but figured you weren't really on there much as you only had six friends."

No, that's about the measure of it. Catherine blinked.

"Then I found your company website — Truscote and Dulson?"

"Dalton."

"Yeah, that's it." Jules gestured at Catherine with her fork and grinned. "Nice photo of you on there."

Catherine knew the one; it *was* a nice photo of her. Jeremy had suggested they get professional shots taken when they updated the website. After her initial reluctance, she agreed. She turned up for the shoot looking austere, wearing a black roll-neck jumper and dark-rimmed glasses framing her face. But right before the photographer released the shutter, she complimented the angles of Catherine's cheekbones and the distinctive blue of her eyes, which resulted in Catherine's lips curving into the smile she'd captured in the photo. She agreed to a drink with her afterwards. They shared a bottle of wine and almost kissed, but Catherine glimpsed the woman's wedding ring and pumped the brakes... *Once bitten!*

When she emerged from the memory, Jules was staring at her with a deep line etched between her brows. "I'm sorry I overstepped. I shouldn't have done that, or at least I should've introduced myself when I first realised—"

"Well, I'm just surprised you recognised me from one photo."

Jules flashed her a sheepish smile. "You are quite distinctive."

Despite the compliment, Catherine's smile faded. Should she be flattered or alarmed by Jules's revelation? She stared at the flickering candle whilst trying to decide. In the low light, shadows danced on the walls, making the already intimate space feel even smaller. When she looked back at Jules, her cheeks were glowing, flushed with either embarrassment or something else entirely.

"I've made it weird, haven't I?" Jules grimaced again.

Silence crept in, putting the conversation in a choke-hold. Catherine stared at the candle again. Hadn't she been just as bad? She'd built the woman's flatpack without being asked, she'd snooped through a stack of postcards, and she'd ogled Jules's underwear, imagined her in it even. A wave of mortification washed over her.

Juniper sauntered back into the room, announcing himself with a meow before dramatically flopping onto the rug. They both turned to look at him as he contorted himself like a furry pretzel and began what could only be described as an aggressive act of personal hygiene.

"Will says he wishes he could do that. Lick his own balls, that is, not Juniper's."

Catherine stifled a laugh, and it came out like a hiccup. Jules met her gaze, her lips curving in a small, uneven smile.

"I'm sorry again," she said, her voice barely a whisper.

Catherine's eyes swept the cosy room. She glanced back at the half-eaten meal Jules had so thoughtfully prepared and their empty glasses on the table. She drew a decisive breath and bunched her napkin from her lap onto the table, before standing to leave.

25

CURSUM PERFICIO

1991

I spent the first two weeks of the summer break helping Dad around the Daltons' estate. After a stressful semester of exams, it was a relief to relax in Dad's easy company. Not much conversation passed between us, but we always reached to turn up the same songs on the radio and never disagreed about the best biscuits to dunk in our tea.

The start of August delivered a blisteringly hot day. Dad and I spent the morning mending the dry stone wall on the northeast corner of the estate. Sweat trickled down my back, plastering my shirt to my skin. Now and then, I'd pause, wipe my brow with a dusty forearm and glance towards the cool, inviting blue of the swimming pool in the distance. The work was slow, painstaking, and had me craving an icy beer in a cool bath.

As Dad pulled the Defender up to the cottage, Jane came trundling down the path from the main house, a broad smile blooming on her face. Her sundress billowed in the slight breeze, and her coiffed blonde hair bounced with each step.

"Yoo-hoo," she called out. "Catherine, I have the best news!"

My heart sank. I loved Jane, but I'd made every excuse to avoid her since my return from university. On the few occasions I'd run out of luck, she'd ambushed me, peppering me with details about Jeremy and Francesca's trip, how healthy they looked, and how loved-up they were when she and Jasper had met them for lunch on the Cote d'Azur last month.

I couldn't bear it.

Yes, time had passed and my wounds were no longer raw enough for the salt to sting, but still I couldn't quite bring myself to be happy for them, especially when it was likely a facade. Francesca might be able to fool the Daltons with her calculated charm, but she couldn't fool me.

I jumped out of the Defender and pushed my hair back behind my ears where it had come loose from my ponytail. "Hey, what's up?"

"Jeremy phoned. They're coming home!" Jane almost bubbled over with the news.

"Oh, right." My stomach dropped. I tried to force a smile, but my face wouldn't comply. I hadn't seen Jeremy or Francesca in over two years, and I had no desire for that to change. If I'd realised they'd be coming back this summer, I would've planned to be anywhere other than on the Daltons' estate.

"Isn't it exciting?" she asked with eyes so wide they looked set to pop out. "I haven't spoken to Jasper yet, but I thought I'd throw a welcome-home supper. What do you think?"

I shifted my weight, feeling the uncomfortable prickle of sweat between my shoulder blades. I could almost hear that cold beer and bath screaming my name. Jane's gaze flittered over to Dad, who was tinkering around with something by the shed.

"Just the six of us, or should I invite the Beaumonts, too?"

"No," I said a bit too quickly. "The six of us would be… nice." I blinked, thankful she'd asked and not just invited them. It was bad enough having to face Francesca and Jeremy, without the hassle of Handsy Hugo in the mix too.

"Good, okay. Well, that's settled then." Jane rubbed my arm. "I wish you'd have let us get you that plane ticket, Catherine. It would've done you good to relax in the sun with your friends," she said, referring to the generous offer they'd made to fly me out to see Jeremy and Francesca. The Daltons meant well, and it was a kind offer, which I'd politely declined by saying I'd agreed to help Dad over the summer break. The reality was, I couldn't imagine a torture more terrible than time alone with Jeremy and Francesca.

"There's plenty of sun here." I swept my arm out at the cloudless sky. "Besides, I've been enjoying catching up with Dad, and mainly been making myself useful, I think."

Dad stood by my side now. He bumped his elbow into mine and smiled down at me.

"When do they get back?" I asked.

"Tomorrow." Jane clapped and exhaled a happy little hum.

I drew a breath. There wasn't much time to prepare myself, but equally it meant less time to spend worrying. Dad and I watched as Jane skipped back to the house.

"Are you going to be okay, kiddo?"

I looked up into his face, his eyes crinkled with concern. Something unspoken passed between us. He knew; somehow he knew.

I tried to speak, but the words caught in my throat.

Dad crushed me into a hug I didn't know I needed as much as I did.

✳

EVEN AFTER ALL THIS TIME, THINKING ABOUT Francesca was like pressing a bruise. The last time I'd seen her, I'd screamed in her face and shoved her. In the time and distance that had stretched between us, I'd grown — older, wiser, and far more resilient. I'd built walls Francesca wouldn't be able to tear down.

Or at least I thought I had.

But as Jasper opened the front door, there she was, descending the stairs with the aura of a fresh breeze off a warm ocean. My mouth went dry.

Gone was the vampy dark hair; now it fell in soft chestnut waves to her shoulders.

Gone was her pale skin; now she radiated a sun-kissed glow.

Gone were the ripped black clothes; now she wore a

gold dress that dripped over her slender frame like hot caramel, the neckline dipping dangerously between her breasts.

Gone, gone, gone was the goth girl I'd fallen for. In front of me stood a woman, refined and expensive-looking. I couldn't tear my eyes away, and the corner of her mouth ticked up as she noticed me gawking. Glancing down at the loose blouse and dark jeans I'd paired with my scruffy Converse, I conceded the point. I may as well have been bare under her penetrating gaze.

I swallowed and reminded myself that I wasn't here to impress her. I was here because Jane had invited me. I was here to welcome my oldest friend back from his extended trip. I was *not* here for Francesca.

"Michael." Francesca kissed each of Dad's cheeks. "So lovely to see you again."

Dad murmured something that sounded like, "Oh right." She smiled and turned to me, her eyes flickering with amusement. "Catherine, it's been too long."

Not nearly long enough, I wanted to say; instead, I reciprocated her air kisses, trying not to inhale her perfume; even that had changed, deeper now — smoky and resinous. We'd barely touched, yet her scent clung to me.

She led the way to the dining room as if she owned the place. I glanced over my shoulder to see Dad and Jasper disappearing into one of the rooms, leaving me alone with her.

"Trusty!" Jeremy bounced out ahead of us. Freckles peppered his nose, and he emanated the sort of serenity only someone who'd been on a two-year holiday could. He wrapped me in a hug, laughing when I stiffened.

Stepping back to take me in, he ruffled a hand through his floppy sun-bleached hair.

He looked radiant. As radiant as *she* did.

Far too fucking radiant.

I wanted them to have been at least a little bit miserable. I'd hoped for dark shadows under their eyes and a prickliness spiking between them, but no, they were every bit as happy as Jane had described.

Francesca drifted through the open French doors into the courtyard, where Jane was tinkering with the table setting. The two of them stood in conversation; Jane looked as smitten with her as Jeremy did.

I stood by as Jeremy wrestled with a wine bottle, uncorking it with a squeaky pop and pouring two large glasses.

"So you're really back then," I said.

"Yeah, yeah. Looks like it. It's been bloody great, but a chap's got to get his head back in the real world sooner or later, right?"

"Yeah, I guess so."

He shoved his hands in his pockets and rocked on the balls of his feet. "I'm coming back to uni in September."

I raised my eyebrows.

"Ma and Pa want to put some money into a practice, you know, invest in our future."

"Great. You two have it all figured out. Good for you."

"No, Trusty. You and me." He traced a finger in the air between us. "They want to invest in both of us. You know they're very fond of you too; they see you as a daughter of sorts. Plus, they think you keep me on an even keel. So they're putting up the money for..." He swept a hand through the air as if envisioning a sign over a door. "Dalton & Truscote. Counselling and Psychotherapy Services."

My mind buzzed. "I, er... I mean, that's a lot. I don't really know what to say—"

"You don't have to say anything right now; it's still years away. You've caught up to me at uni, so we'll be in the same class. We can help each other along, qualify together, and then we'll set up shop."

My gaze drifted back to Francesca, who still held Jane rapt in conversation.

Jeremy draped a heavy arm around my shoulder. "This was all Francesca's idea, actually."

Even though she couldn't possibly have heard it from outside, she spun around at the mention of her name and hit me with a sultry smile. My stomach lurched, and I glanced away.

"What do you mean it was *her* idea?"

"Exactly what I said. She came up with the whole pitch to Ma and Pa. I'll go back to uni and finish my doctorate if they lay down a path for me. She told them I work better when I have an incentive to pull me along." He chuckled. "She's not wrong."

I clenched my jaw. I didn't want to think about the sort of incentives Francesca might offer Jeremy to get him to do what she wanted.

"Why did I get brought into it?"

Jeremy leaned in close. "I think it's a peace offering, Trusty. She's sorry for how things ended between us all. I am too. It's all water under the bridge now though, right?"

My mind whirred into overdrive. I swallowed, trying to wet my parched mouth. I grabbed one of the glasses of wine Jeremy had poured and took a large gulp.

Jeremy's eyes bulged. "Oh, that was for... never mind."

The wine tasted bitter and wrong, and now my mouth was too wet.

"Trusty, are you okay? You've gone awfully red."

My face burned. "I, er... I just need to..."

I turned, rushing out of the room and back through the house until I was outside again. The heavy evening air felt too dense for my lungs. Gasping, I tugged at the collar of my blouse, undoing another button. Then came the soft press of a hand on my back and her honeyed voice in my ear.

"Take it easy, just breathe." She rubbed the space between my shoulders.

I stood, and her hand fell away.

"What are you playing at, Francesca?"

She tilted her head, her lips pressed into a thin line.

"Why did you suggest that the Daltons pay for Jeremy and I..." I gasped for air again.

She stepped toward me, gripping my shoulders until I looked into her dark eyes. "Calm down, will you. Breathe." She took slow breaths herself, drawing the air in and out, in and out. I copied her until my racing pulse calmed and my lungs remembered how to do it by themselves.

"There, that's better." Looking into my eyes, she tucked

a strand of hair behind my ear and touched a cool palm to my cheek. "Walk with me," she said.

Even after all this time, rage bubbled up inside me. I didn't want to walk with her; I wanted to slap her hand away and launch myself at her. I wanted to scratch her insanely beautiful face and tear the luscious hair from her scalp. But, as if enchanted by her siren song, I complied. I hated my feet for going along with her, but our steps fell into sync until we reached Jane's beloved rose garden. I'd spent many afternoons out here pruning and preening these flowers.

Only the distant chirping of birds punctuated the silence between us, which felt as heavy as the air I'd been struggling to breathe.

I risked a glance at Francesca's profile, the sharp angle of her jaw, the way her lip curved up in a half-smirk. She looked composed, amused even. It was infuriating. I wanted to see her fracture with the pain that had broken me.

She stopped and hovered her hand over a vibrant crimson bloom. I thought she was about to pluck it from its stem; instead she turned, her eyes meeting mine, and gestured towards a low stone bench.

"Sit with me."

My brain was outraged that my body yielded to yet another of her commands without protest.

Francesca closed her eyes and tipped her face to the sky, where streaks of pink stretched across it like long, slender fingers.

It was my voice that cracked into the moment. "Why did you plant the seeds about a practice?"

She turned to look at me. "I've missed you," she said.

"What?"

Her wry smile triggered an involuntary reaction that had me no longer wanting to scratch her face but kiss it. I shook my head to recalibrate.

"You have no idea how much I missed you, Catherine."

I swallowed, my mouth suddenly dry again. "But you, you and Jeremy. You're with…"

"It's different." Francesca waved a dismissive hand through the air. "You know it's different. It's always your face my mind drifts to when I need to escape."

I stared at her for a long moment. My eyes on hers, dark with the depths I'd once lost myself in. It would be so easy to fall again. "I, er… I don't understand. What are you saying?"

Francesca released a small sigh, as if exasperated by my unrelenting need for clarification. She reached up and swiped a gentle thumb across my cheekbone.

"I don't want us to fight anymore, Catherine." She leaned closer, her voice a silken whisper that seemed to wind its way around me. "You and me, we're—"

Jeremy's voice boomed from behind, shattering the moment. "There you both are."

Francesca stiffened beside me, and her hand fell away from my face.

"Supper's ready," Jeremy said, drawing nearer.

"We'll be there in a moment." Francesca turned and forced a smile.

Jeremy's shoulders rounded as he sloped back towards the house. Francesca squeezed a hand on my thigh.

"Look, trust me, okay? Whatever's discussed at dinner, I need you to understand that I have your interests at heart too."

I frowned. "Sorry, I don't—"

"Shhh!" She silenced me by pressing her finger to my lips. Holding it in place, she leaned in and softly kissed it. Like a traitorous drum, my heart beat a frantic rhythm in my chest. I hated myself for wanting more, for surrendering so easily. She hadn't even apologised for what she'd done. Yet here I was, entranced and exposed amidst the ruins of my crumbling walls.

Francesca's eyes flicked toward the house. "There isn't time now, but I'll find you later, okay?"

I could only nod. She stood and pulled me to my feet.

A POTENT COCKTAIL OF CONFUSION, DESIRE AND self-loathing swirled in my stomach as I took a seat between Dad and Jasper. Unfortunately, Francesca and Jeremy sat opposite me, affording me a full-frontal view of their saccharine display. Francesca turned on a show for her audience, the sound of her hollow laughter tinkling in the air as she leaned in to Jeremy. She picked a piece of lint off his shirtsleeve, then laid her slender, manicured hand in its place. The intimate moment, played out with such practiced ease, felt like a slap across the face.

I poured a glass of water from a crystal carafe and

gulped it down; the cool liquid did little to quell the heat rising in my cheeks.

Jane's staff bustled around with quiet efficiency, setting down hot, crusty rolls and small plates adorned with tiny works of culinary art. The clatter of cutlery filled the air.

"So, Catherine," Jasper boomed. "Jeremy tells me he's relayed the good news."

"Sorry?"

"We're going to be your first investors — Dalton and Truscote!"

In the Francesca haze, I'd all but forgotten Jeremy's revelation. Now my back was against the wall. Jasper eyed me, awaiting a response.

"Oh, right. Yes, of course. I'm a little overwhelmed, to be honest. It's...it's..."

Dad jumped in where I floundered. "It's very generous of you. Thank you sincerely from both of us. For this and for all the opportunities you've given Catherine."

My heart sank. There was no backing out of it now. "Thank you," I echoed.

Jasper shook his head. "No, not at all. It's our pleasure to see our young people thriving and having such a clear path ahead of them." With great bombast, Jasper raised his glass. "To Dalton & Truscote."

Before the others could lift their glasses too, Francesca chimed in, "I think Truscote & Dalton has a better ring to it." Everyone looked at her.

"You know," said Jane, "it does actually. Truscote & Dalton," she repeated.

Jasper swayed his head from left to right as if weighing the two options. "Yes, yes. And of course, ladies first."

Jeremy jutted out his bottom lip but then raised his glass. "To Truscote & Dalton," he said to a chorus of cheers.

My cheeks flamed. I wanted to crawl under the table and hide. Francesca caught my eye and winked; a gesture probably intended to put me at ease, but it put me more on edge, like I was the butt of a joke I didn't understand.

I concentrated on the food on my plate as the conversation turned to Francesca and Jeremy's travel adventures. Jane and Jasper's faces glowed with adoration as Francesca held court and recounted the highlights of their trip. From Paris to the sun-drenched Riviera, where they'd sipped rosé on the beaches of Nice and Cannes. And from the electric buzz of Barcelona to Rome, where they'd hired mopeds and eaten in trattorias straight out of a Fellini film.

Jeremy nodded enthusiastically and threaded his fingers with Francesca's as she spoke.

"It all nearly ended in disaster though," he said.

Jane leaned in. "Oh, do tell."

"I left Francesca to catch her breath on the Spanish Steps while I nipped off to get a gelato. By the time I returned, the damned thing was dripping through my fingers, but being the generous chap I am, of course I offered her a lick—"

Francesca rolled her eyes dramatically. "He dribbled it all over my silk scarf."

Jane gasped.

"I swear, if looks could kill, it would've been the end of me," said Jeremy.

"I hope you got Francesca's scarf dry cleaned," said Jane.

"No, I went one better." Jeremy beamed at Francesca, and she conceded with a smile. "I bought her a Valentino to replace it."

"Good boy!" Jane clapped her hands.

Jasper chuckled. "Goodness me, wrapped around her little finger, aren't you, son?"

"Quite right," said Jane.

My mood darkened with the sky. As if sensing my struggle, Dad nudged my leg under the table. I looked at him. He raised his eyebrows and mouthed, "Are you okay?"

I gave him a brief nod before returning my focus to the pattern on the plates; it was far more interesting than the insipid travel tales I was being forced to endure.

Truth was, I wished it had been me. Perhaps if I could've afforded to traipse around Europe for two years and buy Francesca designer silk scarves on a whim, then she'd be looking at me the way she was looking at Jeremy. But then, less than an hour ago in the rose garden, she had been looking at me like that; when she kissed the finger she placed on my lips, and when she asked me to trust her. How could I trust her when I knew at least one version of her was lying right now?

The conversation moved on to "unforgettable" Berlin. At this point, even Dad seemed a little mesmerised by Francesca's storytelling. *Traitor.*

"We arrived just months after the wall came down. It was wild. There was this sense of..." She drew a long breath as if more air would help her articulate her point. "...something huge unfolding around us. You could feel the energy of the city being reborn."

Nods and murmurs passed around the table.

"I literally saw Vrubel claim his grey canvas on the East Side Gallery." She fixed her dark eyes on me and said, "*My God, help me to survive this deadly love.*"

I stilled. The moment stretched to the score of my thudding heart in my ears, but then she looked back to the Daltons and seamlessly picked up the thread. "You know, Vrubel's mural... also known as the *Bruderkuss*. I sat and watched him paint it for hours. He was so intense, so lost in his work, like all that mattered was that wall, that kiss."

A burst of laughter tore from my throat. Everyone turned to look at me, but it was Francesca's glare I met — a silent reprimand.

"Sorry," I muttered, once again fixing my eyes on the intricate pattern of the plates.

Jeremy cleared his throat. "It's ghastly, all that graffiti, but I couldn't tear her away."

"It's what helped me to decide." Francesca paused, fanning her fingers at her temples, and everyone leaned in for the dramatic reveal. "I'm going to get into art, albeit curation rather than creation. Just being in the midst of all that creative energy really inspired me."

Jane squealed and Jasper clapped.

For the first time, I saw Francesca's eyes shining with genuine excitement, and everything clicked into place. *It's the lifestyle she's in love with, not Jeremy.* He couldn't see it; none of them could see it, but it fitted with the theory I'd aired to Jeremy before they'd left. *Francesca is a chameleon.*

Our eyes locked again and her lips twitched with a grin. Jeremy squeezed her hand, pulling her attention back to him. She gave him a barely perceptible nod, and he cleared his throat.

"Francesca and I actually have some other news."

"Oh?" Jane's eyes doubled in size.

"We're engaged," he blurted.

The words knocked the air out of me.

Francesca lifted her eyes to me. I put down my fork and glared at her, but she simply smiled.

Jane clutched a hand to her chest. "I wondered. Didn't I say, Jasper?" Jane looked to her husband, who was patting his son on the back. "But there isn't a ring, so..."

"Ah, yes! Of course I proposed with a ring, but Francesca didn't like the one I'd chosen, so we're going to pick something out together."

Jane released a merry laugh and reached across to touch Francesca's arm. "You know what you're doing, don't you?"

"I'll be wearing it for a long time, so it's best we get it right."

Jasper chuckled. "Not a shotgun wedding, then?"

"God, no!" Francesca's lip curled.

Disappointment registered on Jane's face.

"No, one thing at a time," said Jeremy. "We don't

intend to wed until I'm qualified, and the practice is up and running."

"Sounds sensible." Jasper nodded and knocked back his wine. "Perhaps some bubbles to celebrate?"

I tuned out as the conversation continued, seething my way through the sweet course with my thoughts on a loop — Jeremy had bound himself to Francesca, and in a sadistic flourish, she'd bound me to both of them. *I need you to understand that I have your interests at heart too,* she'd said. But I couldn't fathom how any of this was in *my* interest.

When it was an acceptable time to leave, I thanked the Daltons for the meal and, with a tight-lipped smile, congratulated Francesca and Jeremy on their engagement.

Jeremy jumped up and pulled me into a tight hug. "It's all falling into place, Trusty! You're happy for us, right?"

I looked at Francesca over his shoulder, and she stared back, unblinking.

"Yeah, delighted," I said flatly.

✳

ONCE AGAIN I FOUND MYSELF SOBBING INTO MY pillow over Francesca, the pain in my chest returning like an unwelcome guest. I cried until I felt raw and hollow, then surrendered to sleep — deep enough to forget for a while, heavy enough to ache beneath its weight.

I woke to the sound of the front door closing, and the rumble of the Defender starting as Dad left for work, without me — thank goodness. A fresh wave of anguish crashed into me, and I pulled my duvet back over my head, burying myself in darkness. The world outside felt too bright, too loud, too full of reminders.

But then came the creak of my door and the whisper of a voice — small, gentle, and unmistakably hers.

"Catherine, are you awake?"

I froze, as if holding my breath and pretending to be asleep might make her leave, but the weight of her shifted onto the bed. She pressed a hand onto my shoulder and held it there for a long moment.

"I know you're angry with me," she eventually said.

I surprised myself by throwing back the duvet and whipping around to face her. "Angry? You have no idea how I feel."

The muscle in Francesca's jaw pulsed, and she drew a breath through her nose. "Okay then, why don't you tell me? Get it off your chest."

"You slept with my best friend and acted like it was me who'd behaved unreasonably. You cheated on me, Francesca. You cheated on us both!"

She clasped her hands in her lap and nodded.

"Then, you disappeared for two years. Two years! And you have the audacity to show up here telling me how much you've missed me, saying you have my interests at heart, when all along you're engaged to Jeremy. What is wrong with you?"

Francesca tilted her head as if pondering the question. "I meant what I said, Catherine. I missed you. Being away from you for so long was difficult."

I growled in frustration. "Don't piss in my ear and tell

me it's raining, Francesca. From the sound of it, you were having the time of your life. Excuse me if I find your professed pining a little hard to reconcile with the facts."

"You really don't get it, do you?" Francesca frowned and shook her head, her perfectly coiffed hair bouncing with each movement. A brittle laugh escaped her lips. "I'm prepared to sacrifice certain things for a better life. It's been hard work getting to this point, but I've set myself up for the future. And you might be a little more grateful that I managed to do the same for you."

"What do you mean, grateful? You've meddled in my life. I never asked you to do that. What if that isn't what I wanted?"

She shrugged. "You know how hard it is for women to make it in this world. You'd be silly not to take a leg up. It isn't like the Daltons can't afford it."

"You're unbelievable." I pinched the bridge of my nose and sucked in a deep breath, trying to regain some semblance of composure. "So, you're marrying Jeremy for his money, and you think that'll make you happy?"

"Yes, to a degree it will. But I very much plan to enjoy a life beyond what Jeremy has to offer. It's a means to an end."

"You don't love him, do you?"

"Don't give me that look. You're being awfully naïve, Catherine."

In front of me sat what I could have, but it wasn't what I wanted, or what was good for me. Maybe the walls I'd built were stronger than I'd thought after all, although I wished I could tell that to the fat tears rolling down my cheeks.

During my battle of head and heart, my voice escaped as a pathetic squeak. "Please leave."

Francesca released a nasal laugh. "Alright, have it your way. When you've stopped sulking enough to know what's good for you, come find me. But I won't wait around forever."

"Francesca?" I called to her turned back. She spun around, eyebrows raised. "I want my bunny slippers back."

A smirk tugged at her lips. Then, without a word, she left.

EXORCISM

PRESENT DAY

*C*atherine stilled as she caught sight of the woman sitting at the bottom of the stairs, elbows perched on her knees. She'd know her anywhere.

"What are you doing here?"

Francesca stood, a wide grin spreading across her lips as she turned. She looked good, *really good*, in a pair of tailored slacks and a soft-looking chiffon top that fell elegantly around her neck. Her hair tumbled in loose curls to her shoulders.

"Waiting for you, of course." Her lips stretched into a crimson smile.

"How did you get in?"

"The door was unlocked."

Catherine rolled her eyes and muttered under her breath.

"I hope I'm not disturbing anything." Francesca's gaze flicked to the staircase.

"I'm having dinner with my new neighbour."

"How quaint!"

"Yes, well... what can I do for you?"

"May I come in for a moment?"

Catherine's eyes darted to her door. Behind it was *her space.*

Francesca must have sensed the hesitation. "Look, I won't stay long, but there are a few things I need to say."

Catherine sighed and unlocked the door, stepping in ahead of Francesca and hoping to contain her in the small hallway. Francesca had haunted her thoughts for long enough; she didn't want her haunting her home as well. Except now, standing in the boxy space, they were awkwardly close, and Francesca's heady perfume was overtaking Catherine's senses.

"You look nice... I mean, at least better than you did the last time I saw you."

Francesca chuckled. "That was a low bar, but yes, thank you. I feel much better now. Things are looking up."

Catherine unclenched and accepted she'd have to invite the woman further into her home. *Perhaps Penny knows a priest I could hire for an exorcism afterwards.*

"Er, it's just through here. You can help me pick out the most impressive bottle of wine from my collection." Catherine's eyes flicked to the ceiling.

She led the way to the kitchen, internally slapping herself for saying too much already, *because give that woman an inch...*

"Ooh, so you're trying to impress this neighbour of yours."

"Yes, I mean, no. She cooked dinner, so it's only right I—"

"Well, you've always been good at sharing with your neighbours." Francesca winked.

Catherine swallowed, grateful for the space between them now that they stood in the kitchen. Francesca glanced around, drinking it all in. In the soft glow from the under-pelmet lighting, Catherine watched Francesca slowly nodding her head as she leaned back against the marble countertop.

"You've done well for yourself, Trusty."

"*Things* aren't the measure of me, Francesca."

"Don't be so touchy. I'm saying I'm impressed, is all."

Despite herself, the words lifted something inside Catherine. It wasn't that she needed Francesca's approval. *No.* But this was the equivalent of Francesca acknowledging that she'd underestimated her. Recognition that they could have had a good life together if they'd both worked hard. But Francesca had always trodden the path of least resistance, and that path had led her right to Jeremy's trust fund. She'd locked herself away in a gilded cage of her own making.

Catherine pulled out her fully stocked wine drawer. Francesca's eyes flittered across the labels, but she passed no comment.

"Look, I won't keep you from your... *neighbour* for too long. I actually came to say goodbye."

"Oh?"

"We leave for Tuscany on Tuesday."

"Wow, so soon? I know Jeremy has been lining everything up with the lawyers, but I thought it might take weeks yet, months even?"

Francesca waved a hand. "I haven't been involved in any of that, but there isn't anything Jeremy can't resolve over the telephone, and he can always pop back if necessary. The villa is ready now, so why wait?"

Something like a faint sting of sadness registered in Catherine's gut. Her life had been interwoven with the Daltons for so long, and now those ties were being severed as easily as plucking a grape from a vine.

"How do you feel about it all?"

Francesca inhaled a slow breath. "Good," she nodded. "Really good."

"Well, I'm happy for you. For both of you, I mean." She didn't know what else to say. Looking down at her mules, she was jolted by the sudden memory of her pink bunny slippers — Francesca never did return them.

"I wanted to apologise." Francesca's words were so low, for a second Catherine thought she'd imagined them. Her gaze met Francesca's dark eyes. "I also came to say thank you."

"For what?"

"For coming to see me when I wasn't... well."

"It was nothing."

"It was everything." Francesca fixed her with a withering glare. "Believe it or not, seeing you was what snapped me out of it."

"Oh?"

"Yes, seeing you reminded me that a broken heart can heal."

Ouch. Those words chafed an old wound, and Catherine winced. Francesca pushed away from the countertop and stalked towards her with the poise of a panther. She stopped just in front of her, half a head taller, but only because Catherine was still leaning against the worktop and ever-so-slightly reclining away from her.

"You were never very good at understanding me. I meant my heart, not yours. I was deeply in love with you."

"What?" The word escaped Catherine's throat, half-question, half-scoff.

"You were my first love... my first *everything*, actually."

The declaration caught Catherine off balance. Her heart kicked in her chest.

"I thought I had it all figured out," Francesca continued, "but it tore me apart when you chose not to be a part of my life. You were the one that got away."

Catherine searched Francesca's hypnotic eyes and released a shaky breath.

"I treated you badly, and I'm sorry." The words settled between them like dust. Francesca tilted her chin up and, leaning in slowly, traced Catherine's lips with the ghost of a kiss.

"Goodbye, Catherine," she whispered.

Before Catherine dared to open her eyes, Francesca had disappeared from the kitchen, her low heels clicking as she retreated down the hallway. Catherine held her shaking hands before touching a finger to her lips, still tingling with the sensation of Francesca's ghost kiss, just like her ears were still ringing with that apology.

"Oh, and take the Châteauneuf-du-Pape, if you want to

sleep with her," she called out before closing the door and exorcising herself from Catherine's life.

Fuck! Did that really just happen?

A TAPPING AT THE DOOR PULLED CATHERINE FROM her well of thoughts. She hesitated in the hallway, not sure if she could handle another round of Francesca Dalton being... *whatever that was.*

Relief washed over her when she opened the door to Jules standing there instead, shoulders rounded and hands buried deep in her pockets.

"I'm really sorry for being such a creeper and freaking you out, you didn't need to leave..."

Catherine released a breathy laugh. "I didn't intend for that to be a dramatic exit. I popped down for another bottle of wine, seeing as we finished the red."

"Oh? You were gone ages though."

"That's because someone keeps leaving the main door unlatched..."

"Shit, did I do it again?" Jules winced and mouthed, "Sorry!"

"You did, and I had a little visitor to see to."

"Is everything okay?" Jules asked, concern flickering across her face.

Catherine considered the question. Where to even begin explaining Francesca? A long story, maybe for another time, but now she found herself nodding.

"Yeah, it's fine. I'm fine," she said, then surprised herself by asking, "As you're here, do you want to come in and pick a bottle? I have a few that I keep for special occasions."

Jules's face lit up with an adorable grin. "I mean, if you're sure?"

Catherine stepped aside to let her in and then led the way to the kitchen.

"Your home is lovely."

Catherine had received a similar compliment not moments ago, but this one felt different, perhaps because it wasn't laced with surprise.

"I mean, obviously I popped in to get Juni the other morning, but I was pretty frantic so not really paying much attention."

Catherine smiled, savouring the sight of Jules in her space, perhaps for a second too long, before jolting back to the task at hand.

"Oh, the wine is in here." She opened the wine drawer and stepped away to give Jules space to look at the dozen bottles stacked in the rack.

"Ooh fancy! They all look dead posh; are you sure?"

"Honestly, just pick one."

"Okay, er... this one then." She pulled out a bottle and presented it to Catherine, who couldn't contain her laughter when she looked at the label — *Châteauneuf-du-Pape.*

Jules grimaced. "Oh no, have I picked something ridiculous? You really should choose. I probably wouldn't even notice if you gave me the cheap stuff after all those years spent drinking the vinegar we pass off as wine on flights."

Catherine looked from the wine bottle to the woman standing in front of her, all flustered and unsure of herself. Perhaps it was the wine she'd already drunk, or maybe Francesca's visit had stoked her confidence, but with a slow smile, she said, "No, this one's perfect."

WHILST JULES PLATED UP DESSERT — A LEMON tartlet with a heaped spoonful of mascarpone — Catherine uncorked the wine and poured them each a glass. They probably wouldn't finish the bottle; more to the point, they probably *shouldn't* finish the bottle, but she didn't regret opening it. She'd have been silly to walk away from Jules before really getting to know her, plus the woman had owned up to and apologised for the online stalking, which took some guts because Catherine wasn't about to admit to reading her postcards and eyeing up her underwear.

They settled on the sofa, sinking back into the plush cushions once the dessert plates were clean. The slow bloom of alcohol softened the edges, loosening muscles and tongues. Jules was a wonderful mix of curious and captivating. She listened with genuine interest as Catherine talked about Truscote & Dalton and the changes that lay ahead with Jeremy's imminent departure. Catherine tried to sound positive about it all, but in truth, she felt a little rudderless. Swallowing down the onset of rising panic, she quizzed Jules about the places she wanted to visit, hanging on every word as Jules reeled off a short-list of weird and wonderful-sounding cities. She found herself leaning in when Jules enthused about Barcelona — the place she'd called home for over a decade. Her elaborate descriptions of the vibrant culture increased Catherine's desire to visit the city someday soon.

Jules's eyes danced when she talked, and Catherine loved the way her accent wrapped itself softly around some words and fortified others. She could listen to her all day, and she couldn't stop staring at her mouth, which seemed to twitch into a little smile every time Catherine's eyes dropped to it again.

"Where would *you* most like to visit?" she asked.

"Now that you mention it, I've been thinking about Barcelona a lot lately."

"Oh, yeah?" The lines around Jules's eyes crinkled in a way Catherine found incredibly endearing.

"Yeah, not just because of you and those lovely chocolates... okay, maybe a little because of the chocolates..." Catherine grinned. "It just sounds so... different from here. I think I've been in a bit of a rut, and now, with all the changes at work, maybe it's time to spice up my life — take a trip, get a little perspective."

"At least you recognise it and want to change it. It took me years to see that I was in a rut and needed to mix things up." Jules reached out and gently squeezed Catherine's hand. The simple gesture sent a pleasant shiver up Catherine's arm.

"But here you are." Catherine squeezed back. The warmth radiating from Jules was intoxicating.

"Here I am." Now Jules was looking at Catherine's mouth, and biting her own bottom lip, and it was *so damn...* Juniper chose that precise moment to jump up into the space between them. They laughed as he stretched up and softly headbutted Jules. He kneaded his claws into one of the scatter cushions before curling up on it.

"I think that's Juni's unsubtle way of telling us it's time for bed." Jules's voice was husky, her gaze still locked on Catherine's. The air crackled with the electricity between them.

At the mention of bed, Catherine stifled a yawn, her restless nights finally catching up with her.

Jules brushed a warm hand over Catherine's knee. The sensation sent a wave of heat rippling through her. Suddenly, she was wide awake again, senses alive to the woman in front of her. She could only hope her face was behaving itself, because her body certainly wasn't.

Before she had time to stop it, her reckless mouth was asking a question her brain hadn't yet processed. "Do you have plans tomorrow?"

Jules glanced up as if checking a mental calendar. "Er... no, actually. No plans."

"Okay, I'd like to take you somewhere that wasn't on your list."

A stunning smile widened across Jules's face. "I would love that."

"Great. Good, yeah. Okay... next question. Have you ever been wild swimming?"

27

WILD KISS

Catherine woke from the best sleep she'd had in a long time. No weird dreams about Francesca, no spiralling thoughts about Jules, just a deep, delicious slumber that had wrapped around her like a weighted blanket. Warmth spread through her chest as she stretched amongst her pillows and thought about how the evening with Jules had panned out.

When it came to saying goodnight at the top of the stairs, Jules softly gripped her shoulders and grazed a chaste kiss on Catherine's cheek, and somehow it had been exactly enough, whilst leaving her wanting so much more.

And they'd made plans... for today. Wild swimming. As her joy crested, a wave of self-doubt crashed in. Jules was impossibly attractive, and although Catherine looked after herself, she was at least eight years Jules's senior. The other woman would probably be repelled at the sight of Catherine's fifty-six-year-old body in a bathing suit.

Christ, what was I thinking?

That was the problem, though; last night it hadn't been her brain doing the thinking. With just a hint of touch, Jules had set her alight. Panic had Catherine picking up her phone to text Penny.

> Help! Accidentally offered to take Jules wild swimming. Today!

> Now she's going to see me in next to nothing, looking about as attractive as a wet mop.

> What do I do?

Penny instantly responded with a large laughing-face emoji. *Great.* Catherine sighed and flopped her phone, screen down, onto the bed. She pinched the bridge of her nose, wondering whether she could summon a migraine or some other such excuse to get out of the plans they'd made. Her phone pinged.

PENNY:

> Stop being ridiculous, babe. You've got a great body — flaunt it. She'd be mad not to bang you the second you slip out of your Dryrobe x

"Oh my God, Penny!" Despite herself, Catherine grinned at her phone as another text pinged through.

PENNY:

> Wear the black cozzie, your tits look great in that one xx

> P.S. Lawrence says hi.

Why is my best friend such a pervert?

Hi to Loz xx

Okay, that's good. I can do this.

With Penny's bolstering pep talk — if you could call it that — front of mind, Catherine bounced out of bed to prepare for the day ahead. Even though she normally didn't bother until after a swim, she showered because she wanted to shave *everything*. As with the lacy underwear, she had no expectations other than being prepared should she need to be.

She planned to take Jules to the secluded spot she'd discovered last summer, when she'd forced herself to go on a solo hike for blog content inspiration. It would be ideal for wild swimming and perfect for a picnic on a second date. Catherine pulled on her nicest, most flattering hiking clothes, then rummaged around in the depths of her closet for her picnic blanket.

"Aha!" She pulled out the folded tartan rug and threw it into a bag with her usual swim kit, making sure to pack her black bathing suit, because who was she to ignore Penny's advice?

The morning light inflated the day with possibilities and an air of everything that could go right... *or wrong.* But Catherine shrugged off the weight of her expectations and power-walked to M&S to source some delicious picky bits for the picnic. Of course, she panic-bought too much of everything from stuffed vine leaves to marinated mozzarella, at least three different dips, and several cans of gin and tonic in every flavour they stocked.

Back at home, she set her bags by the main door just as Jules was making her way downstairs. Catherine felt her face splitting into a smile as the other woman reached the bottom step. She wore Lycra pants with bold patterns, brighter than anything Catherine owned, and a loose white T-shirt that flowed over her form. Her hair was bundled into a high ponytail, and she fidgeted with the pair of oversized sunglasses perched atop her head.

"I'm blaming the wine, but I really didn't think this through," Jules said, her cheeks turning a deeper shade of pink. "I don't even know what to wear for a wild swim. It's not a naked thing, is it? I texted Will, but he replied with a screen full of aubergine emojis, whatever that means. Do I need a towel?" She gestured to the bulging holdall flung over her shoulder. "I packed two just in case."

Catherine couldn't help but laugh. Jules was even more nervous than she was.

"Stop worrying; it's fine! No, it's not a naked thing. Yes, you'll need a towel. And if my friend Penny is anything to go by, I think Will is being naughty with the aubergines."

Why are we like this? We're just two grown women, hanging out for the day. At this stage, they were little more than new neighbours getting to know each other.

Jules puffed out a breath. "Okay, good. That all sounds good. Do we need snacks?"

"All sorted." Catherine pointed to the bags she'd set down by the door.

"I'm impressed. Aren't you Ms Prepared?"

"It's Doctor Prepared, thank you very much."

"Of course, my bad, Doctor!" Jules said, with a playful elbow-nudge.

Catherine tried to hide her smile at the face Jules made when she realised the sleek black car parked across the road from their building was hers. And she took great satisfaction watching Jules's reverie as the engine roared to life.

"Of course this is what you drive." Jules laughed as she relaxed into the passenger seat.

Catherine arched an eyebrow. "What does that mean?"

"Nothing." Jules grinned and turned to look at the sun-drenched landscape rolling by.

The hazy light gave the day a blurring, dream-like quality and Catherine smiled for no reason other than it suddenly felt like she'd been dropped into a high-definition version of her own life with Jules filling the space Catherine hadn't considered as empty, at least until recently. She focussed on the soft cadence of Jules's voice as she talked about the trails she'd hiked around Mount Tibidabo and Montserrat, her enthusiasm infectious.

"God, I'm so sorry. I haven't stopped yammering on."

"It's nice listening to you."

Twenty minutes later, they arrived. Catherine pulled into a dirt lay-by under the canopy of a towering oak tree. She shrugged on the backpack containing the picnic and shouldered her other bag with the blanket and swimming kit.

"Can I help carry something?"

"Don't worry, it's not far."

They fell into step on the well-worn trail, relaxing in

the sounds of the forest — nothing but birdsong and the gentle crunch of the path underfoot as they wove their way through the woodland. They reached a fork in the path.

"This way," Catherine whispered, with a soft touch to Jules's shoulder.

Sunlight filtered through the canopy in flickering patches, casting golden freckles over the mossy ground. The air grew cooler, the earthy scent thicker and the ferns denser, forcing them into single file. Catherine led the way, stepping over roots and ducking under low-hanging branches.

"Ah, shit," Jules yelled.

Catherine spun around to see her snatching at a bramble caught in her hair. Her sunglasses clattered to the ground as she twisted around, trying to liberate herself.

"Fuck."

Catherine dropped the shoulder bag and dashed over to help her.

"Here, let me..." She reached up and carefully untangled a lock of Jules's hair from the prickly branch. "There you go; you're free."

"Thank you." Jules reached up to tame her hair back into its ponytail.

"It didn't cut you, did it?"

"It's stinging a bit here." She turned her head and touched her finger to a scratch above her temple.

Catherine moved closer and swiped away a strand of Jules's hair to reveal a thin red line dotted with blood. "Ouch! Yeah, it got you."

Jules's lips twitched with a grin, and Catherine became aware of how close they were standing, but she was rooted to the spot, mesmerised by the way the dappled sunlight danced across Jules's face and illuminated the green flecks in her hazel eyes.

A twig snapped in the woods, and Catherine stepped back, bending to retrieve Jules's fallen sunglasses.

"Before we trample them," she said, handing them over.

"Er, thanks. Thank you. Yeah." Jules's words came out breathy and stilted.

"Shall we?"

"Yeah."

They continued along the path for a short while, pushing through the exertion as the barely visible track ascended to higher ground. They were both panting by the time Catherine stopped to catch her breath. She puffed out a reassuring, "Not much further now," when in truth she couldn't actually remember how much further it was.

Jules hung her head and held up her hand. "God, this better be worth it."

After another few hundred metres, the trees thinned, and the ground levelled out. Guarded like a secret by sentinel pines was an untouched lake. The smooth mirrored surface reflected the cloudless sky. No signs, no other swimmers, just them at this perfect spot on this beautiful day.

"This is just — wow!" Jules's mouth hung open. She dropped her bag and stepped closer to the water's edge. Catherine smiled as she watched her taking it all in because somehow this place was even better than she'd remembered it. She tugged the picnic blanket out of her bag and rolled it out on the grassy bank before sitting down to chug some water and take off her boots, grateful to wriggle her toes in the cool grass.

Jules came bounding over, her face beaming as she flopped down next to Catherine on the blanket. "This place is unreal; it was so worth hiking up that bloody hill."

"Do you need some water? Or gin, I brought gin."

Jules lifted her sunglasses to squint at Catherine. "You mean to tell me you hiked up that hill with a picnic blanket and a bottle of gin?"

"No. Not a bottle of gin. I didn't know what flavour you liked so…" She rummaged in her backpack and pulled out several cans.

Jules laughed. "You're… funny."

No one had ever accused Catherine of that before. Penny was funny; Jules was funny. Catherine was poised and stoic, and really no fun at all. Or perhaps she'd never let herself go enough for anyone to really see her because, admittedly, she was hilarious in her own head.

"What's the saying — never gin before a swim?"

Catherine grinned. "That's not a thing."

"Well, it should be." Jules stood and started stripping off her clothes. Catherine gulped, trying and failing to avert her eyes as Jules peeled off her layers until she was in nothing but a bright red swimming costume. Her body was taut under the tight material, leaving little left for Catherine's imagination to fill in.

Shit. Why didn't I wear my costume under my clothes?

"Are you coming in?" Jules smiled down at her before taking long strides back towards the lake; her smooth, tanned legs seemed to go all the way up to her armpits. Catherine wasn't a prude by any stretch, but sometimes being in her own awkward skin was exhausting.

She stood, slowly stripped off her own clothes and folded them into a neat pile. She turned away from the lake, flinging the Dryrobe over her shoulders as she removed her underwear and shimmied into the black costume. Not that Jules was looking anyway, perhaps she'd sensed Catherine's awkwardness and given her space. *Or perhaps she's just not interested in you like that?*

Jules looked absorbed in the moment as Catherine stepped up alongside her. She didn't want to startle her or shatter her peace, so she curled her toes into the mossy bank. Patterns of light skipped over the water.

Jules let out a hearty laugh. "Are you trying to summon the courage too?"

"Ha! No, I do this all the time, and often on much colder days. It'll be lovely once we're in."

"Why doesn't that fill me with confidence?"

"I thought you Scots were meant to be made of hardy stuff."

"Ach! I'm a city lass. I didn't grow up frolicking in freezing lochs!"

Catherine chuckled. "It shouldn't be too cold."

"Says the Ice-Bath Queen!"

"Think of it like a wild kiss." Catherine inhaled, and Jules turned to look at her, a questioning eyebrow arched.

"It might take your breath away, but I can guarantee it'll leave you wanting more."

Jules stared at her for a moment, her lips slightly parted before they split into a grin. "Right, er, yeah... it sounds a bit like you're romanticising hypothermia."

"I'll go first," Catherine said, enjoying the opportunity to show a little bravado. Hyper-aware of Jules's gaze, she squared her shoulders and moved with confidence, and, she hoped, a little grace.

The shallow water warmed her toes, her ankles, then her calves as she waded in. By the time it reached her thighs, the water was colder, but at this point the coolness was a welcome relief against her hot skin, flushed from the proximity of Jules and how brazen she'd just been with that kiss analogy. *What has gotten into me?* But it had been worth it to win that look on Jules's face.

The lake lapped higher. Catherine restrained her gasp as the water swallowed her waist.

"What's it like?" Jules called out.

Catherine took a second to steady her breath before answering. "It's perfect. Come on." And before her rational brain could kick in, she pushed off from the bottom and surrendered her weight to the water. Her nipples pebbled under the thin fabric of her swimsuit.

"If I die, I'm going to haunt you." Jules dipped a toe in.

"You won't die!" Catherine smiled to herself as Jules picked her way into the water with a distinct lack of grace, muttering expletives with every step and splash. Like Penny, Jules was unapologetically herself — a perfect blend of rough and smooth — and it was as refreshing as the cool water. Then with a splash that echoed around the lake, Jules was gone, the mirrored surface rippling in her wake.

A long moment passed, and Catherine stilled. "Jules?"

Shit. Catherine thrust her feet down to reach the bottom, but she still couldn't see any sign of her. "Jules?" Panic made her voice hitch as she called out, louder this time, with frantic eyes scanning the surface until Jules emerged with a whoosh, her hair slicked back and cheeks flushed. "Wow, that was—" Jules finished her sentence with a triumphant whoop and swiped the water from her face.

Catherine clutched her chest and drew a long breath into her lungs. "Oh my God, I thought —"

Jules swam over with a confident stroke, and Catherine realised it was the cold she'd feared, not the water.

"Were you worried I was going to haunt you?" Her lip curled into a half-smile, and she gave Catherine a little splash.

"No. I just wasn't expecting you to put your head under."

"You've just got to take the plunge sometimes, haven't you?... All or nothing," Jules said with a look so intense Catherine almost forgot her own name.

So much for that bravado.

"It's not too cold for you?" Catherine asked, treading water and trying to defy the heat rising within her again.

"No, it's lovely. You were right; once you get over the initial shock, you realise it's exactly what you needed."

Are we still talking about the lake? she wanted to ask,

but Jules had drifted so close she could feel the warmth of her; so close she could see the droplets clinging to her lashes. Surrounded by nature, her eyes looked more green than hazel, and her gaze flitted down to Catherine's lips.

"I don't want to make things awkward between us," Jules began, "but I—"

A loud rustling and the low hum of voices stole the moment. They whipped around to see a small huddle of women dressed like they were on safari, not a woodland hike. The squat woman at the front of the group held out her arms when she spotted them. She turned and said something to the others, who hung back chatting between themselves as the squat woman lurched towards the shoreline and stood with her hands on her hips.

"Ladies! I hope we're not disturbing anything." She held up her right hand and splayed her fingers into a Vulcan salute. "We come in peace." A large carabiner loaded with keys swung from her belt loop.

"The name's Parker. I'm the group lead for the West Warwickshire Women's Wild Swim Chapter, or as we like to call ourselves, 'The Blue Tits'." She splayed her hands at her chest and her face rumpled in laughter. "We've hiked over eight kilometres to get here. Most of us are from Leek Wootton, apart from Glenda, she lives in Dorridge, but that's a..." She continued on, but Catherine's attention drifted to the women behind Parker, who were now sat on the ground tugging off hiking boots and stuffing them with their socks.

"They're not coming in here with us, are they?" Jules muttered out of the side of her mouth.

"It looks a bit that way," Catherine whispered back, disappointment dropping like a stone in her stomach, as the women continued to strip down to their underwear — *God, no!* — strip *out* of their underwear. Catherine's eyes doubled in size, as she tried to look anywhere but at the unholy amount of flesh revealing itself in front of them, lumps and bumps in every size.

The water rippled as Jules convulsed with barely restrained laughter.

"What do we do?"

Jules's eyes glinted with mischief. "Do you speak any other languages?"

"Sorry, what?"

"Never mind. Just stay quiet, I've got this," Jules winked before calling out across the lake.

"Guten Tag," she said with an enthusiastic wave. "Ich verstehe nicht. Was haben Sie gesagt?"

"What are you doing?" Catherine hissed.

Parker stepped back, hands dropping from her waist. "Oh, you're German? Or was that Dutch?"

Jules yelled back, "Können Sie das ein bisschen langsamer wiederholen, bitte? Oder sprechen Sie Deutsch?"

"Er, sorry I don't, er..." Parker turned to the other women, arms flapping as, presumably, she tried to establish whether there was a German speaker amongst them. In the meantime, one of the women, maybe Glenda of Dorridge, let out a roar as she ran splashing into the lake with reckless abandon.

"C'mon, girls," bellowed Maybe-Glenda, and the others followed like a full-frontal flash mob.

Clearly conceding her quest to communicate, Parker shrugged and stripped off her own clothes to join her shrieking sisters.

Jules gave Catherine a shrug. "I'd hoped it might scare them off, but nope."

With an unspoken consensus, Catherine and Jules swam back to the edge, trying and failing to contain their laughter as Parker splashed by, mustering an "Entschuldigung," as she passed.

They scooped up their things and ran, giggling into the woods, Jules's hair hanging in red ribbons, water coiling down her back as she charged ahead.

"Ouch, shit!" Jules hopped on one foot after treading on something.

"Wait," Catherine puffed through her laughter. "Let's get some shoes on at least."

Jules leaned against a tree, catching her breath as Catherine pulled out her Dryrobe and chucked it on a tree stump, where she sat to dry her feet and pull on her boots. She looked up at Jules, who was staring at her with an odd smile.

"Here, sit on this while you get yours on."

Jules pushed off from the tree. Her mouth twisted into a grin when Catherine stood. "That's a good look on you."

Catherine glanced down at herself. She looked like she'd stumbled out of a wrestling ring. But rather than shying away from it, she put her hands on her waist and owned it. "If you're lucky, I'll wear my robe like a cape.

Now get your shoes on; we've got a new picnic spot to find."

They hiked through the woods, putting plenty of distance between them and the Warwickshire Wild Women or whatever they were called, Catherine with the Dryrobe draped around her shoulders, and Jules who'd just pulled her white T-shirt over her wet swimming costume. Catherine tried not to notice the two round puddles soaking through. She also tried not to think about how see-through the T-shirt would be when Jules took her swimming costume off, or how cool the skin of her breasts would feel on Catherine's lips. *Stop it*, she scolded her dirty mind.

"What about here?" Jules stepped off the worn path and into a small sun-drenched clearing. She stretched out her arms and turned a full circle. "We can dry off in the sun."

"Yeah, looks perfect."

Between them, they draped the picnic blanket over the ground. Jules flung a towel over her shoulder and gathered up her strewn clothes. "Just nipping off for a wild wee."

While she was gone, Catherine set out the picnic. The ice-packs had done a good job of keeping everything cool. She cracked a can of pink G&T and gulped down a mouthful, trying to work out whether pink was meant to be a flavour or a colour.

Jules returned, dressed, her wet hair still hanging loose but tousled and slightly drier. Those round wet patches were pulling far too much of Catherine's attention than was decent. Jules's lips twitched as if she'd noticed, but she said nothing.

"Here, have a gin." Catherine passed Jules a can, and for some reason announced, "It's pink."

"Thanks," Jules cracked the can and took a sip. "And thanks for all this. What a lovely way to spend the day."

Catherine reached to open the olives.

"Although if I'd known you were going to try initiating me into a naturist colony, I never would've agreed."

Catherine laughed. "I had no idea we'd be swarmed by bloody naturists. I didn't know where to look. Outside of an art gallery, I've never seen so many boobs at once."

"Ha! The look on your face was hilarious."

"I'm pleased my discomfort amused you so." Catherine tried to suppress her smile by popping an olive in her mouth. "So, are you fluent in German, or just subterfuge?"

"I know my way around a few languages. It was handy for work. And that little trick got me out of a few situations over the years. It's only backfired the once so far."

"Oh? What happened?"

"A couple of years ago I pretended to be French to avoid the advances of a sleazebag at a bar, except he overheard me later on ordering drinks in English. The cheeky bastard called me a lying bitch and threw my drink over me."

"Oh God, that's awful."

Jules shrugged. "Nah, it was fine. He got chucked out, and the owner felt so bad about it he let me off my bar bill at the end of the night."

"Still, what an awful way to behave."

"I've had worse at work. From the rude and entitled, right through to drunks who can't keep their hands to themselves… and that's not just the passengers!"

"Blimey! I'm sorry to hear that."

"Occupational hazard. See, I told you it wasn't at all glamorous. But don't worry, I usually got my own back." Jules scooped up some dip with a tortilla chip.

Catherine's eyes widened, but she dared not ask. Instead she said, "Well, here's to your fresh start. Hopefully, there'll be less groping and more glamour!"

Jules tapped her can to Catherine's. "Ha, yeah. Cheers to that."

2 8

CHOCOLATE CAKE

The last dregs of daylight were draining from the sky by the time Catherine pulled up outside their building and cut the engine. Her skin tingled from the sun, and her body hummed a happy tune from all the time outdoors. *No, from all the time in the presence of Jules — the least you can do is admit it to yourself.*

Their time together was slipping away like a Sunday afternoon, and her chest ached for more. She wished they were still in the lake trying to ward off the indecent invasion of nudists, or laughing and debriefing over cans of gin and picky bits in the forest, but *all good things...*

Jules stifled a yawn against the back of her hand. "God, I'm shattered. It must be all that fresh air! I'll sleep well tonight; that's what they say, isn't it?"

Catherine yawned in response.

Jules unclipped her seat belt and Catherine wanted to clip it back in to keep her there for longer, just the two of them in this joyful little bubble of her car, where life wasn't complicated and she couldn't fuck it all up by sleeping with her neighbour. You'd think at her age, and with her experience, this wouldn't be so difficult.

But Jules was already closer than she should be. Jules lived in her building and literally slept in the room above her. And Catherine hadn't let anyone get this close since... *Francesca*.

But that was then, and this was now, and she so desperately wanted to bottle the precise moment Jules twisted around in the passenger seat to face her. As if watching it all from a distance, Catherine turned her own head. She never wanted Jules to stop looking at her the way she was right now, both soft and searching.

Jules's lips hitched into a smile that felt like a dare, and even though she was still, her entire presence seemed to lean in. Every synapse in Catherine's brain lit up with the desire to close the space between them. Her entire nervous system hummed with the command to cup Jules's face in her hands and capture her lips; to reclaim the breath Jules was so effortlessly stealing from her. But Catherine couldn't move; she sat frozen on the knife-edge of indecision.

Jules spoke before Catherine could act. "You've probably had enough of me for one day... but if you don't have plans this evening, do you fancy ordering a takeaway and finishing that bottle of wine we opened last night?"

Catherine may have restrained her internal screams of delight, but she lost the battle with the smile that spread thick and fast over her lips. "Yeah." She nodded slowly. "I'd really like that. I mean, it was a nice bottle of wine; it'd be a shame to leave you to drink it on your own."

And just like that, the evening took on a new shape. Her Saturday night wouldn't consist of eating leftover picnic snacks as she attempted to channel all her pent-up energy into a new jigsaw puzzle. It would've been futile, as she'd have fixated on every creak and crack from above until her imagination took the reins and galloped off.

AFTER A REFRESHING SHOWER AND A CHANGE OF clothes, for the second night in a row Catherine found herself at the top of the stairs tapping on Jules's door.

"It's open," Jules called from within. Catherine moved inside, and Jules met her in the hallway, waving a small stack of takeaway menus.

She'd changed too and looked adorably cosy in leggings and a plaid shirt. Damp hair hung loose over her shoulders, and her skin still glowed from the heat of her shower.

"Pizza, Chinese or Thai?"

Catherine shrugged. "You choose; I'm not fussy." She bent down to say hi to Juni, and he wound around her feet as she followed Jules through to the lounge. Catherine instantly felt just as at home as she had the night before. Jules had lit the candle, and two glasses of wine sat waiting on the coffee table.

Jules patted the sofa next to her, and as soon as Catherine sat, Juni jumped up and insisted she continue fussing him.

"He's not like that with anyone else, you know."

"Really?" A little bubble of pride rose in Catherine's chest as she softly scratched Juni's ears.

"Yeah, really. He even hisses at Will." Jules glanced back at her phone. "Don't know about you, but I'm famished. I'm going to go with pizza. Shall I just order one big veggie one and we'll share?"

"Sounds good to me. Let me give you some money, though."

Jules shot her a withering look and tapped their order into an app. Juni made himself comfortable on Catherine's lap and, with all his purring, it took her a second to realise her phone was buzzing in her pocket.

PENNY:

How was the big date? x

Swarmed by skinny dippers! But all's well that ends well. I'm at hers now x

Penny responded with a stream of aubergine emojis. Catherine scoffed a laugh and quickly locked the screen.

"What's so funny?" Jules passed Catherine's wine to her and sat back as she sipped her own.

"Oh, nothing. Just my silly friend." Catherine's phone buzzed again, and even at a quick glance, the long string of splash emojis had her blushing and turning the screen face down.

"It just occurred to me that I don't have your phone number." Jules folded her legs underneath herself. "Like right now, if I needed to get hold of you, how would I do that?"

"Well, I'm right here, so…"

"No, but I mean if you weren't here, then what?"

"Well, you know where I live."

"Alright, smart-arse. I mean if you were out, or I was out. Say I'm at the shop and decide to thoughtfully check whether you need anything, you know, like a cup of sugar."

The corners of Catherine's mouth twitched. "A cup of sugar, from the shop?"

Jules smiled and shook her head. "Okay then, a bag of sugar."

"I don't take sugar; it's unlikely I'd ever run out."

"God, you're actually really annoying."

"Thank you, I do try." Catherine bit down on her grin. "I mean, you could always leave me a note."

Jules narrowed her eyes. "Right, so I'm standing in Tesco Express and suddenly overcome with the desire to do my neighbourly duties—"

"Neighbourly duties?"

"Yeah, to check whether you've run out of milk or you have the munchies, and you want me to write you a note?"

"Yes, I see your point. That would be inefficient."

"Too bloody right."

"Okay, well in that case I can give you the number for a great psychotherapist."

It took Jules a second, but she laughed. "Well, I think I have PTSD from the near-miss with the naturists today, so I could probably do with a little therapy."

"Any time. Although it'd be a conflict of interest now."

"Why?"

"Because I know you."

"Do you?"

"Well… a little, I guess."

"Do you know how much I wanted to kiss you earlier?"

"I, er…"

"I don't want to make things weird between us, but I think it's best I tell you that I like you. And if you don't feel the same, then at least it's out there in the open, and I can move past it."

"No, I like you too… I really do."

"Good, okay." Jules nodded. "That's good. Phew, it's not just me then."

"No, I wanted to kiss you earlier too."

"And… what about now?"

"Yes, also now, but…"

"What?"

"Juniper's asleep," Catherine whispered.

Jules laughed and kept her eyes on Catherine, taking a slow sip of wine before placing her glass on the coffee table. She leaned over, scooped Juni off Catherine's lap and popped him onto the floor, and with a disgruntled meow, he sauntered out of the room.

Jules scooched closer. She gently prised the glass from Catherine's hand, placing it down before meeting her gaze with an unmistakable look of want.

Catherine swallowed. "I think I've run out of excuses."

"I think you have, too." Jules leaned in, her lips so close Catherine could almost taste the kiss. The air between them fizzed with desire, and Catherine's body thrummed at the sensation of Jules's breath so close to her lips, their noses nearly touching. She reached up, cupped Jules's cheeks, and closed the gap. Soft and slow, until Jules's hands found her neck, her fingers threaded in her hair and the kiss deepened, grew urgent. Jules pressed forward and Catherine yielded, slipping beneath her, breathless and wanting. The room narrowed to just the crush of their lips and the heat between them, and Catherine released a soft sound — half sigh, half surrender.

"Is this okay?" Jules murmured.

Catherine answered by fusing their lips together again because it was more than okay; it felt fucking amazing. She wasn't thinking about what came next. She wasn't thinking at all. Just feeling — the heat of Jules's skin, the press of her warm mouth, and the way her own heart felt like it was trying to climb out of her chest.

But then her brain kicked in with the unhelpful vision of someone else sharing this intimate moment with Jules whilst she sat trapped in her apartment below listening to the creaks of the ceiling, and the moans of pleasure beyond.

"What is it?" Jules pulled back, swiping a thumb across her kiss-swollen lips. Catherine didn't know what to say, so she said nothing. She just looked away, embarrassment prickling as it unfurled inside her.

"Did I do something wrong?"

"No, sorry. It's not you. It's just..." She couldn't think with Jules's body pressed against hers and the taste of Jules still on her lips.

Catherine shifted a little awkwardly and Jules withdrew her weight, putting distance between them; only a small gap, but it may as well have been a canyon, because Catherine instantly mourned the loss of where their bodies had pressed, and couldn't fathom her way back to that closeness now.

A deep wrinkle formed between Jules's searching eyes.

"I'm sorry," Catherine said. "I get a little caught up in my head sometimes. I don't mean to get ahead of myself, but what if things go sour between us?"

"Sour? We've literally just kissed. I don't see—"

"No, I don't mean right now, I mean like in a week, a month, or further down the line." She gestured with her hand to an imagined spot in the distance. "This is my home; this building, I mean. If things were to go awry between us, it would make things very uncomfortable."

"I see." Jules passed Catherine her wine and collected her own before moving back to the far end of the sofa. "Well, I hadn't really thought that far ahead."

"No, unfortunately my mood-killing mind likes to calculate all the eventualities. Thus far, precisely zero percent of my romantic relationships have lasted longer than a few dates... so I don't like our chances."

"Huh! That's an odd take." Jules puffed out her lips. "Do you always put your umbrella up before it rains?"

Catherine felt ridiculous. She'd exposed herself as the nutcase she was, and she'd blown this glimmer of a chance with someone she really liked. Her overthinking weirdness had crushed the moment, and Jules would run a mile. She'd be mad not to — in fact, if she didn't, Catherine would question Jules's sanity.

Suddenly the room felt too small, her feelings too big. "I should go."

It wasn't a question, but Jules answered by looking back at her with a brightness in her eyes that held Catherine in place.

"It's such a shame to deny yourself something because of what *could* happen. You know, like being presented with a delicious piece of chocolate cake but turning it down because you *might* get a stomachache." Jules shrugged.

Catherine scoffed. "That's hardly the same thing."

"Isn't it?" Jules cocked her head. "What's that saying about vulnerability?"

"Oh God, don't you start quoting Brené Brown at me too! My friend Penny, she—"

"Probably has a point." Jules chuckled, and her gaze drifted into the middle distance as she took a long sip of her wine. "You know, I moved away all those years ago because of how uncomfortable it made Mum when I came out. I was hurting, too scared to push past the pain and shame of her disappointment." She fixed her gaze back on Catherine's. "But I see now, if I'd given her a chance, things might've turned out differently."

"You courageously took your happiness into your own hands."

Jules shook her head. "I rejected her before she could reject me."

"Again, understandable."

"But not brave!" After a beat, Jules drew a breath. "So, I'm saying, maybe you should at least try the damn cake."

Catherine exhaled a laugh. "That's all well and good, but what if things don't work out? Then someone else comes along and devours the cake, and I have the misfortune of overhearing... their enjoyment."

Jules hummed. "Okay, I can see why that would be awkward. But you realise that could happen anyway, right?"

Catherine frowned and Jules continued, "I mean, you could resist the cake now, then someone else could come along and eat the cake later, anyway. You'd still feel awkward because you almost had the cake..." Jules's mouth twitched. "You could taste it on your lips, and yet you didn't let yourself enjoy it because you were worried someone else might."

"Well, when you put it like that..."

The sound of the door buzzer jolted them out of the moment. Jules slapped her thigh and got up. "Pizza's here." She bopped out of the room, and Catherine took the opportunity to compose herself, straightening her ruffled hair and crumpled clothes.

Miraculously, she hadn't blown it. Rather than giving up, Jules had taken the time to understand and to reason with her. And *somehow* she'd calmed the chaos within, talking her down from the virtual ledge — the way Catherine did for others in her day-to-day, but that very few people could do for her.

Jules returned with the pizza box stacked with plates, serviettes and a smaller box on top.

"Right, let's eat before I start chucking more food metaphors around." The mouth-watering pizza smell wafted out as Jules flipped the box open on the coffee table and gestured for Catherine to go first.

As they ate, Jules resumed the conversation as if she'd never left the room, taking all the awkward edges off.

"I understand your reservations, Catherine, but I want you to know I'm not a reckless person. I haven't had many relationships, but the ones I've had ran their course — no dramas. I'm pretty much friends with all my exes, not that that's an exceptional achievement by lesbian standards, but..."

Catherine finished her mouthful, surprised by the urge to weigh in with her own dating resume. "I got hurt quite badly when I was younger. Since then I've struggled to let people in, you know?"

Jules nodded as she bit off a long string of mozzarella.

"I have had relationships..." Catherine hesitated. "Perhaps *situationships* would be a more accurate term? Just someone to enjoy a meal with, a conversation and wherever else it led." She winced, waiting for Jules to react, but she didn't; she just nodded along as she finished her pizza slice and grabbed another. "But beyond that, I haven't been very brave with my heart. I've just never really let anyone in, and also by that I mean..." she widened her eyes, "I've literally never invited anyone into my home before."

Jules raised her eyebrows. "What, really... no one? Ever?"

"No. I didn't want anyone else's mess in my space. Emotional or physical. And so, I've always dated on neutral territory, or gone back to theirs, where I could leave if things became... uncomfortable."

"Well, you haven't left yet, so..." Jules sat back and patted her stomach. "I hope you saved room for dessert!"

"Dessert?"

A devilish grin crossed Jules's lips, and she jutted her chin toward the coffee table. "Open the little box."

Catherine untucked the lid of the small container and peered inside. She wouldn't have been able to stop the smile rising on her lips even if she'd wanted to.

Two sumptuous slices of chocolate cake sat nestled in the box, adorned with a glossy frosting that she had to resist the urge to dip her finger into. The cake looked delicious but stoked her hunger for something else.

Jules edged closer and almost purred in her ear, "Still want to resist?"

Catherine responded by placing the box down and capturing Jules's lips with her own.

✵

AT THE TOP OF THE STAIRS, THEY TANGLED together in a slow kiss that tasted of red wine and chocolate buttercream. How easily Jules had dismantled Catherine's barriers, and how quickly they'd melted into one another. And yet, there seemed to be a mutual desire to take things slow. Neither of them wanted this thing between them to burn too bright and too fast; better to kindle it and let the embers slowly ignite, so they prised their lips apart, and drew an invisible line — boundaries were not yet discussed, but there was an unspoken understanding that they would be.

Jules gently pushed Catherine away before gripping her shirt and pulling her back for one more kiss until all that remained was the sweet torture of anticipation. They hadn't made any further plans, but they had swapped phone numbers, and that last kiss felt like a promise.

Safely stowed in her own apartment, Catherine slipped into bed and turned off the light. She tossed and turned, the sheets twisting around her legs, each movement a fresh reminder of Jules's touch. The delicious pressure of Jules's mouth on hers, the heat of Jules's body as she pressed into her, and the lingering scent of her perfume.

Sleep seemed impossible as she lay there replaying the evening, tallying all the times they'd kissed, her lips still tingling as if Jules had left an imprint. Her body ached with want as she tried and failed not to think about Jules undressing above her. Her brain unhelpfully supplied images of Jules in a swimsuit with droplets of water beading on her alabaster skin. *Fuck.*

This was going to be okay; she was going to be okay. And if things didn't work out, then that would also be fine. Romantically, things hadn't worked out with Penny, and they'd quickly moved past the awkwardness. Granted, Penny didn't literally live above her, but she remained a big part of Catherine's life, and Jules was as outgoing and easy to get along with as Penny. *It's going to be fine.*

Her phone pinged, the screen lighting up with Jules's name. Catherine's stomach twisted as she read the text; her mind instantly leaped to the worst.

JULES:

This feels weird…

She replied quickly, giving her mind minimal runway to take flight with its usual catastrophising.

Sorry, what does?

JULES:

Having you so close, but also way too far away x

Catherine exhaled a laugh at the thought of Jules lying above her right now. They were only metres apart; she was sure that if she listened hard enough, she'd be able to hear the other woman breathing.

It's like we have fancy bunk beds x

JULES:

Ha! Yeah! Shame I can't hang my arm over the edge and hold your hand :(

As if Jules could see her, Catherine smiled at the ceiling like an idiot. At the very least, she imagined Jules might feel her vibes radiating through the rafters.

Another text pinged through.

JULES:

So, Dr.T… I know you're off the clock, but I need a little help

Sure

JULES:

What advice would you give to someone
too worked up to sleep?

It would really depend on why the
individual is so worked up

JULES:

Let's just say the person in question just
shared the most incredible kiss with a
really hot woman and, for some reason,
sent her home before letting her finish
what she'd started. So, worked up in a
good way.

Catherine's pulse quickened. Should she reply with her
therapist hat on? She could advise on calming down the
nervous system with progressive relaxation and breath
work... or she could flirt back, because Jules was *definitely*
flirting, and the subtext had heat surging through Catherine. Before she could overthink it, her thumb made quick
work of typing a sufficiently flirtatious response, then
hovered over the send icon.

Fuck it. She hit the button, and the message swished
off into cyberspace; split seconds later, it showed as read.
The ceiling creaked, summoning the mental image of Jules
shifting with rising arousal; the mere thought had
Catherine pulsing with want. The three dots bouncing on
her screen suddenly felt like foreplay.

JULES:

And how might one achieve this
'afterglow effect' you speak of?

As if she needed any more encouragement, Catherine

pictured the sparkle flashing in Jules's eyes and that mischievous twitch at the corner of her gorgeous lips.

> Well, if you want to find out, you'll need to reach between your legs and touch yourself.

> Slowly!

JULES:

Fuck yes!

Okay, I'm doing it. I'm touching myself.

> Good, now tell me how it feels.

JULES:

Mmm, it feels good. I'm imagining it's your hand, not mine.

> Not that I wouldn't like it to be my hand, but try to focus on the feeling, not the fantasy.

> Describe exactly what you can feel.

The ceiling creaked again as if the joists were groaning with the weight of their want, bracing against the strain of their desire as it crackled through the wall cavities. For a long minute, Catherine thought Jules wasn't going to reply; perhaps she'd surrendered to the self-pleasure Catherine had instigated. But then her phone pinged.

JULES:

I feel soft and hot...

> ...And?

Jules replied in fragmented words, as if that was all she could muster the concentration for.

JULES:

Smooth… swollen, wet and…

Ready

Fuck. Catherine slipped a hand between her legs, where her fingers met the heat Jules had just described. She brushed a fingertip over her swollen clit and almost vaulted off the bed with the charge of it.

JULES:

Are you touching yourself too?

Catherine had never sexted with anyone before. It was obscene, yet overwhelmingly erotic, and she didn't want it to end.

I am. Just the thought of what you're doing has me so close.

JULES:

Oi! Feelings, not fantasies, remember? :)

I want to know what you feel like. Tell me.

God, it's like I've been live-wired. I can barely touch myself.

JULES:

Fuck, this is so hot!

God, I want to come down there and…
fuuuuuck!

The creaking intensified and grew rhythmic. Catherine

had been right before when she'd assumed she'd be able to hear the bed above her rocking with sex, but she'd never imagined it would be her lying beneath and making it happen. It took all her restraint not to press the dial button so she could hear Jules panting as she climaxed.

She squeezed her eyes shut and gave in to her own pleasure, rubbing the flat of her hand against herself with slow, rhythmic pressure until her orgasm peaked and broke in gentle waves. The whoosh of her pulse in her ears replaced the creaking from above. And then there was silence; a soft, profound calm.

Even with the entire floor of a building separating them, the moment felt as intimate as it would if Jules had been lying spent beside her.

Catherine's phone pinged, and she untangled it from the sheets. The sight of Jules's name on the screen lit her up like luminescence.

JULES:

Sexting counts as taking it slow, right?

29

FORBIDDEN FRUIT

*W*hen Catherine awoke, her lips were already curving into a smile before her mind had caught up. Within seconds, her evening with Jules flooded back and it felt like her whole body was grinning in the afterglow. She stretched languidly and glanced at the phone still curled in her fingers.

No new messages.

But it was early, and they'd had a late night after all.

Shaking off the restless energy, Catherine set out on her usual morning walk. As if manifesting her mood, another glorious spring day bloomed. With an extra bounce in her step, she power-walked three laps around the park. She'd only meant to do two laps, but she'd lost count because all she wanted to do was charge home and consume the woman who lived above her.

She couldn't wipe the dopey smile from her face at the thought of lazy Sunday mornings in bed with Jules. A breakfast of coffee, croissants, and delicious orgasms. Yes, they were taking it slow, but her mind kept racing ahead, wanting to skip to the good parts, even though this was dangerous. She hadn't let herself get swept up in someone like this since... *Francesca.*

Had Francesca showing up the other night really brought the closure Catherine had needed all these years? Or had the arrival of Jules into her life altered Catherine's brain chemistry?

Perhaps it was a bit of both. Either way, it felt good; and far from the usual heaviness that followed a date with a woman who wanted more, at which point Catherine always stepped back. Measure and poise were her whole personality, which had been good for her career, but not her love life. She'd never allowed the temperature with anyone to rise above tepid, lest she get burnt... again. Even on the odd occasion when she'd been tempted to turn up the heat, she'd steadied herself. *Measure and poise.* But Jules shone hot and bright like the sun, and it seemed worth risking a little sunburn just to bask in her warmth for a while.

On the way home, Catherine swung by Snoots for a coffee and a croissant. She contemplated returning with the same for Jules, then decided against it. Best not to seem too keen, even though she was itching to see her, imagining her with mussed hair and a sleepy grin draped over her kissable lips. Besides, Catherine didn't know how Jules took her coffee yet. A fact that would have usually dampened her mood — another surface-level connection with a stranger, but with Jules that part made Catherine almost giddy with excitement. She couldn't wait to peel back the layers and discover all of her.

Catherine caught herself whistling as she turned her key in the lock. After a cursory glance up the stairs, she retired to her own apartment.

The day passed in a tedium of chores, which although mundane, Catherine was grateful for — a way to pass the time and busy her fidgety hands. Several times she caught herself freezing at a sound from above, sending her thoughts skittering like marbles — *What's Jules doing right now? Is she thinking about me too? Does she regret last night? Why hasn't she texted yet?*

To stop herself incessantly checking her phone for messages, Catherine pushed in her earbuds and listened to one of her favourite well-being podcasts, which she often drew inspiration from for *Om-the-Go*. After a short while, the usually calming chatter was putting her on edge, so she shuffled a playlist of recently added music instead, only to be confronted by *Spice Up Your Life*.

She smiled, turned it up, and sang along as she flung open the windows and dusted the lounge. It was in the briefest pause between tracks that she heard the faint thudding. She pulled out her earbuds and turned her ear.

"Sounds like you've been taken hostage by the Spice Girls! Should I send for help?"

On hearing Jules's muffled yell, Catherine spluttered a giddy laugh.

"Hold on," she called out, gathering enough restraint to steady herself before flinging the door open.

The sight of Jules leaning against the banister dressed

in a plaid shirt and jeans made Catherine's stomach flutter. She'd pulled her hair up into a neat ponytail, accentuating her neck and jawline. One side of her mouth ticked up, which was probably in response to the way Catherine was eye-fucking her.

"I was beginning to worry Ginger Spice had you tied to a chair or something."

Catherine clicked her tongue. "No such luck."

"Oh, you like a bit of Ginger, do you?"

"What's not to like?"

Jules conceded with a slight nod and held out a cup to Catherine. "I brought you some sugar."

Catherine smiled and shook her head. "Why? I don't take sugar."

"I know, you said. But I do, and I was hoping you might invite me in for a cuppa."

Catherine tensed, but the silence that followed wasn't awkward — it was charged, like the pause before a song's chorus.

Here was Jules, attempting to blithely crash through another boundary wall. And whilst the woman had freely waltzed in to retrieve Juni a few days ago and came in to pick wine the other night, this was different because Jules now knew what it meant to be invited into Catherine's space.

In the seconds that followed, uncertainty crept into Jules's posture. "Too soon?"

When Catherine didn't answer, Jules shuffled her feet.

"I wondered if I was pushing my luck, but I really wanted to see you, and I finally came up with what I thought was a good enough line... you know, with the sugar." She held out the mug again, a soft, hopeful look replacing her cocky grin from before. Catherine had built her walls so high, others rarely expended the effort to climb over. But here was Jules, persevering.

"Come on in." Catherine stepped aside, the move so out of character even the voice in her own head gasped.

Jules raised her eyebrows. "Really? You're sure?"

"Yeah. I'll get the kettle on."

As Catherine prepped tea, Jules leaned against the kitchen counter and gently plucked threads of conversation. The words were mostly lost, like Catherine was hearing them underwater, but she noticed how Jules's lovely face lit up as she recounted an anecdote about Will falling in a muddy puddle at a music festival.

"You're not really listening to me, are you?" Jules exhaled a soft laugh.

"Sorry. I, er..."

"I've been told before that I talk too much."

"No, I like it. I got distracted thinking about just how much."

"Is that really what was distracting you?" Jules stepped towards her and leaned in so close her breath felt warm on Catherine's cheek.

Catherine swallowed as her pulse picked up pace. "I was also distracted by how much I like having you here." Her gaze dropped to Jules's mouth, and the air between them thickened with want.

The kettle clicked off, breaking the spell, and Catherine

moved to pour the tea, grateful for the excuse to steady her hands and slow down the moment.

Jules didn't press, only smiled and stepped away.

"Why do you have wooden fruit?"

"Huh?" Catherine glanced around to see Jules leaning over the decorative wooden fruit she kept in a bowl in lieu of the fresh stuff. "Oh, that! I guess it doesn't go bad."

"It doesn't taste good, though." Jules ran her fingers over the curve of an everlasting apple.

Catherine shrugged. "I've never tried it."

"It's the ultimate forbidden fruit." Jules smirked.

In the lounge, they relaxed side by side on the sofa. Amidst the comfort of the cushions, the tension eased from Catherine's muscles, and yet again Jules slotted into a space Catherine hadn't perceived as empty before.

Jules's fingers brushed the rim of her mug. "So, should we talk about what 'taking it slow' actually means for us?"

Catherine squinted into the rose-tinted light of the afternoon flooding through the windows. "Yeah, because so far all we've done is the opposite of taking things slow."

"All things considered, I think we've both shown admirable restraint."

Catherine's laughter rang out. "I'm not sure all that kissing and then sexting each other until the early hours quite ticks the 'restraint' box."

"Well, you've clearly no idea how close I was to coming down here last night."

Catherine tried to hide her grin behind the steam curling from her mug.

"It's going to take the self-control of a saint, but I've

given it some thought and I'd like us to get to know each other before we... you know."

Catherine slowly nodded. "Yeah, I think that's a good idea. We should date each other properly and see where things go. And not that I, er... regret last night, but perhaps we should avoid sexting for now."

Jules placed her mug down and edged closer, so close Catherine caught the spicy scent of her perfume. "Do you want to avoid kissing too?" she asked in a low voice.

"No, that would be..." Before she'd finished her sentence, Jules had closed the distance and crushed their lips together in a rush of warmth that had Catherine's pulse whooshing in her ears.

Catherine set her mug of tea aside, freeing her hand to clutch at Jules's shirt and pull her closer. Jules responded by deepening the kiss, her breath hot and uneven as she tilted her head to capture Catherine's lips more fully.

Heat surged between them, and they'd cross the line if they didn't stop now. They parted, breathless and grinning, because they'd broken the rules before they'd even finished making them.

"So much for having the restraint of saints," Jules said.

Catherine released a shaky laugh, her fingers still curled in Jules's shirt. "We just failed spectacularly."

Jules leaned back against the cushions, creating space between them, though her hand stayed close, her fingertips grazing Catherine's knee.

"It's the first day of my new job tomorrow."

"Oh! Why didn't you say?"

"I just did."

Catherine leaned to pass Jules her mug before sipping her own lukewarm tea. "Are you nervous?"

"A wee bit, but also eager to get the first few days over with. No one likes being the new girl."

"There's our next date then. At the end of the week, I'll take you out for dinner to celebrate. We can go to El Vino's and you can help me with the menu again."

"Sounds lovely, as long as you promise not to wear your frowny face this time."

"I promise."

"And how strict are we being in the no-sexting rule?"

Catherine shook her head. "No sexting. You can keep all *those* thoughts to yourself, but do bear in mind I can hear the ceiling creaking when you move in bed."

Jules's eyes practically doubled in size, and a blush crept up her neck, staining her fair skin a delicate pink. "No, you cannot!"

Catherine grinned, reaching for Jules's hand and threading their fingers together; a gesture somehow both chaste and charged.

"I have this mindfulness micro-blog I write for work..." Catherine shook her head. "Oh, actually, never mind... it's silly."

Jules squeezed her hand and smiled. "Go on, say what you were about to say."

"The last couple of days spent with you have been... I've been really present in a way that I haven't for such a long time. It's like I've finally got out of my own way. Holding back isn't about restraint, although it kind of is too; it's..."

"I get it; it's about enjoying where we are now and not rushing."

"Yeah, exactly."

They held each other's gaze. For the first time in a long time, Catherine felt seen, understood. But as the moment stretched, Jules's smile drained from her face.

"I... I need to tell you something. I wasn't completely honest with you before." She bowed her head, breaking eye contact and flooding Catherine with unease.

"You know how I told you I'd looked you up..."

"Yeah."

"Well, I stumbled across your blog."

"Oh, okay." Catherine nodded. "You already knew about my blog?"

"It's really good. I mean, I've enjoyed reading your posts." Jules chewed her bottom lip. "But there's more..."

Catherine angled her head.

"I messaged you a few times."

Catherine frowned. "You messaged me? When? What about?"

Hesitation hovered in Jules's voice. "I don't know why I started, but I enjoyed chatting with you, so, it just sort of continued. I wanted to tell you who I was, but the longer I left it, the weirder it seemed to just say, 'Oh, by the way, my mum used to be your neighbour, and we spoke on the phone when she died.'"

"I really don't understand."

Jules's forehead wrinkled. She held up her hand and gave a small wave as if introducing herself for the first time. The blush on her cheeks deepened. "I'm... Betty77."

Catherine carefully put down her cup. No sudden movements — she might startle the stalker.

Jules looked at her through wide eyes, as if she'd just read Catherine's mind. "I see how this might look to you now. I really clicked with you online, I didn't imagine it'd be even better in person." Jules reached her hand into her hair. "I want to be completely honest with you... about everything. I know it doesn't make things any better, but I suspended my account as soon as I knew I'd be moving in above you."

"Why Betty?"

"Sorry?"

"Why was your username Betty?"

"Oh, it's just what Will calls me sometimes. He's Wilma, I'm Betty... You know, *The Flintstones?*"

Catherine blinked.

"It's just one of those work things that stuck, it isn't—"

"I feel like a fool. You lied to me, Jules."

Jules held up a hand. "Technically, I didn't lie. I know I've done things all tits about, but... I like you, Catherine. I really like you. I felt it back then, and, my God, I feel it now. I don't think I've ever been drawn to someone like this before... it's... you're..." Jules's shoulders sagged as words deserted her.

Catherine shook her head. She'd managed to shrug it off when Jules had told her she'd looked her up online, but now unease welled inside her. This was worse; this was much worse. She'd been manipulated and lured into conversation. On the surface it all seemed fairly benign, but still, red flag. *Big red flag.* Catherine didn't need one of those waving in her face to recognise it; she'd seen plenty throughout her career, and she'd survived Francesca.

Jules stood. "I should leave."

Catherine nodded but didn't get up to see her out.

Her stomach ached with disappointment as the front door clicked to a close — the sound of something ending before it had really begun. Catherine picked up her phone and texted Penny.

> Woman down. Help!

Penny called right away. After listening to Catherine's frantic retelling, she let out a low whistle and muttered, "What in the Kathy Bates?"

"That's not helpful, Pen."

Penny chuckled. "Look, we're just heading out to dinner, but I'll be home tomorrow. Loz has to pop into the office, and he says it'll be a late one. Come over; we'll order something in and chat it through, okay?"

"I feel so foolish."

"I know it's hard, babe, but try not to overthink this. Put it out of your mind, can you do that?"

"I'll try."

"Good girl. See you tomorrow."

Catherine hung up and looked around her apartment. She'd lived there for over a decade and always felt completely at home. Jules had been in her flat for less than an hour, and now the place felt emptier without her, though Catherine knew the space hadn't changed; she had.

The anxious energy buzzing through her would best be dispelled with a walk. Before heading out the main door, she glanced up the stairs — she now officially lived beneath a woman she would have to actively avoid, so why was she still being pulled in her direction? She yearned to know what was happening beyond her neighbour's door. Was Jules feeling as hollow as she was?

Catherine couldn't shake the look of vulnerability etched on Jules's face as she gave her full disclosure. That, and the shape of her smile, the taste of her kiss. *Unhelpful.*

"So, all along Jules was the same person you'd been messaging online? The one I'd warned you about getting too close to because they were probably-most-definitely an axe-murderer?" Penny collapsed back into the plush cushions of her sofa with a whoosh of a laugh. "Bloody hell! I mean, you couldn't make that up."

Catherine buried her face in her palms and nodded.

"Although, actually it's a bit like that movie."

"What movie?" Catherine asked through her fingers.

"Er... Tom Hanks and the cute blonde woman." She squeezed her eyes shut and clicked her fingers, "*You've Got Mail.*"

"It's nothing like *You've Got Mail.*"

"It is a bit."

"No one is falling in love with Meg Ryan or saving an indie bookshop from a greedy corporation."

"No, but you spent months exchanging cute messages

with a woman you didn't know you were already connected to. And now, she lives above you and wants to bone you."

"Penny!" Catherine tried and failed to hide her grin behind her empty glass. "You're supposed to be helping me figure out what to do about my stalker-cum-neighbour situation."

Penny gulped down her last mouthful of wine and sat up to refill their glasses.

"Babe, I'm trying to help you re-frame it. You met someone online, had a genuine connection with them, and they turned out to be a real living, breathing, as-gorgeous-as-the-sun woman... and you don't want to date her because?"

"Because what she did was very intrusive. She sort-of-stalked me and drew me into talking to her..."

"And then turned out to be better than anything you could've even dreamed up, no?"

Catherine lifted her shoulders, but she had to admit Penny was right. In the ridiculously short time she'd known Jules, Catherine's overriding feeling was that she wanted more: more time, more information, more of everything and anything Jules had to offer.

"I mean, she's really hot! She can sort-of-stalk me whenever she likes."

Catherine hit Penny's arm. "Penny, stop. Be serious for once. It's a red flag. If a patient came to me with a situation like this, I'd tell them to run a mile."

"Okay, fine." Penny shrugged. "She didn't need to 'fess up to you, but she did. That's got to go in her favour."

"Yeah, but that was only because we almost slept together."

"She still didn't need to tell you. She could have had her wicked way with you, and you'd have been none the wiser."

"Hmm." Catherine pressed her lips together.

Penny held up her hands. "Admittedly, what she did at the start was a bit creepy, but she had her reasons. She came to protect her mum and stayed for the sparkling conversation. We've all done our fair share of weird shit, right?"

Catherine blinked.

"Okay, you're an exception. But you know from your job that most people do weird things."

"Yeah, and then they go and get help."

"I think you seriously need to ask yourself whether you're just getting in your own way again. Like, are you so intent on looking out for red flags you're dismissing all the green ones?"

Catherine sipped her wine and slowly nodded as Penny's words settled in her mind.

30
EVERYTHING, ALL AT ONCE

*D*espite Catherine's concerns about having to contort her routine to avoid Jules, she didn't see her over the next few days — barely even heard her moving around upstairs, no matter how hard she listened. It was almost as if Jules was making an effort to be as quiet as possible. It was at once relieving and disappointing. And it wasn't as if the physical absence of Jules did anything to remove her from Catherine's every waking thought.

Like a piece from one of her puzzles, Catherine's life clicked back into its routine — *sleep, walk, eat, work, eat, repeat.* She moved through the motions, but the rhythm felt off, and she couldn't subdue her yearning for the new beat Jules had introduced. She nodded along as her clients shared their intimate thoughts, scribbling notes that were little more than doodles on the page, reflecting her own internal chaos more than theirs.

On Friday morning, Stephanie sauntered in and

dropped a hefty brown envelope on Catherine's desk. She peeled it open, unsure how to feel as she held the wedge of legal papers that would finalise the practice's transfer of ownership to her.

After signing off the end of an era, Catherine sighed and clicked the lid back onto her fountain pen. It felt like an occasion worth marking. The conversation with Jules at the Glasshouse flared in her mind. Jules had leaned in and trusted the universe when a new opportunity had presented itself. Catherine would be foolish not to do the same.

On her way home, she stopped at El Vino's to book a table for dinner. She avoided the possibility she might be dining alone on a busy Friday night; that was a chance she was willing to take. She also stopped by the florist and picked out a bouquet of white roses, orchids, and lilies.

Catherine intended to leave them at Jules's door, but as she reached the top of the stairs, the main door opened and Jules entered the hallway below, wearing her signature red coat and holding a bouquet. Jules moved to Catherine's door and set the flowers down on the mat. She started when she turned and saw Catherine on the bottom step.

"Well... this is awkward."

"Jules, I—"

Jules held up her hands. "Oh, I get it. I'd have been freaked out too if I were you. I acted like a total creep, and I should've been honest with you sooner. You deserve better, Catherine, and I'm sorry."

Jules collected the bouquet from Catherine's doormat and held it out to her.

Green flag. Big green flag.

Catherine smiled and held out her own strikingly similar bouquet. They awkwardly jostled the flowers between them, and Jules frowned. "Why am *I* getting flowers?"

"For a couple of reasons. Firstly, congratulations on making it through your first week in a new job. Secondly, because I wanted to apologise too."

"What for?"

"On reflection, I was too harsh on you. You probably won't believe me given everything that's already happened between us, but I struggle to trust people, to let them get close to me..."

Jules raised her eyebrows.

"For some reason, I let my guard down with you, in a way I haven't done in such a long time. But because of that, I probably overreacted; what you told me shook me more than it should have."

Jules's lovely lips curved into a soft smile, and Catherine's chest tightened; she'd missed that smile, those lips. "So, maybe we could start over? You can pretend your new neighbour isn't an unhinged psycho-stalker... and I'll pretend to be normal for five minutes?"

Catherine laughed. "Sounds like a plan. Can I take you out for dinner tonight?"

"Yeah, I'd really like that."

"Good, because I booked us a table for 7 p.m."

"Ha! Okay, well it's a date then."

Yes, *a date.* This time Catherine would relax; she'd wear her normal underwear and try to focus on the green flags.

Luckily, Catherine had thought to book, because when they arrived at El Vino's, the small restaurant was already packed with patrons. The air hummed with conversations, the clinking of glasses, and the tantalising aroma of garlic and olive oil. Mateo shepherded them into the reserved candlelit corner and returned seconds later with water and a bowl of Picos de Pan.

Catherine deferred the menu selections to Jules, who decisively ordered things Catherine hadn't even considered or noticed on the menu before. Mateo scribbled on his little pad, nodding frantically and punctuating Jules's words with, "Sí, sí, sí."

Jules's accent slid seamlessly from Scottish to what Catherine assumed was Catalan. The woman exuded confidence that was undeniably attractive. Catherine sat back and took a long sip of water, letting her eyes drink Jules in; her copper hair seemed aflame in the candlelight as she communicated with Mateo.

"¡Muy bien!" Mateo said and shuffled off to the kitchen. Jules smiled as her gaze settled back on Catherine.

"What? Why are you looking at me like that?"

Catherine shrugged and smiled back at her, feeling the blush creep up her neck. "No reason."

Jules squinted suspiciously, the grin not leaving her lips.

First out came a carafe of pale-coloured wine, followed by a parade of delicious tapas dishes. Catherine didn't stand a chance of remembering the names, but the tastes wouldn't be as easily forgotten. Each bite was an explosion of flavour. She'd trusted Jules to lead the way and found herself transported on a culinary adventure. The metaphor had not escaped her.

Jules rested her chin on her hand; her hazel eyes looked darker in the low light. "I love watching your face as you eat," she said.

"Oh, have I got food on my chin?"

Jules giggled. "No, not at all. You just look like you're savouring every mouthful. Like you said in your Yoda-Nigella blog, I suppose. It's captivating... and kind of hot." Her eyes dropped to Catherine's mouth and, not for the first time that evening, heat surged through her. If Catherine wanted to make it through the meal, she needed to compose herself. She collected the napkin from her lap and dabbed the corners of her mouth before moving the conversation on to Jules's first week in her new job.

"Yeah, it was good." Jules nodded and sipped her wine. "I'll be honest and tell you I was pretty distracted for most of the week because of what happened with us."

"Oh no, I'm sorry that was on your mind instead of focussing on your work."

Catherine grimaced, but Jules leaned forward and cupped a warm hand over hers. "It wasn't your fault. But it did have me wondering whether I'd made a huge mistake and should just go back to Barcelona."

Catherine shook her head. "I don't want you to do that."

"Good, because my first week went really well. Turns out being distracted by you stopped me overthinking being a total noob. I was able to hang my hat on twenty years of first-hand experience, so I ended up being the go-to trainer by the third day."

"Did it feel strange working at a normal altitude?"

"Ha! Yeah, but I'm so glad to be done with all that flying. I can't wait to take trips for pleasure now." A disarming smile lit up Jules's face. "We should do that."

"What?"

"Go somewhere together. Book a trip and explore somewhere new."

Catherine almost spluttered her wine.

Jules winced. "Too soon?"

"A little, perhaps. But yeah, I'd like that. One day. Where do you want to go — Tbilisi?"

Jules cocked her head. "I don't know where that is."

Catherine laughed. "You have the guidebook, so I thought it might be..."

"Well, if I bought the guidebook, I must've liked the look of the place. I'll look it up."

"I already did; it's in Georgia. Think — ancient buildings perched on cliff sides, vibrant markets, and, most importantly, good wine."

"Cool, okay. Well, Tbilisi it is then. I'd also love to show you Barcelona; you'd get a proper local's tour. And after that, we could visit Will and Phil—"

Catherine spluttered again, and Jules grinned.

"Will's husband's called Phil?"

"Yeah, and their last name's Hill."

"Seriously?"

"No, it's Jones actually." Jules laughed. "They have a beautiful place in Lisbon. We could definitely take advantage of that."

"Sounds good. Well, whilst we're compiling a list; there's somewhere I'd like to go. An old friend I promised I'd visit."

"Tell me more." Jules sipped her wine.

"My friend Mei. I haven't seen her since university, but we sort-of stayed in touch online."

"Is she one of your six Facebook friends?" Jules teased.

"Quality, not quantity." Catherine stifled a grin. "Mei is adorably eccentric; you'll love her. She lives in Hong Kong now."

"Great, we'll add it to our shortlist. If you send me some dates, I'll book the flights. I still get a decent staff discount, so..."

"Wait, didn't we just say it's too soon?"

The corners of Jules's mouth twitched.

Catherine released her breath. "You're kidding, aren't you?"

"Yeah." Jules winked. "For now." *Green flag.*

As they stepped outside, the last streaks of dusk faded like brushstrokes against the cobalt sky. Cheeks flushed from the wine, food, and Jules's company, Catherine was grateful for the cool evening air against her hot skin.

A comfortable silence settled between them as they fell into step on the short walk home. They rounded the corner onto Lansdowne Crescent with its row of Regency terraces standing tall like stuccoed sentinels. Jules exhaled a breathy murmur that sounded a lot like "Wow."

Catherine followed her gaze, looking at the familiar buildings with renewed interest. The neat iron railings, sash windows, and elegant facades took on a more muted glow in the last traces of twilight. It really was rather lovely.

"Leamington still surprises me," Jules said.

"Me too."

Jules swayed into her and used the movement to not-so-subtly capture Catherine's hand in her own. The manoeuvre took Catherine by surprise, but not unpleasantly so. Holding hands with Jules felt good; it felt really good. She pressed into Jules's arm and let the world beyond them slip out of focus.

They arrived home too soon. The soft comfortable silence galloped away with Catherine's racing heart as she unlocked the main door and pushed into the hallway. Jules followed her into the shared space, pushing the door to a soft close behind her. The hallway felt too small and too big all at once.

"So..." Jules said, burying her hands in her coat pockets and jangling her keys.

"So..." Catherine said.

"Thank you for giving me a second chance."

"Likewise."

Jules grinned, and Catherine noticed a smudge of chocolate on her top lip.

"You've got something here..." Catherine touched her own lip, "...from the churros."

"Oh?" Jules touched her mouth but missed the spot. "Did I get it?"

"Let me." Catherine stepped into the space between them and reached up to rub the chocolate away. Jules parted her lips and captured Catherine's thumb between her teeth.

The air charged with possibility; a wild look passed between them, and everything sped up in a rush of breath, lips, and frantic limbs. Jules tasted of chocolate and cinnamon sugar, and Catherine fell into the kiss like it was muscle memory.

In the frenzied moment, they stumbled back until Jules pressed Catherine against her own front door, sliding searching hands up her neck and into her hair.

"Fuck," Jules panted when she broke the kiss.

"Yeah." Catherine's entire body ached for the woman in front of her.

"Do you...? Shall we...?" Jules glanced around at the staircase. "I should probably..."

"No." Catherine wasn't done with her yet. She gripped the lapel of Jules's coat and pulled her back in for more.

"Fuck, Catherine. If we don't stop…" Jules rasped between kisses. "You have no idea what you're doing to me."

"Oh, I do," Catherine said in a low growl.

Jules peeled herself away. "Okay, well you need to go in there, and I need to go up there, and…"

"Stay with me."

"Sorry, what?"

"Please. Stay tonight."

"Are you sure?" Jules kissed her again, and Catherine had to break away to answer.

"Never been surer." And even though she'd neglected to wear her nice new matching underwear, this was the truth.

CATHERINE SURFACED THROUGH THE HAZE OF sleep to Jules peppering kisses on her shoulder. She arched into the warm body behind her, relishing the soft press of bare breasts on her back and the curve of Jules around her as they lay nestled together like speech marks.

"Mmm, morning." Catherine couldn't hide the smile in her voice even if she wanted to.

"Sorry to wake you," whispered Jules.

"You can wake me up like this whenever you want."

"No regrets then?" Jules kissed her shoulder again.

Catherine twisted around to face her. With mussed hair and smudged makeup, Jules looked the most undone

Catherine had ever seen her, but even more devastatingly attractive for it.

"No, no regrets. You?"

Jules moved on top of her and answered with a kiss that awoke the rest of Catherine's body, making every nerve ending pulse with want. Jules pressed a thigh between her legs, adding pressure to the aching core of her need, and Catherine moaned into her mouth. She luxuriated in the feeling of being adored in her own bed, between her own soft sheets. Why hadn't she relinquished control years ago to experience this? The answer was beyond her, but Jules had certainly been worth waiting for.

Jules reached for the lube, a knowing grin lifting her lips. "May I?"

Catherine responded without hesitation, rocking into her with a slow, deliberate motion that drew Jules closer. Catherine gasped as the cool gel met her heat, and with skill perfected the night before, Jules slipped two fingers inside her. Within minutes Catherine was teetering on the edge of climax, but rather than giving her the release she needed, Jules eased the pace and pressure, drawing out the delicious anticipation. Catherine arched beneath her.

"We did things your way with the sexting; now we're going to do it my way, okay?"

Catherine swallowed. She was at this woman's mercy, literally putty in her hands, as Jules's slender fingers found a new rhythm inside her, her thumb circling Catherine's clit with gentle precision.

"I want you to look at me as I make you come."

Catherine obeyed, her heart hammering against her

ribs as she opened her eyes to the sight of Jules above her, pupils blown and fiery red hair, hanging wild and free. The ravenous look on her face unlocked a whole new level of want in Catherine.

"Good, that's good," Jules breathed against her ear. "I hope you don't have any other plans today because I'm planning to make you come so much you'll forget your own name."

Oh, fuck. Catherine moaned in rapture, waves of pleasure building with each stroke. With three more thrusts, Catherine was lost in a blissful release. Her body convulsed with pleasure and the world narrowed to this single, exquisite moment as she came undone by the fingers of the woman whose name she was screaming.

When it was over, she collapsed back amongst the pillows, grateful it was her neighbour in her bed or else she'd have to pop around and apologise for all the noise.

Spent and breathless, Catherine covered her eyes with her arm. Jules gently tried to prise it away.

"Don't be embarrassed. Fuck, honestly, it was as hot as hell hearing you come like that."

Catherine turned her head into the pillow and groaned.

"I've never screamed like that before."

Jules dropped next to her, wriggling down until they were eye-to-eye. Her perfect fingers trailed down Catherine's arm, sending another shiver of delight through her.

Catherine bit the inside of her cheek to stop her smile breaking through. "Stop looking so pleased with yourself," she said, even though her body still hummed with pleasure and Jules had every right to be pleased with herself. "Where's that lube? It's my turn to make you scream."

"Trust me, you won't be needing the lube." Jules pushed Catherine's hand into the wetness between her legs, stoking the fire again.

A thunderous noise from above jolted them from their reverie, and they looked at each other wide-eyed until another rumbling stampede pounded across the ceiling.

"Shit — Juniper!" Jules groaned as she sat up. "You'd think it was a baby elephant up there, not a five-kilo cat."

Catherine chuckled. "I told you, you can hear everything!"

"Oh my God! Yeah, you really can," Jules grimaced and laughed. "He'll be hungry and wondering where I've got to. Do you mind if I…"

"No, not at all. How about you go see to Juni, and I'll make us some breakfast?"

"Sounds perfect." Jules leaned in and kissed her again.

Catherine watched as her neighbour pulled on her underwear, and an idea came to her that was uncharacteristically springing out of her mouth before she'd even thought it through.

"Seeing as we left him on his own all night, why don't you wedge our doors open when you come back down?"

Jules cocked her head. "You wouldn't mind if he came exploring?"

"Technically, Juni stayed over before you did."

"Ha, yeah, okay… and you're really okay with that?"

Catherine slowly nodded as if weighing the idea.

"Yeah, I am. More than okay," she said and realised she meant it.

"Alright, let's give it a go." Jules's smile didn't budge as she threw on her clothes. Catherine was sure she had the same silly grin plastered on her own lips.

Dressed but gloriously dishevelled, Jules crawled up the bed and placed a soft kiss on Catherine's forehead. "I'll be back soon, lover," she purred.

Catherine's heart stuttered at Jules's choice of word.

It was new; it was all so new, but it felt good; everything so far with Jules felt good. *Less thinking, more feeling,* Catherine reminded herself as she gripped the front of Jules's shirt and stole another kiss before she left.

Excitement fluttered in Catherine's stomach as she busied herself preparing breakfast. Hopefully, she wouldn't disappoint Jules with her lack of culinary skills, but she couldn't really fuck up scrambled eggs on toast too badly. She whisked the eggs and dropped a quick text to Penny.

Jules stayed over!!!

PENNY:

OMG! That's amazing. Proud of you x

She's bringing the cat over for breakfast!

PENNY:

I think that's the most lesbian thing I've ever read… And I'm sure there's a joke in there somewhere about eating pussy x

Penny followed up with a string of confetti emojis, then

an aubergine and a splash. Catherine laughed, slipping her phone back into her dressing gown pocket just as the front door opened.

"Hey, I'm back," Jules called out.

Catherine met her in the hallway. Jules had removed last night's makeup and tied her hair back. Anticipating the unspoken casual-cosy dress-code, she'd changed into a well-worn sweatshirt, paired with pyjama shorts and socks. Jules smiled and glanced down at the furry grey bundle nestled in her arms.

Warmth spread through Catherine like wildfire, her insides aglow — because this was it, this was everything, all at once.

Maybe it was too soon. Maybe it would all go tits up, but she owed it to herself to take a chance, and so far, Jules had been a pretty safe bet.

atherine buckled her seatbelt and looked at the empty seat beside her. A steady stream of passengers boarded the plane, their hurried footsteps thudding through the cavernous cabin, passing by the premium seats and into the endless rows of economy.

Catherine glanced at her phone; ten minutes until the scheduled departure time. After switching her phone to flight mode, she dropped it back in her bag, severing the last tendrils of connection with the outside world. Not that she was expecting to hear from Jules, anyway.

Outside, a high-vis mob of ground crew scrambled around the plane with rehearsed efficiency; a silent ballet of pre-flight preparation. Catherine eased back into her seat and closed her eyes against the artificial lighting of the cabin. She tried to conjure the serenity of their destination — white sandy beaches stretching into sparkling azure waters, balmy air carrying the scent of salt and tropical flowers. Beyond the visual, she longed for the kiss of the sun on her skin, the soft whisper of the breeze, and the simple joy of someone to share it all with.

A loud clunk rattled under the belly of the plane, jolting her back to the present. She glanced outside again as the funny-looking airport vehicles, like oversized mechanical insects, scurried away. Still, the seat beside her remained vacant. A nervous flutter began in her stomach.

Catherine raised a hand to flag the attention of a fresh-faced air steward, but he barrelled past her, completely engrossed in his pre-flight checks. She arched around, searching the aisle as the last straggle of passengers boarded.

Then came the bounce of her laughter, a familiar, melodic sound that chased away Catherine's anxieties. She turned back to see Jules stepping onto the plane. She caught Catherine's eye and mouthed, "Sorry. I'll just be a sec."

Catherine felt her presence like a calming breath.

Jules's gorgeous red lips stretched into a wide smile as she eased herself into the vacant seat.

"Sorry, that took longer than I thought. It's Gregor's first proper shift, and Mandy collared me to show her something on the system. How do they cope without me?"

"It's fine, although you had me wondering for a moment whether I'd be adventuring around Barcelona on my own."

"Now, why would I let you do that?" Jules grinned, and Catherine's heart tripped over itself, in the way it often still did in Jules's company.

The months since Jules first stayed over had blurred by.

Catherine's adjustment to being the sole owner of Truscote & Dalton had been swift and painless. She'd dropped the Dalton, hired a new, competent PA, and brought in two new psychotherapists to take on Jeremy's caseload and ease her own. All of that gave her more time to work on the things she enjoyed — including her blog, which was ever-popular with a dedicated following eager for her insights on mindfulness, as well as the occasional recipe (supplied by Jules).

Meanwhile, Jules had happily settled into her new job and life in Leamington.

Jules and Catherine had tried to take things slow, set boundaries and make rules, but Juni had moved fast. Like a cute, furry tyrant, he claimed their entire building as his territory, demanding free rein of both their apartments by yowling until they'd not just stopped locking their front doors, but they'd had to prop them open. His reign was absolute; his demands non-negotiable, and his fluffy presence a constant, comforting weight.

They still had their own space but made time and space for each other. It worked. The rhythm of their lives had found a comfortable cadence, a gentle ebb and flow between independence and intimacy.

Friday nights were spent at Jules's apartment. Jules cooked; Catherine brought the wine. They'd debrief on their work weeks and plan their weekends with Juni curled up and purring between them. Lazy Sunday mornings were spent in Catherine's bed. When they'd worked up enough of an appetite, she'd make breakfast, or they'd meander to Snoots for coffee and croissants.

Even their best friends had seamlessly integrated into their lives, perhaps because Penny and Will were actually the same person in different bodies, with an embarrassing penchant for aubergine emojis, a lack of volume control, and an unwavering loyalty that made their presence as comfortable and familiar as their own living rooms.

Life, it seemed, was good — better than Catherine could have hoped.

"What are you grinning about?" Jules fixed her with a hungry stare. Her eyes dropped to Catherine's mouth as she leaned in. Catherine's breath caught, but before their lips met, a loud wolf-whistle shattered the moment.

"Oh, piss off, Gregor, you cheeky little shit." Jules laughed. "Where's that fizz you promised me?"

The fresh-faced steward winked. "It's on its way, boss! First things first," he said with a flourish, before launching into the safety briefing under Jules's appraising eye. Catherine barely registered the words, instead fixing her attention on Jules, who was watching Gregor with a mixture of amusement and barely concealed affection.

"How did he do?" Catherine asked.

"Good," said Jules. "He's stopped getting himself tangled in the life vest, at least, but I'm not sure where he picked up the jazz hands from. They get camper and camper every intake, I swear."

Catherine laughed.

"Anyway, just to be on the safe side, I'd better check your seat belt."

"You can't really get them wrong."

"Oh, you'd be surprised." As the plane taxied down the

runway, Jules reached over and adjusted Catherine's seatbelt, the click of the mechanism cutting over the whirr of the engines. Jules's slender fingers trailed across the buckle. Her hand hovered dangerously close to Catherine's groin before coming to rest on her thigh. The warmth of her touch spread quickly, igniting a familiar heat. Anticipation thrummed through Catherine.

"Was that just an excuse to touch me?"

"Might have been," said Jules, with a playful glint in her eyes, but beneath it, Catherine sensed a matching current of desire. "Excited?"

"Sorry?" Catherine blinked.

"About our trip," Jules clarified, her gaze steady, her smile softening. The subtle shift in tone, from playful flirtation to genuine enthusiasm, tugged at Catherine's heart.

"Right. Yes, *that*. I am excited about that." Catherine recovered, her cheeks flushing slightly.

The thrill of their upcoming adventure returned with a surge.

Jules took Catherine's hand and threaded their fingers together. The roar of the engines intensified as the plane pushed against the wind, gathering speed, and then, with a lurch, soared into the air.

Fall in love one heartbeat at a time.
Let the experience seduce your senses:
First… notice the shift in the air when they enter the room, how your body leans instinctively closer. Let anticipation hum quietly beneath your skin, delicious and slow. Then… savour the contours of their presence, the cadence of their laugh, the softness of their glance, and the way their hand hovers just close enough to stir your pulse. Now… surrender. Allow affection to unfold slowly, each touch a spark, each word a caress, each silence heavy with promise.
Falling in love mindfully is not about restraint.
It is an indulgence.
It is being fully present with another soul and fully awake to pleasure and connection.

BETTY77:

Aww… who's the lucky lady?

DR.T:

Oh, look who's back online and up to her old tricks.

Sorry, I don't indulge internet stalkers with private information about my love life.

BETTY77:

Huh! From what I heard, a certain internet stalker is often indulged with more than just private information!

DR.T:

No comment.

BETTY77:

Is "savour the contours" a euphemism?

DR.T:

You tell me.

BETTY77:

Ha, classic shrink move.

Yes, I believe it's a euphemism.

DR.T:

And what makes you think that?

BETTY77:

Because I believe a certain internet stalker got to savour a certain doctor's contours last night.

DR.T:

Perhaps you could let a certain internet stalker know that if she would ever like to do that again, she'd better stop mocking my micro-blog.

BETTY77:

Haha! I'm not mocking it… It's cute.

And timely advice for someone who's in love!

DR.T:

Who might that be?

BETTY77:

I'll tell you when you get home ;)

P.S. Don't be late, I'm making risotto x

DR.T:

I'm on my way x

ACKNOWLEDGMENTS

Firstly, a big thank you to you… yes, **YOU**. I hope this book entertained you, surprised you, and maybe even nudged you toward discovering more indie authors. We're the wild ones — unfiltered, unstoppable, and gloriously unruly. We tell our stories without waiting for permission, without shrinking when someone louder tries to take up all the space. Every time you choose an indie book, you're helping prove just how powerful our voices really are.

I owe HUGE thanks to the following:

Sophia — It was a pleasure collaborating with you again. Thank you for polishing all the smudges and making her shine!

Sam — Smashed it again, didn't you? Thanks so much for everything, you're brilliant!

Team Beta (Shannon, Sam V, PD, and Janie) for your input and enthusiasm at such a critical stage of the process. With a special shout-out to *Sam* for helping to… ahem… *lubricate* the story. Thanks for being my author bestie; I love our chats.

Team ARC — I'm genuinely so grateful for your support and cheerleading. You guys are the best.

The lovely folk at KDP — I'm still pinching myself about the Kindle Storyteller Award. It gave me such a huge shot of validation, as well as the momentum to push on and keep dreaming big. I'm grateful for your continued support and the opportunities you've sent my way.

Everyone who has supported me in ways big and small — whether you bought a book, left a kind review, or simply asked me how my writing is going… thank you. You have no idea how much these tiny nudges help me (authors are notoriously needy — well, *this* one definitely is). Your encouragement means more than you know.

ABOUT THE AUTHOR

Pip is an emerging queer author of contemporary sapphic fiction. Her work explores themes of love, loss and transformation, by blending emotional honesty with warm, character-driven storytelling.

Pip won the 2025 Kindle Storyteller Award with her sophomore novel, *Pyg,* a loose-retelling of George Bernard Shaw's play, *Pygmalion*, told through a modern queer lens. Pip plans to continue writing funny, flawed sapphic protagonists because queer characters deserve expansive, richly layered stories that are full of possibility.

Pip lives in Warwickshire with her wife, and their two 'kids' Mouse (the cat) and Roux (the dog). When she's not hanging out with her imaginary friends, Pip loves travelling, being in the mountains, making delicious food – and eating it, pouring good wine – and drinking it.

Great news! You've taken the first step — you've read my book, or at least you're reading this bit (*who starts at the back?)* Here are **THREE** more simple steps you can take to support me:

1. DROP A REVIEW

If you enjoyed this book, please drop a review on Amazon, Goodreads, or wherever you normally review things. Even just adding a star rating (5 would be great!) and saying, *'I loved it, what an incredible read!'* could be enough to encourage someone else to take a chance on my books.

2. SHARE THE LOVE

Let other people know you enjoyed my books. Sing a little song about them on social media (please tag me if you do that)! If you enjoy my books, you'll likely know other people who will too. Books make great gifts... just saying.

3. FOLLOW ME

Follow me on Amazon and you'll be notified every time I have a new release. Pop onto my socials, like and (even better) share my posts to make the algorithm really fall in love with me. Also, don't forget to sign up to my newsletter to receive exclusive content and stay up to date with all my latest news.

Pip x

www.ingramcontent.com/pod-product-compliance
Lightning Source LLC
Chambersburg PA
CBHW020902060726
47591CB00004B/1047